P...

Death Lov...

Berkley Prime Crime titles by Mary Jane Maffini

ORGANIZE YOUR CORPSES
THE CLUTTERED CORPSE
DEATH LOVES A MESSY DESK
CLOSET CONFIDENTIAL
THE BUSY WOMAN'S GUIDE TO MURDER

The Busy Woman's Guide to Murder

Mary Jane Maffini

BERKLEY PRIME CRIME, NEW YORK

THE BERKLEY PUBLISHING GROUP
Published by the Penguin Group
Penguin Group (USA) Inc.
375 Hudson Street, New York, New York 10014, USA
Penguin Group (Canada), 90 Eglinton Avenue East, Suite 700, Toronto, Ontario M4P 2Y3, Canada
(a division of Pearson Penguin Canada Inc.)
Penguin Books Ltd., 80 Strand, London WC2R 0RL, England
Penguin Group Ireland, 25 St. Stephen's Green, Dublin 2, Ireland (a division of Penguin Books Ltd.)
Penguin Group (Australia), 250 Camberwell Road, Camberwell, Victoria 3124, Australia
(a division of Pearson Australia Group Pty. Ltd.)
Penguin Books India Pvt. Ltd., 11 Community Centre, Panchsheel Park, New Delhi—110 017, India
Penguin Group (NZ), 67 Apollo Drive, Rosedale, North Shore 0632, New Zealand
(a division of Pearson New Zealand Ltd.)
Penguin Books (South Africa) (Pty.) Ltd., 24 Sturdee Avenue, Rosebank, Johannesburg 2196,
South Africa

Penguin Books Ltd., Registered Offices: 80 Strand, London WC2R 0RL, England

THE BUSY WOMAN'S GUIDE TO MURDER

A Berkley Prime Crime Book / published by arrangement with the author

PRINTING HISTORY
Berkley Prime Crime mass-market edition / April 2011

ISBN: 978-0-425-24060-1

To Giulio, for endless support

Acknowledgments

In writing the Charlotte Adams Mysteries, I've come to love and admire the cozy mystery community that is so supportive of this genre. I am grateful to my author colleagues and to the many readers who make it all so much fun. Of course I will always appreciate the leagues of professional organizers who make such a difference to people's lives.

My wonderful friends Mary MacKay-Smith and Linda Wiken and my daughter Victoria Maffini continue to make time for me and my manuscripts and never fail to be there with support and that all-important ingredient: fun. Of course I love them. Many thanks also to my buddy Nikki Bonanni for digging up elusive facts on such short notice. My husband, Giulio, manages to be smart, brave, and even nonchalant despite living with a woman who knows hundreds of ways to kill people. Once again, my patient editor, Tom Colgan, as well as Amanda Ng and Kaitlynn Kennedy of Berkley Prime Crime, and my agent, Kim Lionetti, offered good-natured and efficient help throughout the process. Closer to home, I continue to be indebted to Ottawa Therapy Dogs for allowing my spoiled princess dachshunds to bring joy to others and to open my eyes to what a difference a dog or two can make. Let's hope they can inspire Truffle and Sweet Marie. We all know that any errors are mine alone.

Make life better. Forget about doing things right.
Concentrate on doing the right things.

1

Nine-one-one?

Calling me?

As often as I have had to dial 911 over the past two years, this still didn't make sense. And yet, Mona Pringle's voice was clear on the phone. Even if the call display said BLOCKED NUMBER.

"Charlotte? Are you there? It's Mona Pringle. We went to St. Jude's together. Don't you remember me?"

I hadn't needed her to tell me who she was. There wasn't much chance I'd forget my regular 911 operator. That didn't make the call any less surprising.

"Of course I remember you, Mona. But why are you calling *me*? Is there some emergency? What can I do?"

"Well, you can listen, for starters. Just let me talk. For once." There was no sign of Mona's usual calm and soothing tone. She was a full octave higher than normal. She sounded like a violin string about to snap.

"Okay."

Her voice rose another few notes. "That bitch is back."

I felt a buzzing around my temples. Mona worked as a 911 operator for the city of Woodbridge. She'd answered every single frantic emergency call I'd ever made, no matter what time of day or night. She'd pulled a lot of double shifts and more than her share of overtime, without ever losing her cool. I'd never heard her use that kind of language. She had a remarkably stressful job: Lives depended on her response. Had the pressure finally caused her to lose her grip?

"Sorry, Mona. I didn't quite—"

"Get with program. I said she's *back*. And believe me, that means they'll all be meaner than ever."

If Mona was flipping out—and it seemed that way—I didn't want to make things worse by asking stupid questions, but I had no idea who or what she was talking about. Wait, make that shrieking about.

"Did you hear me, Charlotte?"

I held the phone away from my ear. "I did, but I'm not sure who's back."

"Mean girls? Does that suggest anything to you? Who the hell else? How can you forget? Have you repressed your adolescent memories?"

"Gosh, I sure hope so."

Mean girls? I thought hard. Who'd been notably mean in my adolescence? A shorter list might have been who hadn't been. But Mona had been a gentle soul, thin as a clothesline, birdlike, with large hands, knobby knees, and a lively case of acne. She'd kept her head down in high school. She'd never given me or any of my misfit buddies any trouble. I knew she'd been on the receiving end, although not from us.

"Are you there, Charlotte?"

"Yes. Um, when did she get back?"

"I don't know and I wouldn't care except I know she's getting up to her old tricks."

My ploy hadn't worked. No name revealed. Mona was obviously strung out. That seemed like a strong negative in a person who took emergency calls from panicky people.

"That's terrible. Oh boy. Mona? Are you crying? Is there anything I can do?"

"I'll cry if I want to. It's my party, ha-ha. And I doubt there's anything you can do."

"But you've always been so helpful when I've called you. The least I could do is—"

"Get rid of them? Wipe them all off the face of the earth? Exterminate them like the cockroaches they are? Go ahead, do it, Charlotte. Make my day."

"Exterminate?" I blurted.

"That's right."

"Exterminate who?"

"Start with that hag, Serena Redding. I told you she's back, living the good life in a mansion on the edge of Woodbridge."

Serena. Oh. Thoughts tumbled in my head, jagged flashes from St. Jude's. I could still picture Serena with her honey-blond hair, velvety golden tan, that turned-up nose, and round brown eyes fringed with thick lashes. She'd definitely been pack leader, and she and her three followers always seemed to have been sashaying through the halls of St. Jude's as if playing to a swarm of paparazzi. They were gorgeous, smart, and popular, and left a trail of expensive scent in the air as they passed by. Some people admired them. Some people had the hots for them. And some people were scared to death of them. My memory dredged up the image of a scrawny girl with angry red zits stranded in the locker room after her shower. Mona. Not a piece of her clothing in sight. Not even her underwear. I'd come across Mona crouched in a corner, weeping, teeth chattering. Her skin was ice-cold when I tried to pat her shoulder. My own gym clothes were much too short for her thin, awkward body, but they were better than leaving her naked any old day. I'd gone searching for my friend Sally, who was tall enough and generous enough to give Mona something to wear to class. I'd been shaken by the vindictiveness of that trick. The first face I'd seen outside the locker room had been Serena Redding's. She'd been laughing. No sign of her cruel deeds on that lovely face. She was a beauty queen of mean, without a shred of empathy.

I could see how Mona might bear a grudge.

"What do you mean by 'she's back'?" I asked.

"What could I mean? She's here. In Woodbridge. Again. Probably stirring things up as we speak. Oh crap. There goes the line."

"The 911 line?" I squeaked.

"Some idiot probably gave himself a heart attack shoveling snow. When will people learn? Eat fries in front of the TV all your life and then, when you finally stir yourself, make sure you grab a heavy shovel to lift wet snow in the morning, when your blood is thick. Sure, go ahead. Live like an unhealthy slob. Nine-one-one will be there to bail you out. Not like we have anything else to do."

Was this happening?

"You'd better pick it up, Mona."

"Yeah, yeah. I will, but there's more. I have to talk to you."

"Let's talk later. I'll call you back." I was speaking to the dial tone. However, in this case, I was glad. Mona needed to concentrate on her job and not on the return of Serena Redding. I thought back. Every queen bee has her courtiers, and Serena had been no different from any other flourishing monarch. In all public appearances, she'd been supported by Jasmin Lorenz, Tiffanee Dupont, and Haley McKee. They weren't quite as gorgeous as Serena. She had to be number one. But Tiffanee had been particularly striking: waist-length dark hair, almond-shaped eyes, and milky skin. She'd been taller than Serena. Tiffanee must have been six feet. She always walked at the back of the pack, that fabulous hair swaying. They'd called her Princess T. Serena had usually been flanked by Haley and Jasmin. The boys had liked Haley; the flawless ivory skin, the bouncy ponytail, the sexy grin, and perhaps most of all, those curves. Next to Haley, everyone felt too tall or too short or too flat-chested. Everyone except Serena. And Haley had played on that. Jasmin's name had seemed exotic, and she'd been a fairly attractive brunette, but not as dramatic as the other three. Not as nasty either, perhaps the weak link in the chain. At the time, each one seemed to have whiter teeth, lovelier skin, and a more fabulous wardrobe than anyone outside the charmed circle. None of the three measured up to Serena. Her hair could have fueled an ad campaign; her skin glowed. And those clothes— fresh from LA whenever her mother went on a shopping trip. Mind you, we wore uniforms to St. Jude's, but Serena somehow managed to appear half-dressed and provocative, even when wearing our prim little plaid skirts, navy jackets, and knee socks. I remembered football players with their tongues dragging on the vinyl floor as Serena and her entourage swanned by.

Looking back, I asked myself, Why would a beautiful, well-dressed, intelligent girl—the object of major male-adolescent lust in our high school—ritually humiliate a self-effacing, harmless classmate? Everyone must have known. Why had no one done anything to stop it? More to the point, why had *I* let it go on?

—◆◆—

I suppose it was a good thing that Mona had called with her bombshell. It distracted me from the three items clogging my mind.

First was the looming therapy-dog evaluation for my

rescued miniature dachshunds, Truffle and Sweet Marie. Make that reevaluation. Or, to be precise, re-reevaluation. The pooches were now napping on the sofa, snoring softly, their silky fur smelling vaguely like warm toast. They weren't worried. I was.

Second, the next morning I would be launching a five-part course in cooperation with the Woodbridge Public Library: The Busy Person's Guide to Managing Time and Life. The first session kicked off on Saturday morning. It was a new venture for me in my organizing business and I wanted it to go well.

Third, Jack Reilly.

Who was I kidding? Jack was first on the list. It had taken me nearly twenty years to realize Jack was the man for me. He was responsible for me having pets for the first time in my life. He was involved in animal rescue, and I was a sitting duck. He'd been my friend since we were kids, and now he was my hero, my landlord, and also the guy who had saved my life more than once. Of course, I've saved his life too, but only because he'd been in danger saving mine. It's complicated. Jack isn't. Now, if I could just find a way to tell him how I felt. But what if he didn't share my feelings? What if I attempted to nudge the relationship forward and the whole friendship collapsed? That would be a disaster and I wasn't yet prepared to risk it.

At that moment Jack arrived home from CYCotics, his bicycle shop. He thundered up the stairs to my second-floor apartment, bringing a gust of wintry air with him. Jack lived downstairs, but he spent a lot more time upstairs in my home. Perhaps because I had furniture and sometimes food. Or maybe it was the lure of the dogs.

"Ready for tonight? We'll knock them dead." He shook a few random snowflakes from his spiky dark-blond hair, and eased his lanky form onto the sofa, letting the dogs snuggle up. "Still snowing. Brr. I wonder if it will end before June?"

I refrained from commenting that if he didn't like the snow, perhaps he shouldn't wear cargo shorts and Hawaiian shirts twelve months a year. Why not? It wasn't like being nice was getting me anywhere.

Jack, obviously unaware of my grumpy thoughts, said, "Not the best weather for the spring bike sales."

I turned my mind back to the other worries. For instance, the rumor that Woodbridge Therapy Dogs had a "three strikes and you're out" rule. I didn't like to ask, in case the answer made me even more nervous. Speaking of nervous, I wondered what was happening with Mona. I tried calling 911, but was told quite firmly that operators didn't take or *make* personal calls. That made sense, although Mona had called me from work. I took the hint. I found a Woodbridge number for M Pringle on the 411 website (although no home address was listed) and called. I left a soothing message and hoped for the best.

Next, judgment day in a dog-training center. Actually, judgment night. Would Truffle and Sweet Marie make it through the test this time? We'd been training diligently, and after more than a year of trying and two spectacular failures, we were up again. I had a lot riding on it. My beloved pooches were adorable and cuddly—in my opinion anyway—the exact characteristics a therapy dog needs. Unfortunately, they were also inclined to bark. That got them turfed out of the last two evaluations in disgrace. We'd been working on that. All other thoughts flew out of my head as we, the about to be evaluated, faced down the evaluator. I held a trembling Sweet Marie. Jack stood next to me with Truffle firmly grasped in his long arms. That was only fair, as without Jack's interference, I wouldn't have dogs in the first place. This was a far cry from my glamorous evenings back in New York City—stilettos, fashion, and freedom. Oh, and one lying, cheating hound of an ex-fiancé, but let's not dwell on that.

We were surrounded by oversize dogs, the trigger for much of the barking. I tried to minimize the impact of the two whopping golden retrievers, one lazy and serene, the other a bundle of bouncy energy; a Bernese mountain dog; a puffy Keeshond; a Saint Bernard; and a miscellaneous and adorable fuzzy creature of unfathomable breed. Tonight, a combination of whispering in their ears, treats, and one-on-one attention seemed to be working to keep Truffle and Sweet Marie in the game.

"Third time's a charm," Jack said with his usual crooked grin.

The evaluators touched each dog's paws, checked out their nails, and lifted their velvety ears to peek inside. Grooming counts.

Not a growl or a protest.

"Good girl," I whispered, as the evaluators checked Sweet Marie's teeth. I knew Jack was murmuring the same combination of bribes and threats.

Truffle was a bit more of a challenge than Sweet Marie, but Jack kept him under control. Dogs are putty in his hands. So far they'd done every command flawlessly, even the elusive "lie down." I never thought I'd see that day. They'd survived the simulated hospital environment, complete with volunteers in whirling wheelchairs, thumping IV poles, and clomping crutches, to say nothing of the ones who wandered randomly, wailing like zombies. They did well with the fake swarming incidents. The evaluators had explained that these tests were to make sure that a dog didn't flip out in a hospital corridor or dementia unit. I thought I detected a low growl from Truffle as sixteen hands reached out for him, but Jack coughed loudly just in time. Have I mentioned he's the best?

Nearly three hours after we began, we were fidgeting,

awaiting the results. I was surprised to find my heart racing. We had to succeed. I wanted to be part of this program.

I was holding my breath as the evaluator stepped toward me to say that Sweet Marie had passed. Truffle too. I exhaled. I shook the evaluator's hand so hard that she gasped. Jack gave his evaluator a huge hug. She blushed. Women do when Jack pays attention to them, even though he seems unaware of it. I stood and got my picture taken with Truffle and then with Sweet Marie for our photo IDs.

Truffle and Sweet Marie received attractive red scarves with the Woodbridge Therapy Dog emblem. They seemed proud of themselves and also far less surprised than I was. The diminutive red-haired coordinator, Candy Brinkerhoff, was all smiles too. I think she was as excited as we were. We'd been discussing where Truffle and Sweet Marie could do the most good. In some of the local schools, specially trained dogs were part of a program to help children become more confident and fluent readers. I didn't have all the details, but I loved the idea of that. Of course, we would have to wait for our assignments.

Candy said, "I already have a placement for you. They've been waiting since forever and they're very excited."

"Where is it?"

"Truffle and Sweet Marie can do a lot of good at the Alzheimer's unit of Riverview Manor. It's a nursing home downtown. Of course, you know that it's one pooch at a time. Bella Constantine, the program director of the unit, can't wait. She'd be thrilled if you could come by Monday morning at eleven thirty for a visit with either Truffle or Sweet Marie, and she asked me to confirm. I'll be there too, making sure that everything goes well."

After so much time trying, we were off to a flying start. I felt a small swell of pride that we had actually achieved this goal.

"We'll be there." I am pretty sure Sweet Marie wagged her tail.

When we emerged from the evaluation area, Jack and I clutching the diplomas, we each let out a whoop and danced around the parking lot in the swirling snow. Truffle and Sweet Marie barked their pointed little heads off. Why the hell not? They'd been holding it in all night.

— ⚬ —

Of course, the situation with Mona nagged at the back of my mind all evening. I was worried about her. She still didn't answer her home phone when I called again from the parking lot. I wasn't sure what the shifts were like at 911 or when she was on duty. Was she still there? Still freaking and taking that out on unsuspecting callers?

I paced in the lightly falling snow by my Miata and told myself that Mona's meltdown was a type of emergency. I decided to try again. This time I was prepared to use a fake name and disguise my voice. When I got up the nerve to dial 911 from my cell, Mona was still at work and she sounded more like her normal thick-skinned self. She wasn't fooled.

"Is this a crime in progress, Charlotte?"

I guess she recognized the phone number of my cell phone, a sign that I'd called once too often. "No, I just wanted—"

"Hold," she said. "I'm dealing with something here. Prowler."

I gave her time to deal with the prowler.

"Are you okay now?" I asked when she came back on the line.

"Sorry; I kind of lost it earlier, Charlotte," she said.

"Did the heart attack guy make it?" I had to know.

"There was no heart attack. False alarm. Kid dialed the number for a joke. Happens all the time."

"A joke?"

"Sure, we get hundreds of false alarms, mistakes, and stupid questions every single day. I hope you don't think this is an easy job."

"Never crossed my mind, Mona."

"Good."

"Are you feeling better about—?"

"The bitch brigade? No. I hated them. But she can still get to me. She had the nerve to call me and say she wanted to get together, reconnect. She claimed she really wanted to make amends. As if she could ever make amends for everything she did. To hell with that! I told her that I didn't need to reconnect with her, that I wasn't alone and friendless now, that I had you in my corner. I don't know where that came from, but we do talk a lot. Don't we? Even if it is for emergencies."

"That's fine, Mona. I am your friend."

"You know what? I was driving to work this morning and I spotted Serena Redding crossing the street to get into her giant yellow Hummer, big phony smile plastered all over her face. I wanted to drive right over her. I wanted to see that face splattered against my windshield and her—"

"Mona! Don't say that."

"Why not?"

"*Why not?* Be serious. Murder? That's not something you should talk about, especially in your line of work. Even if you are joking."

"Who's joking? I mean it. That fiend caused so much damage to people who couldn't even fight back. Maybe she even got you."

"She didn't. Or at least, I don't remember being bothered too much."

"You'd remember if she had. You saw the kind of things she did to other people. I thought you would understand."

"I know it was horrible. But, Mona, things turned out well for you. You have a good job and a good life." I hesitated. I didn't actually know if Mona had a good life, or even if she liked her job, as our interactions were confined to me calling for police, fire, or ambulance on a far too regular basis. "You wouldn't want to jeopardize all that because of some miserable—"

"Bitches. Just say it, Charlotte. And I don't mind jeopardizing anything if I have a chance to get back at them. Oh dammit, what now? Cat up a tree? Kid locked in the bathroom? Mother-in-law coming for a visit? Grow up, people. Get a life and save one too. Leave 911 for stuff that matters. For Pete's sake. Hold, Charlotte."

I thought hard. I'd been somewhat of a misfit in high school; small, flat-chested, and unfashionably studious. But I'd been lucky enough to team up with four other misfits—my friends Sally, Margaret, Pepper, and, of course, Jack. We'd stood together. We'd been united against cold shoulders, wedgies, and sneers. Except for minor losses, we'd been strong enough to keep ourselves safe from Serena and her pretty little coven. We're all still friends, although it's on and off with Pepper.

Obviously, others hadn't been so lucky. Especially Mona. But could Serena's power possibly extend from our distant teenage past, to mess up Mona's life and career? I'd let her down in high school. The least I could do was offer support now that Serena was back.

As soon as Mona picked up again, I said, "I've always felt bad that I didn't do much to help you deal with those—"

"Bitches," Mona said helpfully.

"I was part of the misfits—"

"Everyone knew that. You had each other for comfort and protection. Nice for the five of you."

I couldn't fail to hear the anger in Mona's voice. "True, and we all had problems fitting in for one reason or another. We kept each other safe and sane. Maybe if we'd thought about it more we could have extended our reach."

"It's all right, Charlotte. You acknowledged my existence. You were always decent to me. And you and Sally helped me out the day they left me naked in the locker room. Margaret let me copy her lab report when Tiffanee ripped mine up and flushed it down the toilet. Jack got my locker door open and helped me out that time Haley squeezed me into it after classes on that awful Friday afternoon. Without him, I would have spent the weekend there. Can you imagine what state my locker would have been in after that? And me too. I couldn't even stand up."

How could I have forgotten?

"And Pepper walked me home one day when they were waiting by the alley with those smirks on their faces. I never found out what they had in mind that time, but Pepper talked about her father being a cop as we walked by them. Loud enough for them to hear. She said he couldn't stand snotty teenagers." Mona snorted. "She kept talking about how much he hated bullies. And how he enjoyed making sure they experienced the juvenile system. How he'd like to embarrass their parents with some names in the paper and he thought an overnighter in solitary was good medicine. I was glad when she joined the police force later. She's a terrific cop. We see each other here in the hallways quite a lot."

I kept my mouth shut. Pepper's dad had been a bully himself and a parent who'd deserved to be embarrassed, although it never happened. There was no way he would have said anything like that. At the time, Pepper must have been channeling her own future police-officer self.

"I'm glad Pepper was there for you."

She said, "You all were at one time or another. They still got to me. It all made a difference. If it wasn't for you guys, I would have been abandoned by the world. And I would never have wanted to help people myself. I wouldn't be a 911 operator today. Gotta go. There's the line again. What now? Some idiot speeding in the snow skidded off the road?"

I sat staring at the phone. Perhaps if my friends and I had been kinder, more inclusive, Mona might have ended up being a tad more sympathetic to her frantic callers. Never mind; I had to admit she was efficient and that mattered too. Now I had a more worrisome thought. The image of Serena's dead face splattered against Mona's windshield while Mona laughed haunted me. But Mona was only fantasizing. Surely she wouldn't actually harm Serena. I climbed into the car with Jack and the dogs and worried all the way home.

— ◆◆ —

Jack and I celebrated the dogs' success and our own part in that achievement by ordering in pizza. I had picked up gourmet dog biscuits for the pooches earlier in the day. Who says life in Woodbridge lacks the glam factor?

It was Jack's turn to call in the order. "Remember anchovies on my side," I said. "And don't make that face."

We'd been working so hard that anything recreational had taken a backseat to training for weeks. It felt so good to chill out a bit. It was a busy weekend for me. I'd worked hard on my five time-management sessions. I was ready with my talks, handouts, checklists, worksheets, audio-visual enhancements, blog sites, Facebook group, and reading recommendations for The Busy Person's Guide to Managing Time and Life.

I wanted to be nicely rested up so my energy would be high enough to keep everyone interested. That's not easy on a snowy Saturday in the library auditorium.

I turned on the television to catch up on the weather while waiting for the pizza. Woodbridge had been suffering under a ton of late-season snow, including some serious snowfall the last week of March. On April 1, people started asking themselves if this was a joke.

"Ack. Who switched the channel to WINY?" I said.

"Not me, for sure," Jack mouthed.

The Busy Woman's Guide to Murder 15

"Where's the remote? I'll be blinded by Todd Tyrell's teeth. You know I hate his program. Let's watch—"

"I didn't switch it. The dogs must have," Jack said, rejoining me. I guess he thought I'd fall for that.

"Did you forget the anchovies?"

Jack plunked his lanky body on the sofa and made a face. "The pizza has been ordered according to your specifications."

I should have bitten my tongue. Jack is just short of a finished thesis for his PhD in philosophy. If he could get his head around those dusty nineteenth-century eggheads, surely he could order a pizza. Even one with anchovies. I'm told I can be just the tiniest bit bossy. I'm trying to fight that. Sometimes, I lose.

Meanwhile, on WINY Todd Tyrell was a vision of barely suppressed excitement.

Woodbridge Police are seeking a hit-and-run driver after an unidentified woman was struck and killed near the corner of Long March Road and Amsterdam Avenue this evening. There were no witnesses to the crime, in which the pedestrian was tossed in the air by the speeding vehicle and left to die on the deserted street. Police are suggesting slippery road conditions may have been a factor. The victim's name has not been released, as police have yet to contact the next of kin.

"That's horrible," Jack said. "Long March Road and Amsterdam Avenue? That's just around the corner from my shop. People drive way too fast for this snow."

"How do they know she was tossed in the air if there were no witnesses?" I grumbled. "I never believe a word that jackass says. How many times has he insinuated that I was implicated in a crime when I was absolutely innocent? That's why I hate this show. Did I say hate? I also meant loathe and detest. Where's the remote? I want to turn it off."

Of course, the remote was nowhere.

Perhaps the dogs had hidden it. I used the prehistoric method of touching the off button with my index finger. But our good mood had been punctured by the thought of a woman who'd gone out for a walk on an ordinary Friday night and ended up dying alone in the snow. Had she just achieved something she'd been striving for? Was she planning on celebrating, hurrying through the blowing snow to get home? To a husband? Children? People who loved her and didn't know she was lying cold and wet on a dark, quiet street?

I shivered.

Jack leaped up to answer the door as the pizza arrived, and the perfume of tomatoes, cheese and, yes, anchovies filled the room.

I dashed into the kitchen and opened a bottle of our favorite cheap merlot to go with the pizza. I filled two glasses and left Jack to put the pizza on plates. He prefers to eat it straight out of the box, but we're working at being grown up. We alternate: box one time and plates another. Grown-ups compromise. Truffle and Sweet Marie got the first bites. A well-deserved reward, with dog biscuits for dessert. Luckily, there wasn't a vet or a nutritionist within spitting distance.

I was just about to bite into my pizza when the phone rang.

Jack said, "Let it go to message."

I would have loved to let it go to message, but it was from Mona.

She said, "Oh my God!"

"Mona?"

"I didn't hit that woman."

"Hit that—"

"It wasn't me. And stop repeating what I say."

"Of course it wasn't you, Mona. It never crossed my mind that you had—"

"It's just that I told you I had that fantasy that I wanted to hit her with my car and see her face splatter all over my windshield and you might have thought I acted on it. Since that seems to be what happened."

"But I didn't think that."

"Well, you know how you're always getting mixed up in murder. I thought you might figure this was just one more to stick your nose in."

"Nope. Not sticking my nose in."

"Are you still dating that detective? What's his name? Oh, right, Tierney?"

"No," I said firmly. "I am not. Not at all."

"Are you still in touch with him?"

"In no way." I hoped that Jack was not paying attention. For some reason, everything about Connor Tierney seemed to set him off.

"Are you sure? He's still with the Woodbridge Police, isn't he? I haven't seen him for a while, but I hadn't heard that he'd left."

This was tricky. Connor Tierney was dealing with a difficult family situation but that was no one's business. "Out of town, I believe, for a few months. I don't have details, but you could try reaching him yourself, Mona."

"Are you out of your mind? Do you think I'm going to call a detective and tell him I was thinking about killing someone who then turns up *dead*? I suppose he wouldn't find that suspicious."

"He probably would, but we don't know who it is yet. There's no reason to believe it's Serena, no matter how much you might have liked that outcome."

"Maybe you're right. But I'm not going to talk to him anyway. But you could stay on top of the situation."

"Actually, I couldn't. We're not on the best of terms right now." And probably never would be. I'd let Tierney know that I wasn't interested in pursuing a relationship with him once I woke up to the fact that Jack was the man for me. Just because Jack was unaware of this didn't mean I was going out with other people.

"Someone needs to."

"It won't be me. And for what it's worth, I don't believe you would murder anyone, Mona."

Jack raised an eyebrow at that.

There was a long pause before Mona said, "Right. I didn't."

"Okay then. I'll let you go back to work and I'll return to my—" Actually, my pizza had lost its appeal. Something about the windshield image and the dead woman.

Mona said, "I just wanted to let you know that I hadn't killed her."

"Good."

She added, "But, one other thing."

I turned around so I wouldn't see Jack staring at me. Reproachful would have been the official name for his expression.

"Yes, Mona?"

"The woman who was hit. Do you think she was Serena?"

"I am certain it isn't. It will turn out to be a tragic accident. Random."

"Oh well. Can't have everything." At that, Mona hung up.

"Don't look at me like that, Jack. She called me."

"You promised, Charlotte."

"I know I did."

"You swore. No more murders."

"Damn straight. No more murders. None." I felt a knot in my stomach. This wasn't a murder. Nothing to worry about.

"Good. You going to eat your pizza?"

"It's all yours, Jack."

How could he eat after that news? I sure couldn't. I was too busy thinking about Mona.

Identify the time bandits in your life and give them the boot.

2

The small wood-paneled auditorium at the Woodbridge Public Library was bursting at its seams. The confined space already smelled of hot wool and simmering boots. Through the long windows, I could see the drifting white flakes as Woodbridge continued to be blanketed in the whitest spring on record. Even so, it wasn't enough to keep folks away from my first time-management workshop. That was a relief.

My organizing business needed a bit of a boost. The Woodbridge economy had taken a slam and businesses like mine had been slammed with it. Having an organizer come in and bail you out seems like a luxury to many people, and people cut luxuries in tough times. Check the magazine covers; everyone wants to reorganize their lives. No one wants to pay for it. I know that having an organized home, business, and schedule saves people lots of time and money. But business was down. Way down. All to say, I figured my series of courses would pay off in more ways than one. I was expanding into the time-management aspect and I hoped the exposure would raise the profile of Organized for Success.

Not surprisingly, every person was female except for one solitary man, who sat there doing his best not to seem out of place. I assumed that his wife had sent him, her own time being too valuable. I thought they all radiated apprehension. But I felt wonderful. This would be the first workshop I'd ever presented. All those people were here to listen to me. I would talk. They would pay attention. I could help them. I found myself beaming at no one in particular.

My friend Ramona's earrings dangled and shimmered as she made her way to the front of the room. She was resplendent in an indigo suede jacket and matching pants, her go-to meeting outfit, she called it. As she tapped the mic at the podium, her short silver hair glowed like a crown in the fluorescent light. "Welcome, ladies and gentleman," she said, "to the first in the Woodbridge Public Library's spring community cooperative programs. Our topic is The Busy Person's Guide to Managing Time and Life. I believe that you will learn how to get control of your days and weeks. Your time spent here will be a great investment. All five sessions are booked to capacity with waiting lists. I believe that's because of our workshop leader. I'm sure Charlotte Adams needs no introduction here in Woodbridge, but she'll get one anyway. After a few hectic years in the financial sector in the city, she returned home to Woodbridge determined to lead a simpler life, with time for friends and community. She now runs her own business, Organized for Success, and has helped hundreds of clients declutter and reclaim their homes. During this course, she'll help you do the same with your time and your life. Please welcome Charlotte Adams."

Ramona stepped back during the surprisingly wild clapping. I believe she's my biggest fan. She gradually edged toward the back of the room and gave me a surreptitious little wave. She was on reference duty that day, as she was most Saturdays, and she wouldn't be able to stay. Luckily, Ramona didn't need any advice on managing time.

I smiled out at the sea of eager faces. Almost everyone in the crowd smiled back at me, with the exception of the pale, blond, rabbity woman in the far corner of the back row, who averted her eyes and stared at the floor. I thought she was trying to disappear into the man's parka she was wearing. Make eye contact with every single person, I reminded myself.

"Thank you, Ramona, and thanks to the Woodbridge Library for its support of this program and our workshop. I'm very happy to be—"

Several hands shot up.

I blinked. Usually the questions follow information. In such a large crowd, it can be tricky maintaining control. That was something I'd have to get used to.

"I'll take one question," I said. "We need to stay on schedule to get everything done. That's something I'll talk about in more detail today. Yes?" I pointed to the most enthusiastic hand waver; a plump, permed grandmotherly type sitting two feet away from me in the front row.

Her happy face lit up as she gushed, "Charlotte! What did it feel like having a gun fired at you?"

"Horrible," I said. "And I—"

I should have said that I was there to talk about time management and not murder. Maybe made a little joke that murder was not my business. However, whatever I might have said would have been drowned out by the barrage of questions from almost all areas in the packed room.

"Charlotte! How many times have you actually been arrested?"

"I've never actually been—"

"Some of your friends have been injured. Do they avoid you now?"

"No. We're lifelong friends and—"

"Have the police started calling you when they need help?"

"The police like to solve their own cases. I like to concentrate on—"

"My neighbor is being stalked. Can you help her?"

"No, she should—"

"I think she needs protection."

"I am an organizer. I can't—"

"Do you own a gun?"

"No!"

"Do you plan to buy one?"

"Never."

"When did Woodbridge become such a dangerous place?"

Ramona stormed back to the front of the auditorium, ready to rescue. But I did not want to be rescued. And as a rule, I don't need to be.

I winked at Ramona so she'd get that point and said, "We are all in much more danger from overcommitment in our lives than we are from mysterious villains. Trust me on that. If you want to find out how to get rid of the time bandits that rob you of your days, the worries that steal your sleep, or the stress that can kill you, let's get started. For everything else, we have the police or *Law & Order* if you want entertainment value."

Ramona nodded approval. She likes to sock it to them too. I needed to stay on top of this crowd. I knew they'd love what I had to share with them. Or at least, I thought I knew that.

"So, here's the road map for today. We'll find out what the real obstacles are to you enjoying your life and why you are failing to meet your goals. We'll see how you can have a better balance in your life and in your family relationships."

Now why did I feel that wasn't quite as entertaining as the idea of me acquiring a weapon and firing at a felon?

— ◆◆ —

I guess I'd overestimated my fun value. To say nothing of the time-management problems of the Woodbridge populace. After the coffee break, I lost about 10 percent of the crowd, including my plump, permed questioner from the front row. I was surprised to note that the pale, rabbity blonde in the back corner returned to her seat. I smiled reassuringly in her direction, but there was apparently something quite fascinating on her shoes. Oh well.

Ramona had rejoined the group for coffee. She said, "Most people love it, Charlotte. A few have decided this kind of workshop wasn't quite what they wanted. They're probably already home watching *The First 48.*"

"That's fine with me. They can have a partial refund. I'm here for the ones who are serious about fixing their lives. We'll have better discussions with a smaller group."

The second half of the morning went well as we focused on finding out what is actually important in each of their lives. Before the break, everyone in the room had identified three goals that they wanted to achieve but had been unable to. Now we were identifying barriers and figuring out strategies to fulfill those goals. I love this stuff.

There were five sessions in total, but the Saturday session was a two-parter, and with luck, this serious group would be back the next week to talk about how they'd put their strategies into practice. I'd help with suggestions for developing good habits, finding support, positive self-talk, and tricks that had worked for others.

At the end of the session, when the would-be time managers filed out of the room, most of them stopped to say thank you. As I straightened out my notes to leave the front of the room ready for the second half of the day, I became aware of a woman sidling up the aisle. It was the blonde from the back row. As she got closer, I could see that her hair was seriously overbleached and underconditioned. Her skin was a flat fish-belly white, with a few angry blemishes, and she didn't meet my eyes. Under other circumstances, she could have been very pretty. I couldn't avoid noticing that her hands were rough and red, the nails bitten to the quick. This woman was a walking advertisement for stress.

I wanted to reach out and give her a comforting hug, but, of course, there was no way I could do that. Pity is not something that most of us seek. As it turned out, that wasn't what she was looking for at all.

"Hello," I said. "I hope the course so far is—"

This time she stared straight into my eyes. "Oh, Charlotte," she said in a high-pitched girlish voice. "Can you ever forgive us?"

I shook my head. "Forgive you?"

"Yes." She stared at the floor and I swear tears formed in her eyes.

"Forgive you for what?"

"We were so cruel. Heartless. And you were just a little thing." She giggled softly. "Of course, you're not very big now."

I said, "I'm sorry, but I don't understand."

"I'm Haley? Haley Brennan? I was Haley McKee? I used to be friends with Serena Redding?"

I blinked. The flawless ivory skin, the bouncy ponytail, the contagious grin were gone, and the sexy curves, if they remained, were buried under a loose sweatshirt that said OFFICE CLEANING SPECIALISTS. At least she'd taken off the man's jacket and was carrying it.

She said, "And Jasmin Lorenz and Tiffanee Dupont were my friends too, of course, to a certain extent, but mostly Serena."

When someone begs your forgiveness and you have no recollection of the incident they want to be forgiven for, that won't bring them any relief. One glance at Haley's pale face and anguished expression and I understood she was desperate to be forgiven. I could forgive her for whatever it was. What the hell. It wasn't going to cost anything, was it?

I said, "It was a long time ago."

"But you must have felt so humiliated."

I resisted the urge to shrug. I'd never felt humiliated by Haley, or Tiffanee or Jasmin or Serena, for that matter. Annoyed and occasionally cautious when they were in the vicinity, but that was it. I'd had a challenge with Helen "Hellfire" Henley, the teacher who terrified us all, but a few mean girls? I couldn't remember anything they'd done that was anywhere near humiliating. Mona Pringle's image flickered in my mind. Now she should be the one being asked for forgiveness.

"I'm over it," I said with a smile. "My life has turned out fine. I love my job, I have great friends, and I enjoy myself. Also, I've learned to not hold a grudge. It's a huge waste of time and energy."

She stared at me. "You don't hate us?"

"Why would I? We're all adults now. We move on."

Of course, looking at Haley I realized that her life hadn't turned out great. She seemed to be at the point of collapse. Could it be guilt? Misplaced if so, as she'd never succeeded in doing me any damage. Of course, she may not have caused *me* grief, but she'd sure brought plenty to other people.

She was weeping softly now. I glanced around. I preferred that the rest of the group not think I reduced one of their number to tears.

I patted her arm, doing my best to appear forgiving. "All in the past. The present's what counts."

"The present's not so great for me, as you can probably tell at a glance. And now Serena's back."

"I'd heard that." Damn. I hadn't meant to blurt that out. "Who told you?"

"I don't even remember," I said, not wishing to bring Mona Pringle into this. For one thing, Haley might need to ask for her forgiveness and I doubted that Mona was in that zone. I tried not to imagine Haley's sad face splattered against the windshield of Mona's car.

Haley stared at me, her large blue eyes magnified by the red eyelids. A few random tears straggled down her cheeks. "How could you forget something like that?"

Because Serena was so unimportant in my life that I had to be reminded who she was? I chose not to say that. "I may have even just overheard it when I was shopping at Hannaford's. But I never had much connection with Serena. I'm neutral on whether she comes back or not. I wouldn't even expect to run into her. What brings her back to Woodbridge? She's been gone since graduation, hasn't she? Are you looking forward to reconnecting with her?"

Oh boy. Wrong question. Haley was horrified and possibly even terrified by the idea of her friend coming back. I could see why. Life had not been kind to Haley, and Serena would be even less so when she got a peek at her. What was the purpose of life's losers except to amuse the strong and beautiful? The blue eyes filled with tears again. I reached over. This time I squeezed her hand.

"Why don't we get out of here and go to Ciao! Ciao! for coffee?" I said, adding quickly as her pallid face fell, "My treat."

"Oh, I don't know."

"I think the library staff has to get the room ready for the children's activities this afternoon. Don't feel any pressure, Haley. We don't have to go for coffee if you don't have the time. We can talk on our way to the parking lot."

She shivered in the hot room. "Coffee sounds good."

—✦—

Twenty minutes later we were each wedged into one of the tiny painted chairs at Ciao! Ciao!, facing each other over a fancifully painted table; bright blue and decorated with what seemed like garden gnomes in the middle of a wild polka. I was drinking a latte and Haley was going for just plain coffee. We each had chocolate biscotti to crunch or dunk.

"You know what? I always thought they were just a waste of money, but that does look delicious," she said as she eyed my latte.

"No one can beat them here."

She glanced around. "This place is so nice. I've never been here. I thought only snobs came here. Not that you're a—"

"Mostly students and professors, artists and some techy types and entrepreneurs who work out of home and like to mingle. I like it too."

With her oversize jacket that also said OFFICE CLEANING SPECIALISTS on the pocket, and her washed-out hair, Haley in fact didn't match the young and hip crowd in Ciao! Ciao! I kept resisting the urge to offer her a makeover. Everything is not about appearances. Haley certainly had changed since St. Jude's; there was no question about that. I put it down to guilt. Perhaps the way she'd treated people like Mona had come back to haunt her. Kicked in the keister by Karma.

She said, "You can't judge people by their looks. That's one thing I should have learned over the years."

I wondered what those years had done to Haley. Nothing too good was my guess, but I didn't want to ask too much. I did notice the rings on her finger. "I see you're married."

She shrugged and glanced away. "Yeah, right out of

high school. One of those unplanned things, you know. We have a fourteen-year-old daughter, Brie. Can you believe that?"

"Wow."

"She's a great kid. She's very smart. She loves poetry and reading."

"That must keep you busy, keeping up with her activities."

Haley gave me a strange glance. "Sure. That and the job. When she was younger, I was able to stay home with her. But now Randy—that's my husband; you may remember Randy from the football team at St. Jude's—"

I made a noncommittal head movement, the type that can be a yes or a no, depending on interpretation. I'd never spent any time thinking about the football team. Except for one guy who'd asked me out and then changed his mind for unexplained reasons, my interests had always been in geekier, smart boys. But as Haley had married one of the players, I chose not to mention that.

"He was a hero," she said, a faraway look in her red-rimmed eyes. "A big man around town. So handsome and nice too. Popular. I was lucky to snag him. Everyone was so jealous."

I nodded. I wasn't interested in pursuing the jealousy angle. Best to avoid that conversational trap.

She continued, "Anyway, Randy had a job in sales. He was dynamite. Things were great. We had a beautiful home, cars, and people to clean *my* house. Randy could sell anything, but the company went out of business and sales jobs in this area dried up in the bad economy."

"Sorry to hear about that."

"It's just the beginning. He has . . ."

I waited until she regained her composure. Whatever he had, it wasn't good.

She pulled herself together. "He has a chronic kidney condition. He's been pretty sick. Medical care and drugs have been killing us. It's been very hard on him. He doesn't have the stamina he used to have. I don't even know how long . . ."

"I'm so sorry."

She nodded. "He doesn't deserve it. He's always been wonderful to everyone. Not like me. But, anyway, we have to keep going. He took over an office cleaning business and I work with him. We have enough customers to keep us afloat. A lot of people know Randy and like him. We even do some weekend maintenance work at St. Jude's. How's that for a comedown for me?" Her lower lip quivered. I glanced away until she managed to pull herself together. "I shouldn't complain. We're lucky. We had a cabin outside of town near the ski hills. We moved there when we lost the house. I mean, we could be living in our car. Also, it's mostly nights so it gives us some freedom. If he isn't well, I can fill in and Brie helps out. I hate that she has to, but we need to survive."

My bet was that Haley worked darn hard too and worried while she did. Working nights couldn't be easy, especially with a sick husband.

I said soothingly, "Mmm. At any rate, I don't want you to worry any more about anything you may have done to me when we were kids. It's all water under the bridge. I'm glad to have reconnected with you."

"I'm surprised."

"At what?"

"That you can. It's just that they were so awful. The things we said, I mean. It takes a big person to forgive that, Charlotte."

Of course, I am a small person. Four feet eleven, to be precise. And I'd been prepared to forgive, although I wondered exactly what they might have said that might have been so awful that Haley couldn't believe I'd forgive her. I resolved not to find out. I was better off not knowing. And it wasn't as though I was going to spend any time with the former mean girls.

"I got a terrible shock when she died," Haley said.

"What? Who died?"

"That girl, the woman who was killed by the hit-and-run driver last night."

I dipped my chocolate biscotti into the latte. "For sure. Sad story, that."

"Did you know she was the spitting image of Serena? I saw her in the photo they showed on the news."

"She was? I saw the news last night, but they hadn't released any information about her."

"WINY had her photo on this morning. They showed members of her family too. That's awful, isn't it? Her sisters couldn't stop crying. It doesn't seem right to me to go up to a person whose sister has just died and ask them how they are feeling."

Just like that toad Todd Tyrell, stalking some grieving family member with his microphone stuck out in the hopes of a sound bite. I said, "I can't believe the media sometimes."

"But, of course, it wasn't Serena. Just some nice woman going home after being out hunting for her cat. That's what they said."

"Did they give her name?"

Haley shook her head. "I missed her name. I just saw the photo and the sisters crying. She was about the same age we are and she resembled Serena. I knew she couldn't have been Serena because Serena was an only child. And I heard she'd moved into a huge mansion out of town on the river."

She shrugged and glanced at her watch. "Oh sorry, Charlotte. I have to get a move on. I need to get the truck back to pick up my husband. We just have the one vehicle and I don't like to keep Randy waiting."

As we parted company and as I hadn't seen her in fourteen years, I figured I wouldn't see her again, except possibly at next week's session. I congratulated myself that I hadn't fallen into the trap of asking what they'd said about me.

"Thanks for spending time with me, Charlotte. And for forgiving me. You have no idea how much it means. I have a lot of regrets. Maybe I'll have them all my life."

I felt the need to cheer her up.

"I guess you can be thankful that it wasn't Serena who was killed," I said. "At least your friend is still alive."

Surprise washed over Haley's pasty face. "She's not my friend anymore. I don't know how I could have been her friend back then. I was under her spell. She was so . . . wicked. I wouldn't have been surprised if someone had killed her." She put her hand to her mouth. "That's awful, isn't it?"

Somewhat belatedly, I clued in that Haley would have been far more thankful if the victim had been Serena. At the minimum, Haley McKee Brennan would have been very, very relieved.

3

"So isn't that weird?" I said to my best friends in the world, Sally Januscek, Margaret Tang-D'Angelo, Pepper Monahan, and, of course, the ever-present Jack. It was getting close to eleven and we were still gathered that Saturday evening, happy to escape from the cares of the world and enjoy one another's company, as we had for so many years, always at Sally's place. As usual, Benjamin, Sally's busy doctor husband made himself scarce in the farthest reaches of the sprawling house. We were clustered around the coffee table in her relaxed living room, still strewn with kids' toys, most of them pointy. Every now and then one of us plunked down on the sofa or on a chair and jumped up with a squeak. Sally just laughed.

Unfortunately, the topic had turned to Serena and her fellow bullies and Haley's hope for forgiveness. I said, "I couldn't figure out what I was supposed to forgive her for."

"Are you serious?" Sally said.

"Why wouldn't I be serious?"

"Jason Gardner, for one reason."

"The football player?"

"Of course the football player. What other Jason Gardner is there?"

"The one who asked me out and then changed his mind?" My heart did a little flip. My first big crush.

Sally gave me her most dismissive glance. "Well, yeah. That's the Jason Gardner."

"Why? Did Serena and Haley have something to do with that? Why are you rolling your eyes, Margaret?"

"Because of course they did. I can't believe you don't know that."

"What?"

I noticed Sally, Margaret, and Pepper exchanging glances. Pepper cleared her throat at last. "I didn't realize you never heard anything about it. They circulated a rumor that you had something, um, contagious and weren't careful about not spreading it."

I opened my mouth, but no words came out.

Jack tuned in to the conversation. "What? That's a horrible thing to spread around about someone. Especially Charlotte."

"No kidding," Margaret said.

Jack was pacing now. "It's so nasty. I can't believe that they—or anyone—would invent that. What kind of creep could even dream up something like that?"

Sally said, "Of course *you* wouldn't, Jack. But Serena and her coven would have. I think it was Tiffanee who had a hankering for Jason. And, funny thing, didn't she end up going out with him?"

I said, "She did, I think. But how could they?"

Sally added, "With great glee. You weren't alone, Charlotte. They started a rumor I'd been pregnant and . . . got rid of the baby. In tenth grade. Me! The baby lover. I'd never even been out with a guy."

"That's right," Margaret said, "you were a late bloomer too."

"We all were," Pepper said. "We were pathetically innocent up against that crowd."

I stared at Sally, tall and gorgeous with her wild, tumbling blond curls and willowy figure, which had always snapped back, even after four children. It was hard to recall the gangly girl with the frizzy ash-colored hair when I saw this beautiful woman. I'd loved Sally for her forthright comments and bravery and the sense of humor that had been very well developed, even as a young teenager. I still did. I turned to Pepper, sleek and professional now that she was back on top of her game on the police force. She'd trimmed down and spent a bit of her salary on clothing and a new hairstyle. Unlike Sally, Pepper didn't thrive as a stay-at-home mom. Perhaps because of whom she'd chosen to marry.

On the other hand, marriage agreed with Margaret. She looked great, but, as always, her expression was deadpan. "And they said that I'd found a way to cheat on the Regents exam in chemistry."

"But you always had almost perfect marks."

"Right, and they put those under suspicion. That exam rumor got right to the administration as it was intended. Somebody made an anonymous call and was believed, unlike me. Luckily, my chemistry teacher knew better. That rumor followed me for a long time, probably cost me a recommendation for a scholarship. I hated those girls."

I guess I'd been out of town for that too. "Why would they do that?"

"I stood up to them once in the cafeteria."

"I remember that," Sally gasped. "It was the time that someone squirted ketchup over some girl's skirt."

Margaret nodded. "Mona Pringle. They did target that poor kid. I couldn't stand there and let that go. But she never tried to fight back."

I said, "What chance would she have had?"

Pepper said, "None. She wasn't any threat to them."

Sally shrugged. "It was just sport for them. The fun of being cruel. And, in practical terms, it would serve to keep other people cowed, so that they wouldn't retaliate. Like Margaret and the cheating rumor."

Jack said, "We all stood up to them in some small way."

"That's right," I said, "you got Mona out of the locker."

"I heard them laughing about it. I just went in and checked. She might have been there all weekend. That was the plan. The expression on her face was one of the saddest things I ever saw. And she wouldn't let me rat them out. She said it would be the worst thing I could do to her. I let it go, but I shouldn't have."

Margaret said, "Charlotte, you, Sally, and Pepper stood up to them too. Remember when you found Mona in the locker room, naked? And you found Sally who could lend her some clothes? And Pepper walked her home when they were waiting for her. But they made Pepper pay for that."

"How?" I said.

Margaret said, "Another rumor. They were specialists."

Pepper said, "Oh yeah. Can you imagine when my father got wind of the story that I'd spent the night with two guys from the team?"

I'd known Pepper's father. "That would have been awful."

"Yeah. I was black-and-blue for weeks and I didn't even know those two guys, let alone would I have done something like that. I found out who started the rumor from Nick. It was Jasmin. She had a thing for him and she actually thought he would think it was funny too. Nick told her what he thought of her and set the record straight too. People listened to him because he was a popular jock. Too late for my father, although Nick did his best to convince him."

Pepper had carried a torch for Nick Monahan all through

high school after that. Now she was married to him. Not
that it was any happy ending.

I said, "But you were still black-and-blue."

Pepper shrugged.

I said, "A lot of this is new to me. It's horrible."

"You had it easy. You were always flitting off with your
mother somewhere exotic. Paris. London. Milan. You
weren't stuck here all the time like us. I remember whole
semesters we never spotted you."

"Hang on. How did you know that they were the ones
who started the rest of the rumors?"

"They made sure you knew they were behind them, in a
way that kept you from doing anything about it. They probably let you know too, but you would most likely have been
obsessing about putting your socks in alphabetical order
and not paying attention."

I turned to Jack. "What about you, Jack? You stood up."

The other three laughed long and hard. In fact, I thought
Sally would choke.

Jack and I both said, "What?"

"Idiot. He was a guy."

"Still am," Jack said, "last time I checked."

I said, "So?"

Margaret said, "They only targeted girls, potential rivals."

Sally added, "And anyone helpless, disenfranchised. Sad."

Like Mona.

"They were typical bullies in that regard," Pepper said,
"and they used it to maintain their power base."

I thought about my earlier phone call. "Right. So I guess
I found out why Haley wanted my forgiveness today. But I
was thinking about Mona Pringle, and the incidents in the
gym and the locker. She's the one they should be asking
for forgiveness."

Margaret said, "No kidding. Poor Mona. They made her
life hell."

Sally squeaked. "She asked you for forgiveness. I can't get over that."

Pepper said, "Amazing. Not that I would forgive her for those bruises."

"Haley was a follower," Margaret added with contempt. "But even so, she was quite enthusiastic about her participation. I think Serena would get her to do some of the worst things and then, because Haley was needy herself, she'd do whatever, and if there'd been consequences, say with the school or with someone's parents, naturally, Serena would have made sure that Haley carried the can. She would have been expendable. And she never would have turned on Serena."

I'd never heard Margaret talk so much in one stretch.

"Serena was too dangerous," Sally said. "Probably still is. You're right about Haley, though, Margaret. I heard that she was the one who called in to say you had been seen cheating. She did great imitations of half the teachers. She could fool anyone. She was very proud of that."

I said, "Well, I guess a lot's changed. Because she sure isn't proud of herself now. I think she's been ground down by life."

"Glad to hear it," Margaret said. "Justice prevails."

I could understand that, but when I thought about Haley's life, I couldn't hate her.

I felt my cell phone vibrate in my pocket. I decided to ignore it. There are rules at our misfits nights. Taking business calls was top of the verboten list. Spouses are barely acceptable, as Benjamin, Nick, and Frank know. The phone kept vibrating, stopped, and started again. The fifth set of vibrations sent me to the kitchen on the pretense of getting some more salsa and cheese.

I checked the phone. Blocked number. On all five calls. I continued on to Sally's downstairs powder room and miscellaneous headless-doll storage area. The phone vibrated again.

This time I answered. Mona said, "I didn't do it."

I said in a whisper, "What is it, Mona? I'm not in a position to talk."

"Whoop de doo. Poor you. What about me?"

I sighed. Maybe all that stress of being a 911 dispatcher had sent Mona over the edge. "What about you, Mona?"

"I didn't do it."

"Yes, you mentioned that. Didn't do what?"

"Kill that woman, of course. What else could I be talking about?"

"Kill that woman? What—? Oh. You mean the pedestrian who died on the corner of Long March Road and Amsterdam?"

"There was only one woman killed in Woodbridge last night, Charlotte. Who else could I possibly mean?"

"I'm sorry, Mona. We've been through all this before. It's obvious that you are very upset, but I am missing something. Of course you didn't kill her. Who would even suggest such a thing?"

"I don't want anyone to suggest it. Don't tell anyone!"

"Well, who would I tell?"

"Your friends. You know how you all practically live in each other's pockets."

"Mona. I'm not about to tell anyone that you killed this poor woman and I have no idea why you would think I might."

"Didn't I tell you I wanted to kill Serena?"

"Yes, but—"

"And this woman was the spitting image of her. I mean a body double. Didn't you see the news? They had her photo."

I felt a little buzz around my head. "I missed the photo. Mona—"

"And didn't I say I wanted to run Serena down and see her body splat up against my windshield?"

"Words to that effect."

"So I don't want anyone to think I murdered this innocent person. That's all."

"Okay. Well, Mona. My lips are sealed. I won't say a word to anyone and I hope you won't try to run Serena down if you do see her."

Mona laughed, a strange, demented, hyena-like chortle. Goose bumps rose on my arms. "Mona?"

"Yes?"

"Are you all right?"

"I'm just peachy, Charlotte. Can't you tell?"

"Promise me you won't do anything . . . inappropriate." Okay, I realized as soon as the words slid out that it was a pretty silly promise to exact from someone who was obviously losing it. The problem was, did Mona present a danger to Serena? I'd just learned that Serena was a nasty piece of work, no question. But splatting on the windshield wasn't the type of tidy solution I'd prefer.

"Sure," Mona said. "You can trust me not to do her any harm. Good-bye, Charlotte."

"Wait!" I must have shouted it because outside the bathroom door, Sally shouted back. "Charlotte? Are you on the phone in there? Or did the killer zombie dolls get you?"

"Ha-ha," I answered. "I'll be fine. I'm fighting them off. See you in a couple of minutes." I changed to a whisper. "Mona? Are you there?"

"Where else would I be? It's not like I have much of a social life. That was all ruined for me when I was a kid."

"What about the other dispatchers? Don't you hang around and—?"

"And what? Compare dead and dying stories? So how many shaken babies today, Sharmaine? How about those heart attacks, Brian? Hey, Jim, I bet you're some jealous I got the guy with the nail in his—"

"I didn't mean to be insensitive. I'm just worried. You seem so upset."

"Oh yeah? Where were you when I needed you? When I was a tormented kid?"

"But I helped you. When you were in the change room that time?"

"Well, it wasn't enough to make them go away, was it?"

"No. And I'm sorry about that. I didn't understand everything they were doing. Honestly. I regret not being more aware."

"You had nothing to worry about, did you? They couldn't get to you, not even that thing with the football guy."

"You knew about that too?"

"Sure, I overheard all the rumors. Everyone at St. Jude's did."

"I didn't even understand they'd done that. But remember, I'm not the villain here, Mona."

"True. Not your fault. You were little and cute and smart and had beautiful clothes and a famous mother."

"Actually, I would have traded places with a lot of people just to have a normal, loving family."

"I doubt you would have. I had a normal family and they just told me to get over it, fight back, tough it out. All that crap. My life was a living hell."

"Oh. I just thought your family would be there for you."

"You know what? Most of the kids who were the most bullied, they had loving families who proved to be useless. And the bullies? They had them too."

"I am truly sorry I couldn't have helped you more. By the way, Haley came to see me and I believe she regrets her part in all that."

"Does she, now?"

There was that laugh again. "Mona?"

"Regrets her part? That's a laugh and a half."

"I don't think life has been all that kind to her."

"Oh, cry me a river. I still remember the time she spilled water on my seat so everyone would think I wet my pants. The expression on her face, drunk on power and cruelty."

Right. That and the ketchup attack. Poor Mona. "She seems very sorry."

"Maybe not nearly as sorry as she's going to be. Goodbye, Charlotte, I'm heading off to work now."

I stared at the phone after Mona clicked off. What did Mona mean? Was there any slight chance that she had actually killed the woman on Amsterdam, and was Serena in some kind of danger from her? Worse, had I drawn attention to Haley, and by doing that, set her up as a target for Mona's revenge fantasy? I like being in charge. I love knowing what to do. But not this time. In this case, I had no idea what was going on or how to deal with it.

I glanced at two headless dollies propped up by the wastepaper basket. The goose bumps were back, bigger than ever.

"Charlotte?" Sally banged on the door. "Do I have to come in there and get you?"

I had begun to wonder if there were enough nachos in the world to cheer me up when I rejoined the gang.

Jack said, "Everything all right, Charlotte? You look . . ."

"I look what?"

"Yeah, you do," Margaret added.

Jack said, "I don't know. Like something's wrong. Are you upset? I can go get some more nachos. You like the jalapeños? I guess I shouldn't have pigged out on them."

"It's okay. I have something on my mind, but it's not nachos. Or jalapeños."

"My money's on those headless dolls creeping you out," Margaret said. "I can never even use that powder room without getting nightmares. I put it down to delinquent parenting."

Sally shot Margaret a dirty look. "Let's see how you do, Miss Smart-Ass, when your time comes."

"Which it won't." Margaret kept insisting on no children, despite relentless lobbying by her parents and Sally. She stuck to her arguments that Frank's family was grown-up and he had no desire to start another one. We all knew that Frank would do whatever Margaret wanted. I was on Margaret's side. Surprisingly, Jack and Pepper, both notoriously baby crazy, kept their noses out of it for once, and that was a good thing.

"Can we watch a DVD now? Are there no more under-dog losers that we could root for?" I said.

Sally wasn't ready to give up yet. "Were you on the phone in there, Charlotte? Because I can see the dolls making you scream, but not leading to a bizarre, furtive conversation."

"Hardly furtive," I said defensively. "Or bizarre."

"You were on the phone," Pepper said. "I recognize your pattern of deflection. So it won't work this time."

"Maybe I was, but that's hardly illegal."

"Unfriendly though," Margaret said. "These nights are supposed to be sacrosanct."

"I know, but it was kind of an emergency. She kept calling."

Sally wasn't letting go. "Priorities, Charlotte. You of all people with your obsessive-compulsive tendencies should know the rules."

"Obsessive-compulsive? A tiny bit overfocused from time to time, I admit, but I'm hardly obsessive-compulsive."

I don't know why they all found that so funny.

"So," Sally said, "since you violated our long-standing

agreement about taking calls, at least you can tell us who was on the phone."

"Someone who was worried about something."

"Oh, *so* not good enough," Pepper said. "We need details. Specifics."

"That's not fair to the person. I promised that I would keep our conversation confidential." At the same time, I kept asking myself, Was anyone in danger from Mona? Should I be confiding in my friends to ensure that nothing happened?

"Maybe we should talk about it. You are with the perfect group. Margaret's a lawyer and she'll keep it confidential. Jack's a philosopher, or just a couple of months short of a thesis anyway. Sally, being a mother of four should give you an edge on figuring out bad behavior. And Pepper's a cop and she may know what to do."

"So what did your friend want that got you so worried?" Jack said.

"She wanted me to know that she hadn't killed that woman."

Pepper's head snapped to attention. "What woman?"

"The one who was killed in the hit-and-run on Amsterdam."

"Why would you think she had killed her?"

"Because she had previously told me if she saw Serena that she would enjoy seeing her splat all over the windshield."

"That's brutal," Jack said.

Margaret glanced around the group and shrugged. "I can kind of understand it though."

Pepper nodded. "Me too, for sure. But it doesn't make it right."

"Not the best course of action," Margaret said somewhat reluctantly.

"Lots of people felt that way," Sally said. "I suppose if

I'd seen Serena sashaying across some street I might have been tempted to press on that old accelerator. Maybe just enough to give her a little scare."

Jack gave her a startled look.

"Right," I said, "but of course the victim wasn't Serena. This person on the phone just wanted me to know that she hadn't, you know, run over this woman by mistake, thinking it was, um, Serena. At least, I believe that's what she wanted. She was kind of over the edge. Strung out. The whole thing was a bit crazy."

"Why did whoever it was call you anyway? What connection do you have?"

"I don't know why she called me. She just needed to reach out, I suppose, and we have a bit of a history."

Pepper said, "No harm done. Anyway, as she was calling to say she didn't hurt this person and I imagine since the death was so horrible, whoever she is probably decided that her fantasy of revenge was a bad approach. Yes?"

I bit my lip. "Maybe."

"What do you mean by 'maybe'?" Pepper said, still with that cop alertness about her.

"Well, there was something else."

"Out with it," Sally snapped.

"I told her about Haley being sorry for the way they treated her . . . this person . . . and she didn't react the way I expected. I'd thought she'd see that we aren't teenagers anymore and we've all gotten past what was done to us."

"Not that you remember any of it," Sally said. "Lucky little skunk."

"I remember some of what they did to her. Her life wasn't ruined, although I could understand how it could have been. It's a shame she's on the verge of a breakdown over stupid events from so long ago."

Margaret said, "Question time. Is Sally the only one who isn't over it? Raise your hand if you would have been just a teeny bit tempted to run over Serena if you'd seen her on the road in the dark with no witnesses. Tell the truth and nothing but the truth, you guys."

Margaret's own hand shot up first. Sally laughed and raised both of hers. "Of course, I wouldn't actually commit murder because I couldn't bear to leave my kids while I served my life sentence. Otherwise, hey. Splat you, Serena."

My eyebrows rose as Detective Sergeant Pepper Monahan's hand inched up. "Not saying I'd do it, just that I can understand the desire."

I glanced at Jack. His hands were poised over the nacho bowl and showed no signs of being raised.

"Charlotte?"

I shrugged. "No. I guess I didn't realize everything those horrible girls were up to. But I get it. Honest. And, trust me, this person got treated a lot worse than you guys or me. Infinitely."

"That must have been Mona Pringle on the phone," Pepper said. "Who else could it be? She's always been a bit peculiar and they sure put her through a living hell. At least she didn't end her own life like some bullied kids."

Margaret said, "Don't bother to deny it, Charlotte. We can tell by the expression on your face that it was Mona."

"Fine, but I didn't *tell* you. She's still really angry at Serena and Haley."

Pepper shrugged. "Haley *was* pretty awful."

"But she's a woman now, with a sick husband and a child who has to help out with the cleaning business. She has her own troubles. She's changed."

Pepper said, "Yeah. I've seen her around town. For one thing, she hasn't aged well, looks like crap."

It was easy for Pepper to judge. She was back to her prebaby weight, working out and sporting a two-hundred-dollar hairdo, with her bad-boy husband behaving himself.

I said, "Haley might have been cruel back then, but I

think she was sincere in her regrets. I'm not the same person I was in high school. We grow up and change and our brains develop."

Pepper sneered. "So what? If you knock off a bank and feel bad about it afterward, does that make everything all right?"

"I suppose it's not impossible that she is regretful," Margaret said.

There was something in her tone. I said, "You don't believe it?"

Margaret shrugged. "She always seemed to be having a good time when she was making someone else's life a living hell. My memory is quite clear about this. So forgive me if I don't shed a tear. Or fully believe her."

"I hear you," Pepper said. "She was a nasty little toad and we all felt the sting, except possibly you, Charlotte, because you weren't paying much attention. I think that was during your phase when you wanted to find your father."

"That wasn't a phase. That was—"

"Haley gave me plenty of grief too," Sally said. "Not just the rumors and backbiting, but she actually slammed me into a bay of lockers once. I could hardly move my shoulder for weeks. I'm with Margaret on this."

Pepper said, "So she's had a rough life. I'm thinking that Serena wouldn't give Haley the time of day now. Maybe Haley's afraid that Serena still has the urge to torment people and she could become a target herself this time. Haley must have all kinds of dirt on Serena. Maybe she's seeking allies."

I turned to Jack. "I suppose you have an opinion on this too?"

"I don't remember these perpetrators that much. Are you going to eat the rest of this salsa?"

Sally said, "Oh, come on, Jack, never mind the salsa. How could you forget Haley? She was the one who brought up the fact you were adopted in front of everyone in the cafeteria. Remember her jeering?"

I blurted out, "I remember that day. I'd forgotten it was Haley who was behind all that. She thought she was going to get to you. But I remember your response, Jack. You said you were lucky to be born with good basketball genes and better chess genes and to have adoptive parents who were better than anyone's biological family. You tossed it back to her. You said if she'd had decent parents who were doing the right job, she wouldn't need to try to make herself feel worthwhile by putting others down. You said you felt sorry for her. You said if she had any self-esteem, she'd find some decent friends."

Margaret laughed. "That's true. I still remember the look on her face. You struck a chord."

Pepper said, "I'm betting if anything bad happened to you from that point until you graduated, you could trace it back to her and the rest of them. They would have hated that they couldn't crush your spirit."

Sally said, "I bet the only reason you were a target was because you were our friend."

"Maybe. Nothing awful happened to me. I don't even remember the details clearly. I mean, it was how long ago? You can't go carrying this resentment and anger around with you. I'm with Charlotte. This Haley girl may have done some evil deeds, but if she's asking for forgiveness, let her have it."

Margaret crossed her arms. "She didn't ask *me* for forgiveness and it'll be a cold day in hell when she gets it."

Jack said, "We've all done things we're ashamed of. Let it go."

"You must be kidding," Sally interjected. "I have my own children and I don't want to forget what it was like coping with those bullies. I want to listen to my kids and pay attention if someone is making their lives miserable."

Pepper tossed in her two cents' worth. "One of the reasons I became a cop was to make sure no one ever had that kind of power over me again."

Jack just shook his head.

Margaret said, "Don't judge us, Jack. You got off easy with that adoption comment. But you were a guy. They didn't find the right way to harm you. Or Charlotte. Girls were their targets. Mona's life must have been unbearable. She might not have been the only one. And you're right, Pepper. I think one of the reasons I went into law was so that I could sue the pants off anyone who ever tried to pull stunts like that."

Sally said, "One of the reasons I got a gun was so—"

"You do not have a gun, Sal," Jack said.

As Sally produced little Madison's water pistol, I sat there thinking. I was pretty sure that Serena and her gang hadn't influenced my career. But it might have had an impact on Mona's. Mona's life had been intolerable. I was now sure that there were many more crimes against her than I'd ever realized. And they had been crimes. Real crimes. Now Mona made her living ensuring that people were helped and rescued when they needed to be. She was good at that job too. Although if she continued to unravel, that could change. Mona could lose the self-respect she'd worked so hard to gain. My thinking had changed a bit. I'd found it easy to feel sorry for Haley when she approached me. Now I wasn't so sure.

*Keep a master list of goals, projects, tasks, and even dreams.
Check it every day and make sure that at least one item
from that list is on your daily To Do.*

4

As we finally headed out to our snow-covered cars, I stood
near Pepper as I swept the latest layer of snow from the
roof of my Miata. "I sure was lucky I invested in snow
tires this year. My all-seasons would have been hell in all
this snow." After years of being on the outs with Pepper,
I felt comfortable with her once again. We'd been inching
toward that for a while, but as the result of events from
the previous June, any hard feelings she'd nurtured were
gone. I felt I could trust her advice. I said, "This is probably ridiculous, but what if Mona seriously intends to harm
someone? What if she is over the edge? We'd feel pretty
bad if Serena was killed or injured, wouldn't we?"

She didn't hesitate. "As a police officer, I'd be appalled
and I'd have no choice but to take action. I'm sworn to uphold the law. Personally though, I wouldn't lose sleep over
any of those bullies."

In the pale light of the snow, Pepper's face was hard. If
Mona did something wrong, Pepper would arrest her with-

out a qualm, but there'd be no tears for the victim. I was beginning to understand that was a common reaction from my usually kind and gentle friends.

I said, "Isn't it better to take action before something happens? Mona's not even herself, she's so worked up. She sounds more distraught and angry every time I talk to her. What should I do? Go over there? I don't actually know where she lives."

"You don't do anything. You don't get yourself all involved. Do not go over to her house or even try to find out where it is. I will talk sense to Mona. I'll figure out if she needs some professional help. She's a trained worker with our department; she works with the police. For sure, she can't be going around talking like that."

"Or doing something that can't be undone."

"Leave it with me."

"Okay."

"Charlotte?"

"Yes?"

"I mean it."

"Hey, fine with me. I have no desire to get any more caught up in this situation. I have more than enough to do this week. I was just minding my own business when she called me. I'm still not so sure why that was, unless she thought of me as a friend. You helped her out and stuck up for her, but maybe she chose not to talk to you because you're with the police. I get that. I feel bad telling you about this situation, but I was concerned."

"Remember what I'm saying. Don't start sticking your nose into an active investigation."

"Don't worry," I said as I got into my car to follow Jack, who had arrived separately in his ancient dung-colored Mini-Minor that evening. "I'm happy to leave you with this problem. I know you'll handle it."

—✠—

It had stopped snowing by the time we approached the yellow Victorian house I loved. I was still thinking about the mean girls and their impact on people like Mona. As we got out of our cars, I said, "We were very lucky in our friendships. You know that?"

Jack turned to face me. "Still are lucky."

"And you're right, Jack. I guess if you can't forgive, it would only bc bad for you."

"Sure. It would blight your existence. Make you bitter. Color the way you perceive life and limit your joy."

Pondering that, I headed up the stairs to take the dogs out. It was a bright, cold April night, with eight inches of recently fallen snow turning our street into a wonderland. That would have been good at Christmas, but it was just plain bizarre at this time of year. It was beautiful though. Quiet, calm, and soothing now that we didn't have to drive in it. The dogs did not share my opinion on the wonderland. They do not do cold and snow. It's summer or nothing for them. This might have been the shortest dog walk on record.

In our brief absence Jack had made himself at home in my living room and Truffle and Sweet Marie flung themselves at him to warm up.

I joined him on the sofa and said, "The others seemed pretty bothered by it."

"Because we were all talking about it. That brought it back. But I bet they don't give it a moment's thought otherwise. We're all busy and successful in our own way, Charlotte. That childish cruelty can't do anyone any harm now."

"Hope you're right. I stirred it up, I suppose, by talking about Haley and the victim."

The rest of the evening, I was distracted by thoughts of

Mona. She had obviously not forgiven her tormentors and just as obviously had no intention of starting now.

Was Mona a danger to anyone in her angry and emotional state? Or was I just being overly dramatic? I couldn't shake the thoughts as I tidied up and laid out my clothes for the morning, or later as I made my To Do list. That's right, even on Sunday, there's always something worth doing. I made sure I had no more than five key items identified, and four of them were just plain fun. That was something I'd come to realize in the past few months. I kept a master list of chores, tasks, goals, and targets, and checked it first. One of my goals was to have more fun. Another was to spend more quality time with Jack. Still another was to try to eat better. Once I hit thirty-one, I started to notice that certain foods stayed with me, in places I'd rather they didn't settle. Oh well, nothing lasts forever.

I set two places for breakfast, something new that Jack and I were sharing in pursuit of that healthier post-thirty lifestyle, not that Jack ever gained an ounce. Breakfast was my job. Jack used to love to cook, but I hated the chaos he'd create in my kitchen and now he seems to have forgotten how to do anything except order out. I wondered if there was a solution to that as I cut up some vegetable sticks for the next day, prepared some juice, set out the cereal box, vitamins, and a bit of fruit. I made sure the coffee was ready to go. I emptied my handbag and put away papers that needed to be filed, added a few things to my ongoing grocery list on the fridge. I washed my face, exfoliated, brushed my teeth, flossed, slathered on moisturizer to prevent dry winter skin, even though winter should have been long gone. All good, but even I knew it was boring.

Jack had been reading a crime novel on the sofa throughout this, one dog asleep in the crook of his arm, the other stretched out against his leg. It was an updated Norman Rockwell picture, even with Jack's soft snores as he dozed off. Still, I couldn't relax. I knew it was because of my Mona worries. I kept expecting the phone to ring. I checked my cell phone. I checked my landline. I checked my cell phone again. No new messages from Mona or anyone else. Jack opened his eyes, yawned and stretched.

I said, "Let's just get the Ben and Jerry's and not talk about this whole bullying thing."

"But you've already brushed your teeth."

"I'll brush them again. What part of 'don't talk' isn't clear to you, Mr. Philosopher?"

We polished off a tub of Ben & Jerry's New York Super Fudge Chunk. It might have been winter outside, but good old-fashioned ice cream met some deep inner needs, for sure—stoked my serotonin and all that. Even so, by the time I said good night to Jack and watched him lope lazily down the stairs to his own apartment, brushed my teeth again, and settled down in my frog pajamas under my snuggly duvet with my two warm little dogs at the end of the bed, all that ice cream hadn't been enough to put Mona Pringle out of my mind.

All night long, I tossed like a stormy sea.

—◆◆—

"What time is it?" I said, staggering out of bed.

I'd been talking to myself, but Jack answered, "Nine."

He was already back upstairs. I pushed aside the recurring thought that it would be nice if he just lived here. No point in making myself miserable. I grumped, "Since when do I sleep in until nine? I am up at dawn every morning, raring to go. People hate me for it. Nine? Are you kidding?"

"First time for everything. I walked Truffle and Sweet Marie for you. They didn't sleep in. I fed them too. They didn't care for the snow much and they're recovering under their blanket on your sofa. Coffee?"

I nodded. I sat in grateful silence as the heavenly scent

filled the room. I would have enjoyed spending the morning in my cozy apartment with Jack, but he had some urgent thing to take care of and needed some time at the shop. He headed off to CYCotics shortly after breakfast, dressed for the tropics as usual.

I glanced at my To Do list. It was full of fun things, but I was sure that I wouldn't be able to relax until I figured out how to handle this situation with Mona. It didn't help that everyone seemed to be telling me to butt out. I tried calling her, with no luck. Mona must have been one of the few stubborn souls without an answering machine.

I checked the thermometer and decided that Woodbridge must have broken the record for cold on this day. I suited up: lined jeans, puffy white parka, and my only pair of warm no-nonsense boots. Lined gloves, a scarf, and my least favorite item of clothing: a hat. The dogs declined to accompany me.

Ten minutes later, I drove by the corner of Long March Road and Amsterdam and turned right. This was the site of the fatal accident with the woman who'd had the misfortune of looking like Serena Redding. I pulled in and sat there thinking. Someone had erected a small wooden cross on a snow-covered patch by the side of the road. Two teddy bears and at least a dozen bouquets of flowers were stacked around it. I got out of the Miata and walked over to them. The snow hadn't been plowed on the sidewalk and it had drifted in front of the makeshift shrine. My feet were still dry, but the drifts soaked my jeans quickly. That didn't seem important right at that moment. It seemed so sad, a person of my own age struck down because she was in the wrong place at the wrong time. I shivered.

A red-faced woman walking a large shaggy dog of no distinguishable type stopped and shook her head. The dog sat obediently beside her while she chatted with me. Her breath left frozen white trails in the air. "The guy just hit her and drove away."

"Yes. It's hard to believe. Terrible thing."

"Did you know her, then?"

"I didn't, but I heard about the accident on the news and I just wanted to"—not the best time for the truth, I decided—"pay my respects."

"Bethann had her issues, but she was too young to die like that."

"Bethann? I hadn't even heard her name."

She sniffed and nodded in the direction of the house. "She was the best of that bunch, Bethann Reynolds."

I decided I didn't want to hear what the neighbor thought of this Bethann, whom I didn't even know, and her family. "Well, I'll be off. Oh. Bethann Reynolds, did you say?"

"Yes. Did you know her after all?"

"Um, maybe. A long time ago. In high school. I have a vague memory of her. Quiet, kept to herself."

"That's her. Very pretty woman, but didn't socialize. Just taught school and came home. No boyfriends that I ever saw. But she was no pushover. I heard she'd just won a lawsuit against a former employer. She told me she was tired of taking crap from people and she was going to take care of herself from that point on. She said people had better watch out. From now on it was just her and her cat. She liked her cat a lot. That's why she was outside with all that blowing snow. Searching for the cat. It was an indoor cat. She'd had it declawed so you can imagine she was in a panic. Didn't think it could look after itself."

The huge shaggy dog whimpered.

"Brutus here was terrified of that cat. Weren't you, boy? You know, I feel bad. I heard her calling for that cat and I didn't come out to help. Maybe . . ."

"It's not your fault," I said automatically. She nodded,

glad to be off the hook. But as I spoke memory fragments were flooding in. Back in high school Bethann Reynolds had been a tall, awkward, and painfully shy girl. She had been very pretty in a pale, anxious way. Did I just imagine she was always glancing over her shoulder? Getting away from high school improved all our looks a lot, in my opinion.

"My own dogs are not good with cats," I said. "Where exactly did Bethann live?"

"You're not one of those reporters, are you?" The dog growled. "Won't give people a decent bit of privacy? Buzzards. Vultures, preying on the—"

"No. I'm not. I'm just an ordinary person."

"You'd better not be lying."

An echoing growl from the shaggy dog.

"It's the truth. I hate those guys," I said, as much to the dog as its owner.

She pointed two houses down to a white house with green shutters. Even from where we stood I could see that the draperies were tightly closed in every window.

"She lived alone with the cat?"

"The mother and one sister lived here too, although they come and go. The other sister lives in Poughkeepsie. They're a bit flaky at the best of times. This is not the best of times, so I wouldn't want to see anyone bothering them."

"Don't worry about that. Thank you." I headed back to my car, snippets of memories continuing to pop into my mind. Unless I was mistaken, back in high school, Bethann Reynolds had been yet another target of Serena and her pals. Now she was dead. So many people had been targeted back then. Did this mean anything? Was it just a crazy coincidence? Life is full of them, but it seemed too close to my conversation with Mona. Of course, Mona would have no logical reason to harm Bethann. But was logic driving Mona?

———

I dropped in to CYCotics to see Jack. The shop opens at eleven on Sundays. I found no Jack, but one of the part-timers who did the bike repairs was on duty, doing spring bike tune-ups for optimistic Woodbridgers. I was surprised because I rarely see these part-time employees. However, this day customer sightings were even more rare. Jack had finished whatever he'd gone in to do and headed home for the day. By the time I trudged up my stairs, he was already settled in on the sofa. He'd taken the dogs out again and made another pot of coffee.

"Sit down. I'll get you a cup. The news is bizarre again," he said as he poured dark fragrant brew into our matching Organized for Success mugs.

"I need to change out of these horrible wet jeans first. And what do you mean?" I yawned as I headed to the bedroom to change and hang up my sodden jeans to dry. "More weird than usual?"

When I returned, Jack handed me a fresh mug and said, "Well, yeah. I think so. Two people killed in Woodbridge in two days. Even though we've dealt with some bad stuff in the past two years, that is still weird."

I took a sip out of self-preservation. "Someone else was killed?"

"If you believe Todd Tyrell."

"Not sure I do and don't even suggest that I might be interested in watching WINY and ruining the rest of this day."

Jack's Y chromosome kicked in and he pressed the remote. Todd Tyrell, who seems to be permanently on the television screen, beamed out, his teeth gleaming like the sun on the fresh snow outside.

In a second shocking incident in less than two days, another Woodbridge woman has been killed by a hit-

and-run driver. Police have yet to reveal the name of the thirty-two-year-old woman who was struck while crossing the street to her vehicle in Ambleside Acres, a quiet neighborhood in the north end of Woodbridge. There were no witnesses to the crime, which police believe occurred sometime after two and before six this morning. The woman's body was discovered by a man walking his dog this morning. For more breaking news, stay tuned to WINY, your window on Woodbridge.

Sometime after two and before six? Who would be out at that time? Woodbridge's few clubs are in the uptown and downtown areas, not in the suburbs. A horrible thought occurred to me. What about Haley? She was connected to this whole business. She'd said she worked nights in her husband's cleaning business. What was his name? Oh, right, Randy. There were a lot of small businesses bordering the Ambleside Acres area, restaurants and offices mainly. Could she have been going from one cleaning job to another, not worrying about speeding vehicles in the middle of the night?

"Jack, what if it's Haley?"

"Haley who?"

"What do you mean, 'Haley who'? Haley McKee, now Brennan. What is wrong with you? Remember we were talking about Serena and her evil cabal? Haley was the one who asked me for forgiveness. We just had this talk at Sally's last night, Jack. Weren't you paying attention?"

He shrugged. "Don't take it personally, Charlotte. Sometimes I tune out when you girls get into certain topics."

"Anyway, Mona was talking about wanting to kill Serena Redding. Everyone thinks that Haley did a lot of Serena's dirty work. Mona hates her too. It would make sense in a demented way. Don't look at me like that."

"I'm not looking at you like anything."

"Are."

"Not anymore, I'm not."

"Fine. I have to get dressed and go see for myself."

"But they won't let you see the body."

"Of course I am not going to try to see the body. I meant go see if Haley's all right."

"Do you even know how to find her?"

"Luckily, I do. I have her address in my attendee file, for the follow-up questionnaire. And I have a perfectly good GPS system. Take that, buddy."

"Huh."

Call me crazy, but I thought it was the only thing to do. I just had to know. I put down my wonderful mug of coffee and headed to my room to get ready. I changed again and put on wool pants this time and a bulky charcoal sweater under my down vest. I had to find a dry hat and scarf. My sturdy and practical boots were still fine. Especially as I was wearing the socks that were good to minus thirty degrees.

As I emerged ready to go, Jack said, "Want me to come with you?"

I did want that. "Thanks. You might want to put a jacket on over that Hawaiian shirt. Just this once." I smiled, but it didn't stay on my face long. "Did you just mutter 'bossy'? Did you?"

Haley's address was in a rural area, outside Woodbridge proper, accessible through a network of back roads. A half hour after we set out, we were bouncing down a rough country road about an inch wider than my Miata, passing snow-covered fields, old farmhouses, the occasional new country home, and even a quick glimpse of one lonely junkyard filled with mountains of old cars. Even with the acres of sparkling snow, the naked trees seemed barren and lonely. I figured the drive would be prettier in the summer when the trees were leafed out and the farmer's fields filled up.

The road had recently been plowed or we wouldn't have had a chance in my low-slung car. We hurtled over one last hill and spotted the sign that said BRENNAN. The long driveway curved and twisted a quarter of a mile to a clearing before a small weathered cedar house, with a few new boards showing pale against the silvery walls, and a red metal roof giving it visual impact. The drive had also been well plowed and the long series of steps leading up to the door had been shoveled clean. A battered white van sported a graphic of a smiling red squirrel wielding a broom. OFFICE CLEANING SPECIALISTS was lettered below it. An even more dilapidated pickup with an attached plow was parked off to the side. You'd have to be able to dig yourself out to live out here, for sure.

As I knocked and stood shivering, I glanced around at the outbuildings—a lopsided garage and an even smaller version of the house, which I took to be a workshop, as there was power running to it. The ribbon of smoke from the chimney told us that someone was home. Not that they answered our repeated knocking. I was too cold to enjoy the scent of wood smoke.

Jack stood around as if it were a summer day, but I was stamping my feet to keep my toes from getting numb and asking out loud if those socks had been a rip-off. I was about to give up hope when the door finally opened. Haley stared blearily out at us. She was wearing the oversize men's sweatshirt that said OFFICE CLEANING SPECIALISTS. Haley's striped pajama bottoms rippled over her bare feet.

She actually looked better half-asleep and without her makeup, even though her face was a bit swollen, her eyes unfocused, and her hair tangled like the squirrel might have nested in it.

Now what? I had just wanted to know that she was alive. She obviously had not been killed, so I didn't have much of a purpose there. Jack had even less.

She squinted at me nearsightedly. "Charlotte?"

"Haley," I said, allowing a huge smile to escape. I can't even describe the wave of relief that washed over me. I reached over and squeezed her rough hands.

She stared at me like I had lost my mind, which was beginning to feel like a possibility. "What are you doing here?"

Jack also gazed at me quizzically, as if wondering the same thing. I said, "For some reason, I just got worried."

"Worried?"

"Yes. I wanted to make sure you were all right."

"Why wouldn't I be all right?" Haley said—at least I thought that was what she said as her teeth had begun to chatter. The door was open and it was damned cold out.

"It was just a silly notion, that's all," I said. "Sorry to disturb you."

She stifled a yawn. "Well, I am awake now. You came all the way out here. You may as well have some coffee."

"Coffee's good," Jack said.

My own teeth were chattering by then. That meant yes.

"You're freezing," Haley said. "Come in. I don't know what I was thinking. We don't get many visitors here and never in the morning so I just didn't—"

Jack said, "That's great," and walked through the door. I followed. The door led straight into the living room. The cozy fire in the woodstove was the focus of the room. A saggy sofa was positioned close enough to warm whoever was lucky enough to sit on it. The room was paneled in pine and the floors were made of wide pine boards. All that wood made the cabin feel even cozier. I liked the homeyness of it.

"Nice fire," Jack said, pointing to the woodstove and

heading straight for it. I scurried after him and got as close as I could. Through the glass front of the woodstove we could see the red-hot logs glowing inside; a cheerful sight.

"Have a seat," Haley said. Jack sprawled on the sofa and I settled in a battered armchair with a crazy patchwork afghan covering the worn upholstery.

Haley busied herself making coffee and soon that scent added to the wood smoke. When the coffee came, it smelled good. It might have been half-strength and it could have passed as last night's dishwater, but, unlike last night's dishwater, it was hot and it was there. Haley settled down and smiled at us, expectantly. Her face was already less puffy and she was obviously more with it than when we arrived.

"I'm sorry," she said, "I just didn't follow what was going on. Explain it again."

"Charlotte thought you were dead," Jack said, blowing on his coffee cup.

"Dead?"

"We're both glad you're not."

"Hey, me too," she said. "But, um, what would make you think I was dead?"

"Silly," I said, feeling my face redden.

"Charlotte lets her imagination run away sometimes. This was one of those times. Great coffee, Haley."

What a liar. He seemed so innocent too.

"Excellent," I said, adding to the lie quotient in the room. "Just strong enough to do the trick."

"I still don't understand why you thought I was dead."

"It's crazy."

She nodded. I guess she already knew that.

"Another woman was killed in the middle of the night. She was walking to her car near Ambleside Acres, probably going home. She was found around six this morning."

Haley's watery blue eyes widened. "Killed? You mean another hit-and-run?"

"Exactly," Jack said. I noticed he wasn't actually drinking the coffee.

Haley's gaze shifted from Jack to me. "I didn't catch the news yet today. We usually finish around three and sleep until ten or eleven. Randy's still sleeping now."

"I hope we didn't wake him up."

She grinned. "An atomic bomb wouldn't wake him up. Don't worry about that. The same with our daughter, Brie."

I felt a bit of relief that I only had to appear like an idiot in front of one person. Jack didn't count. We were used to being foolish in front of each other and so that never mattered. I said, "I knew you worked nights in offices and I knew that there were those couple of strip malls at the edge of Ambleside Acres so I started to worry. What if . . . ?"

"What if someone's trying to kill me too?"

I nodded. "I realize it's silly now. It's just that the first victim looked so much like Serena and I was wondering if it was a case of mistaken identity."

Haley had just started to realize what that might have meant. "You think someone wanted to kill Serena? And me? Because of actions when we were kids? Oh my God, I regret all that so much. Why would someone want to kill me? I'm sorry for everything I did."

"That was my thinking. But it wasn't you, so it was obviously a product of my feverish mind. I am so sorry, Haley."

Haley stood up, walked over to the stack of split firewood, opened the glass-fronted door, and added a healthy top-up to the fire. I liked the crackling noise. She sat down again and said, "But it might have been me. What if this was another mistake? Randy and I do have clients in those strip malls. We just don't work there on Saturday nights."

I added, "We're sorry about this, Haley. I shouldn't have

panicked and alarmed you. I see now that it didn't happen and that's a good thing."

A sound between a squeak and a roar caught our attention and we turned. A large hairy man stuck his head out of what must have been the bedroom door. He stepped into the room and scratched his belly. He spotted us and then scratched his head. He turned to face Haley. "What's going on, sweetheart?"

"Randy," she said. "You remember Charlotte Adams, don't you, hon?" I gave myself yet another mental kick.

He squinted at me. He was a man who had worked all night and found himself with unexpected visitors in the morning before he'd had a cup of coffee. Considering all that, he seemed pretty mild. He said, "Who?"

"Charlotte Adams. From St. Jude's? She almost went out with your buddy Jason Gardner? Remember? Before we were going together. Or we could have double-dated."

He blinked. "Yeah, sure," he said unconvincingly. He managed a teddy bear grin. He was instantly likeable. I would have trusted him with my wallet. I could see how he would have been a dynamite salesman as Haley had said. "How ya doin'?"

I said firmly, "I am doing very well."

Haley hadn't bothered to ask me if I recognized Randy. I did, although time hadn't been kind to him either. The huge football player's body had turned flabby and his dark hair had receded—well, actually descended, because there was lots of it on his chest, arms, and, although I didn't want to check too closely, his ears. He was far too pale, a clue to his health.

Haley inclined her head in Jack's direction. "And this is, uh . . . I'm sorry; you look real familiar, but I don't quite remember your name."

Jack was his gracious self. "Jack Reilly. Don't worry about it. I didn't remember you either, Harley."

"Haley," I said quickly. "It's Haley, Jack."

The hulk squinted at Jack, and then grinned. "Basketball, right? It's all coming back to me."

"That's me."

"You were pretty good. You still play?"

"Not really. I'm into cycling now."

"Cycling," the hulk said, the way he might have if Jack admitted he spent his time doing needlepoint studies of small pastel animals. He turned to me. "Real nice to see you again," he lied politely and shook my hand. "Hope you don't mind, but I'm heading back to bed for a bit. Haley? You need anything?"

She shook her head.

"I always take care of my girls," he said. "But first a bit more sleep."

"I'm up for good," Haley said in a shaky voice. "But Charlotte's here for a reason. You are just going to die when you hear this, Randy."

He stared at her, slack-jawed, before he said, "What?"

"She thinks someone is trying to kill me." Her blue eyes filled.

Randy thumped down on the sofa and fixed his wife with a loving glance. "But why would anyone want to do that, sweetheart?"

5

Home again. Jack, to his credit, did not give me a hard time about my wild idea that someone had killed Haley.

"We're both glad she's still alive," he said, by way of letting me off the hook. "And her husband is too."

"Right. Funny how it turns out that they're still high school sweethearts. You don't think of that kind of thing working out."

Jack gave me a strange look.

"Thanks for coming with me out there. Better safe than sorry," I added gratefully.

"Can we forget about these mean girls now and enjoy our day?" Jack said.

"Oh, sure." I meant it too.

Jack made some more coffee to wipe out the taste of Haley's brew while I checked the phone to see that Sally, Margaret, and Pepper had all called. That was nice. My lovely contact from Woodbridge Therapy Dogs had too. My mother had phoned from somewhere exotic and left an excited message that could have meant either she was getting married again or she had a new handbag. Oh well, I'd find out soon enough. I left the messages and turned to Jack. Jack and I agreed on a winter wonderland walk with wieners once I'd warmed up fully again. We both had some fun reading and some new music to listen to. We don't read the same kinds of books. I favor personal development books; Jack likes mysteries for some reason. I like funky alternative rock; he's into world music. Big deal. We respect each other's choices, more or less.

At some point, we'd decide between an early dinner at one of our favorite restaurants or a movie. Picking the movie would involve flipping a coin, unless we saw two movies. Sunday. I love Sundays. It got off to a rocky start, but it was still the most luxurious day of the week. My To Do list was all fun things. I made a promise out loud to myself and Jack that we'd keep this day to ourselves. I hoped that would continue if "us" ever turned into more "us" than it currently was.

—◆◆—

Jack and I parked near Kristee's Kandees and spent a happy hour strolling through snowy uptown Woodbridge. The dogs cooperated for once. When we'd finished, we headed in Kristee's. I wanted to get a couple of boxes of Kristee's black-and-white fudge, which is my gift of choice for hostesses, people in hospitals, reluctant sources in investigations, bribable police officers, and myself. Just because.

Kristee is never the sunniest of individuals, to understate the case. It's always a surprise that she can turn out such yummy confections when you can practically see the black cloud of misery over her head. Today she scowled as I walked through the door. She extended the scowl to Jack.

"I'm staying outside with the dogs," Jack said.

Truffle and Sweet Marie sniffed the air. They love this

place because Kristee has a special line of homemade peanut butter dog biscuits. Of course, pesky health rules kept
them outside the shop. I think Jack was grateful for them.

"Charlotte," Kristee said. She stretched her lips out to
simulate a smile that could fool no one.

"That must be painful," Jack muttered from behind me.
Out loud he said, "I'd better put some money in the parking meter."

"Don't need to pay on Sunday," Kristee countered. From
her expression she thought that was a bad idea. You might
assume a business person would have encouraged anything
that made life easier for customers, such as free parking.

"How are you, Kristee?" I realized I was dreading the
answer. Kristee could often have a tale of woe that was
entirely of her own making. As long as I'd been coming
there, it was always something.

As usual, Kristee had a bit of icing sugar in her short, dark
hair. She often dyed it blond or red, but her natural dark hair
suited her. She was as plump as one of her hand-dipped choc-
olates and was quite pretty when she wasn't in a sour mood.

"Worse than usual," she said. "I imagine you are too."

"What?"

"Well, you know. Bad enough it's April, usually a good
month for me, with ice cream sales going up, but now with
this bad weather, people are staying home in droves. Also
Serena Redding's back in the area and you know what that
means."

I was surprised to hear Kristee echo Mona's comments.
"I know what it used to mean. But surely people like Serena don't have power over any of us anymore," I said.

She dismissed that with a shrug.

"If they ever did," I added.

Kristee shot me a venomous glance. I turned and checked
the window. I guess Jack had caught a bit of that glance. He
recoiled and appeared to trip over his own feet.

I reminded myself to stand firm and remember the fudge. I thought reinforcements would be good. "Excuse me a minute." I opened the door and told Jack to put the dogs in the car and join me. I was undeterred by the pathetic expression on his face.

As he dragged himself through the door, I said, "We were just discussing Serena's return and whether or not she could still have power over any of us."

Jack said, "Did she have all that much power?"

Kristee said, "Guys have no idea about the kind of control she had over everyone. I'm speaking as a fat girl who still bears the scars."

Of course, that would have been something else I hadn't paid attention to. "Did they make your life miserable too?"

Kristee curled her upper lip. "You mean all the pig remarks? The snorting whenever I tried to take a bite of my lunch. The bacon jokes. The snapping sounds that were supposed to be my waistband popping. I hated every minute I was in that school. Those pig jokes? They were just the warm-up."

I thought I saw a shake in her hand.

I shook my head. "Too rough to talk about."

Kristee curled her lip. "How would you know, Little Miss Perfect?"

"You're right. I guess I was kind of oblivious. I feel bad that I didn't pay attention to what they were doing."

"Huh. They didn't give you any grief. You were always just right, mincing about."

Mincing? "I don't believe I minced."

"Trust me. You were always a little—"

"I'm sorry I wasn't there for you, Kristee," I said.

"Yeah, well. Too little. Too late."

"That reminds me, do you remember the first victim, Bethann Reynolds?"

"Sure. She had a hard time too. But she's another person

like me who got tired of being bullied and decided to fight back. She took her former employer to court and won a major settlement for harassment. It was actually a school board too. When other people don't help us, we can do it ourselves." She flashed me a guilt-inducing look.

"Is that a new kind of fudge?" Jack said, leaning in toward the display cabinet. "It doesn't seem familiar."

Her face lit up. She was quite appealing when she was talking about candy. It was everything else in the world that was the problem. "Triple chocolate truffles," she said with pride. "Dark, semisweet, and white chocolate. I found a new way to make them complement each other."

"Wow," Jack said.

Kristee would have been through hell for sure. I cut her a bit of slack and let the mincing remark go. I supposed there were many things worse than mincing. Being fat at St. Jude's, for instance. That must have been torture. She was right. My remarks *were* too little and too late.

Didn't matter much apparently, because Jack and Kristee had put together a box of the new triple chocolate truffles and I added two gift boxes of black-and-white fudge to the order. And a regular box for us. After all.

I thought that Kristee had mellowed a bit by the time the amount was rung up on the register, but that turned out to be premature. "When I saw the photo of the woman who was killed in the hit-and-run Friday night, I thought it was Serena. I was celebrating right up until I found out that it was someone else. What a letdown. I guess whoever aimed for her didn't do her homework well."

Mona's face flashed through my mind.

Jack sputtered. "Come on, Kristee, that was a tragedy to have a person killed that way. She never did anything to you."

"Yeah, yeah, tragic for Bethann. But not if it had been Serena. If she'd been killed a hundred different painful ways, it wouldn't be nearly enough payback for the harm she did to people. I would have done it myself if I'd had the chance. That all? I have some white chocolate bark with dried sweetened cranberries on special this weekend. Going fast."

"Sounds good," Jack said. "And we'd like a bag of dog biscuits too. The bone-shaped ones."

I said nothing. I just kept wondering if the victim had been mistaken for Serena and if someone I'd known at St. Jude's had taken the opportunity to target their murderous rage at the wrong person. Someone like Mona, for instance.

Kristee finished the transaction and said with an evil grin, "But at least they got Tiffanee. That felt good."

Jack and I said, "What?" at the same time.

Kristee said, "They got Tiffanee."

I felt a chill. "You mean that was Tiffanee who was hit last night? I didn't think the name had—"

"A cop told me this morning, just after I opened. They know these things and this guy has a weakness for fudge. It was her, all right. Bang, you're dead. Now other people tell me that Princess T had been walking around Woodbridge all these years pretending to be a decent person, with her yoga and her sandals and all that BS. I can see through that. I remember the kinds of things she said and did to me. I remember the gloating look on her face. I hope she suffered before she died. I am not going to pretend to be shocked or upset. I hope she saw the face of the person who hit her and I hope she knew why."

Jack and I were very quiet as we walked back to the Miata. Back at the car, the little dogs jumped with joy trying to get at the bag of dog biscuits as soon we got in. I was still too shocked to enjoy the moment. So was Jack.

I realized I was shivering.

"Makes you think," Jack said. "Do you want my jacket?"

"No, thanks. I don't want you freezing. Makes you think what?" I said as I finally pulled out onto the road.

He said, "I didn't know Kristee had such a hard time at St. Jude's."

"I didn't either, but it sounds awful."

"Exactly. How many other lives have been blighted by Serena and her friends?"

"So you're saying how many people might have wanted to kill Tiffanee?"

"Yes. And is that the end of it?"

The car swerved a bit. I couldn't wait to get home. Something told me I wouldn't get an answer from Mona.

——•——

If Jack and I were late in finding out about Tiffanee, WINY was not. Todd Tyrell embraced his inner snowman as he stood on the site of the second hit-and-run. He barely managed to keep the joy out of his voice. "Tiffanee Dupont," he intoned, "was a popular yoga teacher in Woodbridge. Tonight her friends and students are mourning the loss of this beautiful woman and generous spirit."

Tiffanee's image flashed across the screen. I wouldn't have recognized her. She was serene and elegant with her glowing skin and close-cropped dark hair. The waist-length hair I remembered was ancient history, but people would kill to have a neck like that.

I suppose I must have snorted because Jack turned to me in surprise.

"Sorry. I guess I was just remembering that this generous spirit told my first date that I had something contagious. That knowledge is tempering my grief and outrage."

"People change. Look at Haley. And this Tiffanee obviously had too."

"Might have," I sniffed. Todd Tyrell was busy sticking the mic under the noses of Tiffanee's students, friends, and neighbors. They all seemed shocked and some couldn't stop crying.

"They can't all be faking it," Jack said.

I thought back to Tiffanee, prowling the halls of St. Jude's, her glossy waist-length hair swaying behind her like a wall of silk. Of the three bullies, she was the one with the most memorable face and body. Princess T. She had a dancer's moves even then, despite the platform shoes and the skirt that was never regulation length, the one that got her sent home by the principal more than once. Now she was dead at thirty-one. And some people were grieving apparently.

Jack said, "What's wrong?"

"You know, something strange. Pepper must have known Bethann's name. She knew that Bethann also had a hard time with these bullies, yet she never mentioned it. Even when I talked to her on Saturday night."

"That's because she doesn't want you to get involved, Charlotte. And she's right. Don't go snooping."

I ignored that, and tried Mona's number for the fourth time as Todd rehashed the item on Bethann Reynolds, a quiet preschool teacher who'd lived with her mother near the corner of Amsterdam Avenue. Todd had tracked down some of her colleagues and captured their shock and tears too. He intoned deeply, "How ironic that two weeks after Bethann Reynolds succeeded in a harassment suit against her former employers, she should come to such a tragic end."

No answer from Mona.

What the hell was going on? I worried about it all evening even when I did my preparations for the morning: coffee, table set, To Do list, clothing laid out. The works. Jack didn't worry about a thing. He didn't prepare for the morning and he has never had a To Do list.

6

Usually Monday morning is my favorite time of the work-week. Seriously. I don't tell everyone that, as some people get annoyed by the idea. But I love to see a fresh, clean week stretching ahead, full of possibility and promise, with objectives and tasks laid out clearly. Jack likes to say that I lose people the minute I start blabbing (his word) about objectives and tasks, even if they can handle "the Monday thing." Don't shove it down their throats, he usually adds.

Whatever. I was at my desk by seven thirty. The dogs had been walked and fed and were back for their early-morning nap. My week was shaping up. I had five items on my To Do list for that day. My big priority was the work-shop that evening. I'd called it Taking the Nightmare out of Your Mornings. Of course the handouts were all prepared and ready to distribute. My materials were packed and ready to go. I'd practiced my presentation and left plenty of time to run through it one last time before I gave it. I finished up by giving Sweet Marie a bath and a nail trim to get her ready for her first therapy-dog visit the next morning. This was not appreciated, but you can't have it all. Truffle made himself scarce.

I moved on to my next item cheerfully. I had an initial consultation for a condo kitchen at ten in the morning. Of course, I was ready for that. Then the afternoon was blocked off to do a proposal for a couple who had downsized from a sprawling home on a leafy acreage to a compact two-bedroom condo with a view over the Hudson River. They were thrilled to be smack in the middle of restaurants, shops, river walks, and other good things, until they'd woken up to the fact they'd lost 80 percent of their storage space. Too bad the realization came only when their new storage was jammed and they still had more than half their boxes sitting in the living room and hallway. If only they'd called me in before, it would have been a lot easier and cheaper for them. I was used to this organizing problem. They were smart not to try to cram everything into their new place—a tactic that can make a home feel like a secondhand furniture showroom in the middle of the post-Christmas sales.

I had worked with them to estimate the contents of the surplus boxes and had an appointment to return the next week with a plan of action. Setting out that plan was my afternoon's objective. I was humming as I made sure I had everything I needed to get the most out of it. That way, when I got home from the morning's activities, I'd be ready to roll. I spread out my materials, and made another pot of coffee. The dogs repositioned themselves to continue their nap in my bedroom/office. They have their official office sleeping cushion and blanket. I was still humming when the phone rang. I recognized Mona's home number. I'd called it enough the night before.

"Charlotte?"

"Mona?"

"Of course it's Mona. Who else would it be? Don't you have call display?"

I rubbed my temple. I rarely get headaches, but something told me that might be about to change. "I'm glad you called. I was trying to reach you last night. What's happening?"

"Okay. Just wanted you to know, I'm considering going into hiding."

"Hiding? Why?" Couldn't stop myself. I just blurted it out.

"It should be crystal clear, Charlotte."

"Humor me. I seem to have missed out on a piece of the puzzle. Just run it by me again, Mona, if you don't mind. Why would you go into hiding?"

I listened to her long sigh. She said, "Fine. As you know, Serena has returned to the area. I was fantasizing about killing her, but I could never do it. Now other people are dying the same way as my fantasy. When I heard about Tiffanee I was freaked-out at first. It was like being in a nightmare. You know?"

"I can imagine."

"Although Tiffanee deserved it too. Just as much as any of the others."

"No one deserves to die like that. You must be bothered by that."

"I'm bothered because I'm the one who might have done it. Even though I didn't, I never should have shot my mouth off about that bitch Serena and her vile followers."

"Who did you tell? Besides me."

"I'm not sure who all might have overheard me. Did you tell anyone else? I trusted you to keep that private. And yet you sent Pepper after me."

"Did Pepper talk to you?"

"She grilled me, last night. She can be tough and nasty, you know."

I did know.

"I didn't actually send her after you. I was worried after our conversation, Mona. You're a 911 operator. You can't be threatening people and fantasizing about murder. That's not something I could just hear and ignore. I'm your friend, not your accomplice."

"But you knew I didn't mean it. I'm not a homicidal maniac."

"I'm glad to hear that, Mona, but you sounded like you did mean it."

"Did you think I was crazy? Ready to kill?"

"I thought you were under a lot of strain and someone had to talk to you. Pepper is a sensible person in a position of authority."

"Yeah, well. Who else did you tell?"

I had tried to keep Mona's name out of it, but Pepper had figured out who I was talking about. The misfits had mulled it over, but I didn't plan to share that with Mona, who seemed to have gone off another deep end. "Pepper was the person who needed to know, Mona. Where are you now? Can we meet?"

"You must be kidding."

"What? Why would I be kidding?"

"No, we can't meet. People are dying. And it all has to do with Serena being back. I'm going to keep a low profile until it's over."

"What's over?"

"Whatever is going on. Sometimes you're as thick as a brick, Charlotte."

"I suppose that's true, but I'm doing my best. This is all quite surreal. We really should get together."

A cloud of suspicion accompanied Mona's words. "Why?"

"To talk. I'd like to help, but I have to figure out what's going on first."

"Good luck with that. I may be messed up, but I am not an idiot. If it was easy to figure out, I'd have figured it out. Someone's wiping them out and that person is trying to implicate me. That much is obvious."

"But why?"

"That Serena. She's the cause. This whole mess started after she came back and asked me to reconnect with her, wanting to make amends and all that. I said 'to hell with that' and now look."

"But, Mona, you yourself said you imagined running Serena over."

"I said I wanted to see her face splattered against my windshield."

I shook my head at the image in the light of the two hit-and-run deaths. "Just explain. How is someone trying to implicate you?"

"Stealing my things. Probably planning to leave them at the death sites as false clues."

"What do you mean? What kinds of things?"

"Scarves. Gloves. Everyday clothing, but they'd have my DNA on them. Cops can do a lot with that. I'm being set up to take the fall for many, many murders."

"There hasn't been anything about finding that kind of thing at the death sites, as you call them."

"Well, duh. That's because there's serious backlogs at the labs, but you wait."

Was Mona losing her mind? "What do you mean by 'many murders'? Please let me—"

"And then there are all the phone calls with no one on the other end. It's driving me crazy. No time to talk, Charlotte. I need to take action, and I'm not going to be a sitting duck."

"Action? Mona, that's—" I bit my tongue. "Please, let's get together and—"

Mona laughed long and hard before she hung up.

———— ♦♦ ————

I wasn't nearly as clearheaded after I'd talked with Mona. Could she be right? Was someone trying to implicate her? Why? Would there be many murders? Or was Mona losing it? Perhaps she was becoming paranoid, as the result of trauma inflicted years ago and triggered by Serena's return. Was going into hiding a good idea?

Time to rejig my To Do list. Now the day's priorities were:

> Follow up on Mona—how?
> Call Pepper—re Bethann and Mona—bullies?
> Initial consultation with new kitchen client—10
>   a.m.
> Proposal for downsizing project
> First therapy-dog visit!
> Workshop Two—WPL—arrive at 6:30
> Find time to relax

I had seven items on my list by this time. I hate that. Something wouldn't get done. I had to follow through with the kitchen consultation, the therapy-dog visit, and the workshop. And I had decided to put Mona on top of the list. Otherwise, I'd have trouble keeping my mind off her. I hoped I wouldn't get behind on the downsizing plans. Something told me I wouldn't do much relaxing that day, even though I know it's important to keep rested.

There was no answer when I called Mona back, but I'd decided not to let that deter me.

I quickly checked my assembled kit for the consultation about the condo kitchen: measuring tape, my "what to expect" handouts, brochures, and a standard contract to show the client. Everything was packed except my mini-computer. I'd laid out a pair of black dress pants with a pale stripe, and a turtleneck. I'd added a scarlet cardigan in a cashmere blend. Woodbridge in the cold weather takes planning. My winter dress boots have an insulated lining, so they are good to minus twenty. They are old, but necessary. I considered tucking my nifty new tartan lace-up leather booties into my briefcase, but they'd be awkward to put on, so I chose to save them for a snowless day. I packed a pair of black suede pumps with red leather trim.

The only difficult and troubling item on the list was how to check up on Mona. I knew I had to knock that off first. I called once more but Mona didn't answer. As before, there was no answering machine. This time that struck me as odd, since I figured a 911 operator who worked a lot of overtime would need to take messages. Maybe she had a pager or some other form of communication that I was unaware of. I gave Pepper a buzz at the police station, hoping to get her before the day got going, but no luck. The hit-and-runs would have all the Woodbridge investigators scrambling this week. I decided to check in every half hour until I reached her. In the meantime I got myself ready for my morning consultation. But Pepper didn't call back. I knew that the detectives' mornings were often spent in meetings, so I left detailed messages outlining my worry about Mona's mental state and the possibility that her fears were real.

I called Mona four more times, letting the phone ring on and on. I was beginning to take the lack of an answering machine personally. I knew she didn't want to meet with me, but I felt I had to do something. There must be a better tactic than going into hiding. If she needed protection or help, I would have to see that she got it.

But maybe she'd just been called in to work. I wasn't sure when she would switch from night to day shift. I called. Someone who was definitely not Mona answered, "911." I steeled myself. I knew it was the wrong thing to do, calling the emergency number, but what if it was an emergency?

"Is Mona Pringle on duty today?"

"What?"

"Is Mona—"

"I heard you, actually." It was a man's voice, warm and almost friendly, yet with that businesslike firmness that 911 operators require. "You know you're not supposed to call here for anything but an emergency."

"I do know that, but I urgently need to talk to Mona. It's a type of emergency. If you can tell me she's there, I can relax. I am sorry for calling this number. I didn't know what else to do."

I waited.

He said, "Is this Charlotte Adams?"

"Yes," I said. "But it's very important. I need to talk to her."

"Actually," he confided, "I know you are her good friend, so I'll tell you, she was supposed to be in today and she's not here. She didn't call in either. It's not like her. I've been calling and calling."

Her good friend? "You mean she just didn't show up?"

He lowered his voice. "It's a first for her. Mona's very dedicated. I am filling in, but the supervisor is having kittens over it. Anyone else, and her ass would be grass. You hear me?"

"I do. And I know she's not at home." I noticed my voice got higher as I spoke. It was almost in the trill range. "Would any of your coworkers have an idea where she could be? What about you?"

"They don't have a clue, and if I had any idea where she was, I'd get on over there and tell Mona to get her butt in here, but I don't. Do you?"

"No, obviously, or I wouldn't be calling 911."

"I know you're her friend, so if you find her, tell her what I said."

"I will. How do you know I'm her friend?"

"She talks about you. How else would I know?"

"Of course. Are you her friend too?"

"Damn straight. My name's Brian. Does she talk about me?"

"Oh, Brian. Of course she does. I'm glad it's you."

Well, when had I turned into such a total liar? Not that I cared at that moment. The idea of Mona not calling in before missing work was just too bizarre. A few lies were a small price to pay.

"Keep in touch, Charlotte."

"You too, Brian."

After I hung up, I wondered if I should have confided in Brian. He was a 911 dispatcher too. He might be able to help me find her. And he might know how long she'd been acting this way.

———— ♦ ————

Five minutes later, I parked the Miata at the Woodbridge Public Library and headed grimly to the reference section where Ramona was reigning reference librarian on this blowy morning. Luckily, the library opened at nine on Monday mornings. Unluckily, the usual crowd of entitled readers had managed to stagger in and occupy the best spots, reading the *Wall Street Journal*, the *New Yorker*, and *Consumer Reports*. They gave me their normal poisonous glances. Ramona waved and trotted over with a click of her cowboy boots. Her chambray shirt was a lighter blue than she usually wore and the silver earrings chunkier.

"Thank heavens, a friendly face," she said. "Even if a worried one. I am up to my patootie in prima donnas here today and you, Charlotte Adams, are a welcome relief."

"Glad to help." I grinned. "Not everyone's that glad to see me."

"Information needs?" she said. "For here or to go?"

"Here, if possible. Do you know Mona Pringle?"

"Nine-one-one operator. Sure."

"That was just a pro forma question. I am well aware that you know everyone who grew up in Woodbridge."

"Well, maybe not everyone, but I did get around. I've known Mona since the year I had a summer job with the parks department and she was a little kid."

"You have?"

"Sure."

"Did she have rough time?"

The earrings jingled as Ramona nodded her head. "It was like she was a wearing an invisible 'kick me' sign, that could only be seen by mean kids."

"Good analogy."

"Maybe it was more of a 'boot me to the moon' sign or 'beat me up' notice. You get the picture. She was such a nice little kid. I used to remind her that Ramona had the name Mona in it too, so I'd make extra sure she didn't get bullied on my watch."

"Did that work?"

"It seemed to make a difference."

"That's a relief. It's sort of a private matter, but I need to get in touch with Mona. It's quite urgent. I'm sure that she's not at work, and, anyway, I've been told not to try to reach her there."

"I can't snoop into her library records," Ramona said with a frown. "They're confidential."

I gasped. "I wouldn't ever suggest that. Never. I thought perhaps there was some information that was on public record that you could—"

She shrugged. "There are the old city directories."

"Didn't they stop printing those a long time ago?"

Ramona rolled her eyes. "But she had to live somewhere even a long time ago. Just check out the family name and see where the Pringles lived around town."

"Sorry," I said. "I'm a bit panicky and seeking instant solutions."

"Information worth having is not necessarily instant," Ramona said with a big, blue booming laugh. This time the poisonous glances were directed at her.

I checked out the printed *City Directory for Wood-bridge* from the last date they were available. There was one Pringle in the index. On Spruce Street. Not all that far from the library and not all that far from me, for that matter. I couldn't help but observe that it also wasn't all that far from Long March Road and Amsterdam, where the first hit-and-run had happened.

"This is a great start, Ramona," I said as I headed out.

"Let me know if you don't find her. I'll be glad to try to help."

"I hope you won't have to."

⚬⚬

Most streets in Woodbridge are either on their way down or on their way up, depending on how the economic troubles hit the residents and how attractive the new entrepreneurs and artistic types found the area. Spruce Street had been on a steep slide, but seemed to have hit bottom and started climbing up again. Once, substantial homes had been carved into multiple rental units, but the buildings were in good repair, and today I noticed snow shoveled neatly up most walkways.

The Pringle family was listed at 18 Spruce, a white clapboard house, now subdivided. The walkway to what looked like the main floor unit, number 18, was shoveled with clean lines. I figured you got to 18A via the long exterior staircase leading upstairs. There was a crisp path cleared to the staircase. I approved.

But 18B, on the other hand, seemed to be a basement

unit with an entrance on the opposite side of the house. A sign with an arrow read PRINGLE. Although there were dim remnants of footprints in the snow that was continuing to fall lightly, no one had shoveled the short path leading to it.

I was hoping that Mona hadn't taken off already. It didn't seem like her not to clear her walkway. Had she departed in a panic? Where would she go if she did?

A cheerful light shone out of the front window of number 18. The walls appeared to be a warm shade of toast. I knocked firmly and heard someone call out, "Coming," a minute before the door was thrust open. A very pregnant woman smiled at me.

I smiled back. "I'm looking for my friend Mona Pringle. She used to live here when we were growing up and I'm hoping she still does. I've been trying to reach her by phone."

A wonderful aroma of something spicy wafted out the door and tickled my nose, which twitched in response. The pregnant woman wrinkled her own nose.

She said, "Mona?"

"That's right."

"She does and she doesn't, I suppose."

"I'm sorry; I don't—"

She waved her hand apologetically. "Don't mind me. I seem to have the fuzziest brain lately. This used to be the Pringle home, but now it's three units. I'm Caroline Menti. My husband and I bought it and converted it. It's a way to make the mortgage doable."

"Oh. Do you have any idea how I could get in touch with Mona?"

"Sure. We bought it from the Pringles so of course we're in touch." She uttered a merry little trill, as if the notion of not keeping in touch with the previous owners was quite laughable. "Mona lives in the basement unit. She rents if from us now and she has access to the backyard. That seemed to mean a lot to her because you see she grew up here and . . . I'm babbling, aren't I? Well, you could just go and knock on her door. Oh my, she hasn't shoveled. That's not like Mona. She's an up-and-at-'em kind of woman. Maybe she's away." Her forehead wrinkled. "But usually she tells us if she's going away. We take care of Mooch and Pooch. I wonder . . . Oh, I'm so sorry. Do you want to come in? It's so cold out here."

I stepped through the door feeling grateful. The entrance was warm and hospitable and done in a deeper color, burnt toast perhaps.

"Wait here," Caroline said. "I'll check with my husband. Tony! Tony! Tony!"

An answering boom came from upstairs and a large bald man in jeans, a sweater, and bedroom slippers thundered down, also smiling. This was the smiliest house.

"This lady—"

"Charlotte," I interjected, smiling. Why not? It was catching.

"—is looking for Mona and I just realized that Mona hasn't shoveled. Did she go somewhere?"

Tony shrugged. "Mona only ever goes to work." He stuck his head out the door and stared at the snow-covered walk to 18B. He stepped back in and scratched his head. "Can't figure that out."

"When did you see her last?" Caroline said.

"When did it start snowing?" he said. "Friday? Saturday?"

"Thursday," I said.

"You could still see the lawn when I saw her last. We commented on that. Course that was before we knew what was in store."

"Did she mention plans to go anywhere?" I tried to sound casual and conversational. I certainly didn't want them to know why I might be worried.

He shook his head.

"Perhaps I should just go check?" I said. "She might be under the weather and not able to get to the phone."

Caroline gasped. "Poor Mona. I hope she hasn't been down there feeling sick and alone when I could have brought her some soup."

Soup, that was what I'd been smelling. Wonderful home-made soup, like Jack's mother used to make.

"I'll do that, then," I said.

Tony said, "Wait a minute. I'll shovel out a path for you."

"Don't worry about it. I have terrific boots. I don't want to trouble you."

"No trouble," Tony and Caroline said in unison. Tony grabbed his jacket and started to slip his feet into his boots. "I should do it for Mona anyway, especially if she's feeling sick. Although she usually likes to do it herself."

But usually she's not fantasizing about murder, I thought. "That's a great idea." With luck I could get in and either find Mona hiding out at home or locate some clue to where she might have gone.

There were indeed several boot prints in the snow. Small prints, a woman's boot and not a large foot although a bit bigger than mine, in a neat series of trails. They seemed to go both ways, although I thought there were more leading into the apartment than leading out.

I knocked firmly on the door. I kept on knocking and pressed my ear to the door to see if I could hear anything. I called out, "Mona! It's me, Charlotte."

Nada.

Behind me, I could hear Tony shoveling the walkway. He obviously had a technique—scoop, toss, scoop, toss. He wasn't even short of breath as he approached.

"No answer?" he said. "I guess that's a dumb question. You wouldn't be standing here in front of a closed door if there was."

Was Mona inside ignoring my loud knocking the same

way she'd blown off my calls? I didn't plan to give up on this opportunity. "Do you think she's all right? What if she's hurt herself. Or she's sick. I'm worried about her."

Tony looked startled, then said, "Hang on, I'm going to open it."

As the door swung inward, Tony told me to wait, then called out, "Mona, honey, are you okay? Mona? Mona? I'm coming down to check."

He lumbered down the stairs and I scurried behind him. He was a massive man. I had no doubt that if Mona was lying unconscious he could race up the stairs with her. If she'd decided to take that approach to escape whatever demons she was wrestling with. I felt a bit light-headed and realized that I'd been holding my breath. Tony stopped suddenly and I crashed into him. He turned and glanced down. "Sorry," he said. "Maybe you should go first in case she's not dressed or something. I wouldn't want to embarrass her."

He reached forward and flicked on a wall switch. Light flooded the dark room. It was a pleasant space, but it was never going to make a magazine. Still I got the feeling that Mona was comfortable and happy in this little hideaway. A big blue recliner and an overstuffed yellow sofa faced each other across a square coffee table with a stack of books with Woodbridge Public Library stickers on the spines, a stack of magazines mostly to do with animals, and a bookcase jammed with paperbacks. A large fluffy gray cat approached and rubbed against my legs. "Coast is clear in here, Tony," I said. "Just the cat."

Tony ducked to enter the room. The cat flicked its tail and headed straight for him. Tony bent and scratched its ears. A loud rumble of purrs filled the room.

"Hey, Mooch. Where's Pooch?" Tony said.

"There are no dogs here."

"How do you know?"

"We're not being barked at."

"Pooch will be hiding, not barking. Mooch here's the guard cat."

"Oh."

Tony checked behind the sofa and extracted a small quivering dog. He scratched its ears too, and it seemed to consider not dying of fright.

I said, "So both the pets are here. Just the one dog and cat, right?"

"Yup."

"Okay, I see the food in the dishes seems fresh. If my dogs were here there wouldn't even be a shadow left in the bowls. I guess I'd better check the bedroom."

There were two doors off the large living room. I took the left into Mona's bedroom. I exhaled when I saw a rumpled, unmade bed, and a pile of clothing on a chair, but no Mona. Part of me had been afraid that Mona might have harmed herself. But this spoke of what? A hasty departure? A distracted mind? Or just the way that Mona lived? I pulled back the sheets, just in case. No Mona in that room. I glanced behind me at the door. Tony hadn't stuck his head in. Probably holding his breath too. I lifted up the phone receiver, using the sheet to keep from getting my prints on it (funny what getting arrested will do to change a person). Turned out there was an answering machine after all, but it had been turned off. I turned it on, but there were no saved messages.

I pressed "callers" and checked out the list. Most were from me and they hadn't been answered. Mona had received a number of calls from BLOCKED NUMBER.

"Is she there?" Tony called.

"No. Sorry. I was just checking the phone to see if there might be a clue to where she'd gone."

I wasn't sure what to do about the answering machine. I

turned it off again, reluctantly. I was nervous and uncomfortable searching Mona's apartment. It just felt wrong.

"Good thinking. Anything?" Tony said from the door.

"Not too much by way of results. I'd better check the bathroom." Holding my breath again, I reentered the living room, nodded at the ashen Tony, and entered the bathroom. I was able to exhale easily as the room was empty, the shower curtain open. No Mona.

I said, "Coast is clear."

Tony looked around. "I guess that's good."

"I don't know if it is or not. Does she have an address book?"

Tony frowned. "I don't know. We're not close or anything. Just good neighbors. I don't know much about her life."

I wandered back to the bedroom, searching for an address book, without success. "Friends?" I said.

"I don't think she has many. Or any. She works a lot. I mean a lot of overtime."

I glanced around. The furniture was very good quality, sturdy, but several years old. The plasma wall-mounted television would have cost a bomb, but that was about it. "What about her car?"

"It's a two-car garage. She has half. The other tenant has the other half. We have an old clunker and we both work at home, so we park on the side."

"Let's have a peek."

As we emerged from 18B I noticed Caroline's worried face at the window. Tony pointed to the garage. He opened the door using a button on the side. Empty.

"Well, she took her car. She drives a red Aveo, fairly old. But I guess you know that."

I said, "I was worried for a bit. Now I guess she just went out on an errand.

He said, "Nothing to worry about at all. We didn't disturb anything in her place, did we?"

"No. But if you see her, you should tell her I came by and I urgently need to hear from her. Please."

Tony's pleasant worried face changed slightly, a wary expression creeping in. "Urgently? Is there something I should know?"

"We just need to talk."

"Do you want to leave your number?"

"She has both of them actually. But I'll leave them for you, in case. Well, just in case you ever need them."

Tony said, "If you talk to her, tell her we'll take care of Mooch and Pooch."

As I left, Tony stood staring at my card. Caroline waved from the window.

Where was Mona?

*A well-organized kitchen can be a major time-saver and
stress eliminator in your busy life. Invest in simplicity and
order in the kitchen. It will repay you every day.*

7

My consultation was at ten in a trendy brick condo town
house near the waterfront. I did my best to put Mona's
bizarre situation to the back of my mind and concentrate
on getting through the appointment. It wasn't like I had a
plan for the great Mona hunt. As I pulled up and parked, a
woman radiating equal parts anxiety and eagerness stuck
her head out of the glossy black front door and waved. If
she kept holding her shoulders so stiffly, she'd need a mus-
cle relaxant before the day was done.

I'd always wanted to get a peek into one of these homes.
My would-be client had salt-and-pepper hair cut in a geo-
metric bob. It suited her. She wore a loose black cashmere
tunic and black leggings, with a pair of ankle boots in a soft,
scrunchy, cream-colored leather. Whatever she did with her
time, she was normally an in-charge gal; I could tell by the
confidence in the outfit and the haircut. But today, like most
clients she had that sheepish expression. Mainly because
their disorderly secrets are about to be displayed to me.

I held out my hand. "Hi, I'm Charlotte. I've always wanted to see what these beautiful town houses are like inside."

She hesitated, then shook my hand. "Thank you for coming, Charlotte. I'm Hannah Yaldon. I love my new house except for the hidden bits in the kitchen."

I grinned to put her at ease. My job is a pleasure for me, but my arrival is often horribly stressful for clients. Imagine showing off your most embarrassing secrets to a near stranger. "Kitchens are often a calamity. They make people's daily lives wretched," I said, using words my mother might have come up with. "I love helping to fix them. It's often quite a lot of fun, once we get over that initial hump."

I noticed her shoulders relax slightly. A good sign.

She said, "Come in. Would you like a glass of water? I would have made coffee, but I can't find some of the key ingredients."

"We know you have water, so . . ."

"Exactly. And I have a pound of Kicking Horse and I have no idea where it is, or the grinder, for that matter."

"Water's fine. And finding the coffee and grinder will be a great motivator." I wasn't kidding. On a day like today, hot liquids could be a lifesaver.

"Well," she said, as I slipped into my shoes. "Let's get on the hunt."

We strolled through the sparsely furnished living space. The twelve-foot ceilings, exposed brick wall, freestanding gas fireplace, fabulous L-shaped chocolate-brown leather sofa, and clear acrylic coffee table were all I had time to notice. It was free of knickknacks, reading material, and anything extraneous, except for a sculptural orchid on a plinth. Our heels clicked on the wide-plank flooring as we headed to the open-concept kitchen. I noticed she slowed down as we got closer. I kept walking. The sooner we confront the disaster, the faster the client starts to feel hope again. I'm all about hope.

I glanced around the gorgeous room. No upper cabinets at all. Nothing rested on or above the pricey quartz countertop except a stainless steel range hood that reminded me of a work of art. The undermount sink was also stainless, and the cooktop blended into the counter. Nothing cluttered those sparkling surfaces.

I spotted the stainless oven and had to assume that she had refrigerator drawers and a freezer drawer. This proved to be true as my water was produced from a filtered container.

"Is the dishwasher also a drawer model?"

She nodded.

"Lots of lovely appliances. No top cupboards at all?"

"Just below."

"It makes my mouth water," I said, speaking the absolute truth. "People would kill for this kitchen."

"Until they tried to make a meal in it," she said with a bitter laugh. "Then they'd kill the designer."

"Ah. Not so easy to work in?"

"Fine until you need to find something."

"Mind if I check out your storage?"

She winced and I said, "It will have to happen sooner or later."

"It's so embarrassing, that's all. My husband loves order and simplicity. I like to cook and, well—"

I waited her out.

"Fine," she said. "Let's get it over with. I feel like I'm at the principal's office."

"Don't let yourself think that way. I'll be working for you if you want to proceed. Not the other way around."

"Okay. Go ahead."

I reached over and opened the nearest cupboard door before she changed her mind. A tumble of plastic containers landed at my feet.

She put her hands over her eyes. "I wish you hadn't started with that one."

I picked up an armload of empty yogurt containers and put them on the counter. "No point in replacing them."

I reached for the next cupboard door and heard her groan.

I said, "If it's any consolation, your storage seems to be set up for appearances rather than efficiency."

"I know."

"And it is gorgeous."

"It *is*. Until I start cooking."

The second cupboard was jammed with cookware: pots, pans, lids, baking dishes. Lots of everything, including an untidy pile of recipe books and clippings.

"You could open a store," I said. "What an array."

"We combined two households. Neither of us wanted to give up our favorites. I had no idea what a difference a small kitchen would make."

"Right." I reached over and opened the oven. Sure enough, there were the dishes that had probably been in the sink just before I arrived.

She gasped. "I am so mortified."

"Don't be. I find that in fifty percent of my kitchen jobs. Of course, it's only a matter of time until someone turns that oven on at the wrong moment. But you won't have that problem after we finish."

"Do you know every little trick I've tried?"

"Probably. But you might have tried something I haven't seen before. I'm always ready to be surprised. You'll relax a bit more when I've checked everything. There will be nothing to hide and we can move on." I whipped over the first drawer. Jammed with cutlery. Three or four sets at first glance. The second, third, and fourth drawers were overflowing with utensils, enough for three kitchens. Typical when households merge.

Hannah's cheeks were as scarlet as my sweater by this time. "Don't worry about it," I said. "I've seen all this many times."

"I can't believe I'm so disorganized. Makes me wonder how I can believe that I am capable of running a design business," she said with a self-disparaging grin.

I paused. "What is your business?"

"UBER. We do contemporary furniture, lighting, and custom design. We are uptown in a converted house near the old Dutch church."

"That sounds great, and if your home is anything to go by, you're terrific at your job."

"Except that I am a total incompetent here. That must be obvious."

"Nothing to do with competence. Too much stuff, too little storage. That's the problem. I can see that it's isolated in the kitchen. That often happens when two households come together."

"In this case, in one much smaller home."

"Exactly, but it won't take long to put it right if you decide to use my services. You could manage it yourself, I'm sure."

"I want you to do it. Today if possible."

"We won't be able to do it today. But if you want to pursue the project, I can leave you with homework. I have some time available later in the week. We should be able to get everything done soon if I can round up my helper. Sound good?"

"Sounds like a relief."

Five minutes later, we'd signed my simple contract and I'd gone over the basic plan. I'd asked Hannah to pick a charity to donate her surplus kitchenware to. She said, "I support the community kitchen. It helps needy families learn to cook inexpensive and healthy food. They might need items for the kitchen."

"That's a lovely idea. You'll have plenty to give. In a kitchen like this you need to get rid of everything you don't use and eliminate duplicate items. I saw about six spatulas."

"I'm sure there are more."

"You can get a head start with your utensils drawers. Figure out the most you'd need at a time. I'm guessing two. And give the rest away. It's easier to wash a spatula occasionally than to dig through all this every day when you need something. It's one of the easier decluttering jobs, because there probably won't be that much emotion tied up in those utensils, but in case there is, be tough with yourself. And honest. There's a huge payoff."

"But I don't have a spare minute to do it. I should be at the shop already."

"Not a problem. We can find another slot time for our appointments. And we can always do the sorting for you, if we can agree on a few principles." I whipped out my agenda.

"It has to be midweek evenings for me. I'm building my design business and I need to be there during the days. I use the evenings for in-home consultations."

"Evenings are bad for me this week. I'm doing time-management workshops Monday, Wednesday, and Friday and I have a commitment on Tuesday night. What time do you open your shop? Perhaps I could come in before you go to work?"

Ten minutes later we had found enough common time to fix the first two appointments. Eight a.m. Tuesday and Thursday. Why not?

"It's short notice, but I'll try to arrange a helper and bins tomorrow." I glanced around and realized the only place the bins could stay was in the flawless minimalist living room. Oh well. They wouldn't be there for long. "I hope you will be able to stand the bins for the duration of the project. Short-term pain for long-term gain." I knew Lilith Carisse, my all-around assistant, could use a bit of extra work to get her through the college term. Sometimes her three part-time jobs weren't enough to support her. Lilith would love to see the inside of this jewel of a house. And she'd become faster and more efficient than I was in a purge.

I took the time to peer in all the cupboards and to get down on my knees with my digital camera to take shots of the shelves and their crowded contents.

As we said our good-byes, Hannah bit her lip. I'm used to that. There are often anxieties and second thoughts that surface after that contract's signed. She said, "There are many things we don't use often. I'd hate to get rid of them and then need them. Some have sentimental value. I have some of my mother's cooking paraphernalia from back in the sixties."

"Don't worry about that. We'll find a way for you to keep what's loved and useful. As for the rest of it, if you choose a small kitchen and you don't want any more cupboards, you have to be ruthless with the everyday items. You'll be making the decisions, not me. And if there are utensils you use once a year, set them aside and we'll find a place where you're not tripping over them for the other three hundred and sixty-four days. We'll take it item by item. Most of the items won't have sentimental value. You won't hate the process as much as you think and you'll love the results."

She managed a smile. I recognized that glimmer of hope.

I love this job.

<hr>

As soon as I was back in the Miata, I left a message for Lilith Carisse and tried Mona again. No luck. And of course no answering machine picked up. I was home again soon enough, although the driving was slushy and miserable. Keep smiling, I told myself. No point in fussing about what you can't change, like the weather. I was looking forward to my therapy-dog meeting.

I was surprised to find Pepper waiting for me in my driveway. She stepped out of the unmarked dark sedan that we called her detectivemobile. She wore a long black coat with a stylish cut and a flattering collar. Her new layered haircut suited her and her skin was glowing. Pepper was an excellent detective and she loved being a cop, even if she missed Little Nick during her shifts. Little Nick's dad, "Nick the Stick" Monahan, for long, complicated reasons that gave me a headache, was taking leave to care for him.

I glanced at her feet. I was in the market for a new pair of winter dress boots now that the sales were on.

I waved and grinned. "Where did you get those great boots, Pepper? I—"

"We better talk inside," she said grimly. "Over coffee."

I felt my heart sink. I'd told Pepper about Mona's outbursts. Had she been arrested? Or worse, had Pepper found proof that Mona was responsible for the hit-and-runs? Don't jump to conclusions, I reminded myself. Pepper was still suffering from terrible headaches after her head injury the previous June. Or her mood might have to do with "Nick the Stick." Her handsome and useless husband never failed to present a new challenge to Pepper, especially now that he was on suspension from the police force. Pepper's official story was about Nick's desire to be a stay-at-home dad. No one was buying that. Pepper was quiet on the way up, and the only sound was the clatter of our heels on the wooden stairs. The dogs greeted us with enthusiasm and joined Pepper on the sofa while I made the coffee. I found a stash of sugar cookies left over from the last batch my friend Rose Skipowski had made for me, and I put them on a plate.

When I arrived back bearing coffee and cookies, I noticed Sweet Marie and Truffle had burrowed in to cuddle Pepper, their faces resting on the thigh of her dark wool dress pants. She had a pained expression on her regal face. She's not the type for pets.

"Don't worry, I have an excellent lint brush," I said.

"What are you talking about?"

"Dog hair on your thigh. I thought that's why you have that expression."

"If only." Pepper picked up her cup of coffee. She takes it black, no sugar. So do I. "Here's the thing—"

I blurted out, "I am worried about Mona. I'd like to talk to her. Did you get a chance to talk sense into her?"

Pepper can't lie to me. We've been friends far too long. She scrunched up her face. I knew she was toying with a fib, and thought the better of it.

"So did you?"

"Yes, I did. That's why I'm here."

"You found her?"

"Found her? She's not lost. What are you talking about?"

As much as I felt I owed Mona some loyalty, two people were dead. And Mona was in a state. I wasn't a cop, as people kept pointing out to me, but Pepper was.

I said, "There was another hit-and-run."

"Of course, I know that. I'm investigating the hit-and-runs. What do you think detectives do here in Woodbridge?"

"Do you think Mona is behind the hit-and-runs?"

"No, I don't."

"Do you think someone is trying to set her up?"

Pepper wrinkled her nose. "What do you mean?"

"She's getting prank calls. And she thinks someone is stealing her stuff and has left the items at what she calls the 'death sites' to implicate her."

"That's just nuts," Pepper said. But her expression told me that had hit a chord.

"Did you find a scarf or gloves? That kind of thing at either location?"

I could tell that they had. "Have you sent those items to the lab? Do you think they could implicate—"

Pepper held up her hand. It was enough to silence me.

All that natural authority. "You don't have to stick your pointed little nose into this situation. We are on top of it."

"I'm glad you're on top of it, Pepper, and I never doubted that." This wasn't entirely true, but it should have been. I realize I have to stop trying to control everything.

"If it puts your mind to rest, Mona had nothing to do with that second death, and I doubt if she was involved with the first one either."

"How do you know?"

"Because I was talking to Mona right around the time that Bethann Reynolds died. It was just a fluke that I ran into her in the women's restroom at the station. And she was working the night shift when Tiffanee was killed. Present and accounted for."

"That's a relief. But you understand, Pepper, the way she talked about them, I had no choice but to follow up."

"God knows she had reason to hate that gang, but she didn't do it. Can you accept that?"

"But the second victim was Tiffanee Dupont, one of her tormentors. What are the chances?"

"I am well aware of who it was. Mona didn't do that." Pepper got to her feet and headed toward the door.

"And do you think that the two cases are connected? Do you think that Bethann was killed because she looked so much like Serena? It was uncanny. I saw her on television." I kept talking as Pepper bent to put on her snazzy boots.

"Charlotte, pull yourself together. Bethann Reynolds had a superficial resemblance, shoulder-length blond hair, that's it. She wasn't glamorous like Serena. In fact, if you think back, she was bullied at St. Jude's too. Right now, we're not seeing a connection." She slipped into her elegant coat and buttoned it.

"But you know it can't be a coincidence. They would have gone to school together. Isn't that too weird?" I didn't let her narrowed eyes get to me. Not after all those years.

I said, "This is very scary. I was so worried about Haley yesterday that Jack and I went out to check on her."

"Why would you think that it would be Haley?"

"Because she was one of the original bullies."

"And you got it into your head that Mona had decided to knock them off one by one. Well, she didn't, so move on."

"Fine, but something is very wrong with Mona. She's not at home, she won't answer her home phone, her message machine doesn't pick up, and she's not at work although she's supposed to be."

Pepper left me with a parting shot as I walked her down the stairs to the front door. "Don't contact Mona. Don't go by her house. Don't call her cell. Don't call her workplace. If there's any other Mona possibilities that I have failed to anticipate or articulate, don't do them either."

"Fine. I have plenty to do. And I know you have things well in hand."

"Right. Let's see. Have I forgotten anything? Oh yes. Hit-and-run victims. Don't walk down their streets. Don't pat their dogs. Don't do anything that might make me forget that I am sworn to uphold the law."

*The biggest time-saver of all is a two-letter word: No.
Practice saying it until you can get the hang of it. Make it a
game and role-play with a sympathetic friend.*

8

The dogs eyed me suspiciously. As Truffle and Sweet Marie are a bonded pair, I'd needed some kind of good plan to deal with separating them during the therapy-dog visits. I couldn't leave Truffle alone in the apartment without a bit more trouble than usual. Luckily, Jack had agreed to have Truffle visit him at the shop, where there are endless buckets of dog treats as far as I can tell.

We dropped Truffle off quickly and made our way to Riverview Manor, a purpose-built facility near the river, in the rapidly gentrifying downtown sector. A few minutes ahead of schedule, we pulled up in the parking lot of Riverview Manor. Sweet Marie was adorable in her jaunty red scarf and the ID disc that announced I AM A WOOD-BRIDGE THERAPY DOG. She was still sulking over the bath and manicure, but she knew she looked good. Still, as it was once again snowing, I carried her until we reached the walkway. If she appreciated that, it wasn't at all obvious.

At the door, once we signed in, a cluster of women in

crayon-colored scrubs waited to welcome Sweet Marie. She took to them. She has learned over the years that ladies often have treats. Program director Bella Constantine was there as promised, arms outstretched, silver helmet of hair perfect. Tiny red-haired Candy Brinkerhoff stood smiling broadly behind her, happy doing her duty as the therapy-dog coordinator, integrating us into our first assignment.

Bella squealed, "So glad to meet you, Charlotte! We are so excited about having Truffle and Sweet Marie on board. I realize that you can only have one at a time, but I suppose you could alternate them."

"Candy said you are in charge of a mild dementia unit?"

"Yes. Mostly Alzheimer's patients."

"Sweet Marie is a bit more cuddly and relaxed so I picked her to go first."

I was glad that Candy was along to help me learn the ropes, as this was unlike any volunteer work I'd done before. She'd already given me some useful information about Alzheimer's and its progress. Bella handed me a bit of homework: a sheet with instructions and advice to make visits go smoothly for the volunteer and the residents.

Once we were in the secure unit, Bella and Candy rigged up a small cart and blanket for Sweet Marie and pointed out the features of the unit. I was much more nervous than I expected to be. This was my first experience with any kind of dementia. Bella led the parade, exuding affection and competence. "Give it time. It may take a while for people to be able to see Sweet Marie. They may not react to you or me or the pooch today. Some people don't like dogs so we'll ask each person and take it from there."

With Bella leading the way and introducing us, we made our way through the unit. Many of the residents were walking around, others sitting in chairs along the corridor. Some were watching old movies on a large-screen televi-sion. Others were wandering. Family members seemed to pop in and out, sitting with their loved ones. I saw a number of volunteers smiling and having a good time. The walls here were decorated with bright canvases, acrylic paintings of flowers and animals, plus abstracts in vibrant colors.

"Done by our residents," Bella said with pride. "We have an art program staffed by volunteer artists. Everyone loves it. We have an art show and sale. I'll let you know when it's on. I'm sure you'll want to buy something to support us. You'll notice the fabulous mural painted on the walls and door from the units. Our volunteer art coordinator did those. It makes it feel a lot less like a secure unit, although it is."

I turned and glanced back at the wall and the door we'd come in. Sure enough the mural turned a bland bit of institution into a lush green garden surrounded by trees. It was quite a powerful transformation.

"I love it."

Bella nodded. "Some things make a difference in how you perceive the world around you."

Ten minutes into the job and already I'd learned something valuable. Bella laughed and enjoyed talking to the residents. She was free with the hugs. She spoke to everyone by name and was up-to-date on what was happening to each one.

Of course, she knew who the good dog candidates were. She told me not to worry if someone didn't react to Sweet Marie or didn't seem interested. "It can take a while, and dogs are not for everyone. Some never will respond. But you will be doing a lot of good for the ones who can interact with this little darling. She will leave good feelings swirling behind her."

We didn't get far before we hit pay dirt. A sprightly man with no hair and a smile as big as his chair lit up at the sight of my little dog. He reached out toward Sweet Marie, and Bella expertly guided his hands. Bella said, "Joe, this is Sweet Marie and Charlotte. They're here to visit. Let's see if she wants to be stroked." She did. In fact, the pooch was a lot less nervous than I was. By the time we'd reached the end of the hallway and visited a few rooms, we'd met plenty of dog lovers and Sweet Marie had been patted and talked to. Her tail was still wagging. I had to admit the smiles were worth all the effort.

As we neared the end, Bella said, "You'll find that there are some weeks that are better than others. When a resident doesn't feel well, he or she may not be able to respond. People won't remember you or Sweet Marie as a rule, so don't let that bother you. It's just beyond them. But some of them will start to find the experience familiar. Those positive feelings are so good for our fragile residents. You'll see it in time."

As we exited, Bella thanked us and said she was so happy we could do this. "We've been waiting for a therapy dog forever. Too bad you couldn't bring in the two of them." Candy shook her head and I could tell they'd had that chat before.

In the hallway, Candy told me that the initial visit had gone very well and Sweet Marie had been amazing. She said she'd be glad to accompany us on another visit and I was grateful. Another barrier passed. I hoped I would be able to do it well and make a difference.

For an entire hour, I had been too busy to think about Mona.

The door to CYCotics jingled as I opened it. I was holding on to Sweet Marie's leash and bearing two large lattes from Ciao! Ciao! I also had a small bag of dog treats for the little hero and for the poor abandoned brother, in case Jack had run out of them. Truffle jumped off the desk chair and bounded toward us barking in reproach. I trotted back to the Miata to get the beef-and-barley soup and crusty rolls that had been the day's special. I'd had soup on the brain since my visit to Mona's that morning. Of course, I had Mona on the brain too.

Jack was standing and examining what I knew to be a snowboard. He said, "I'm thinking about bringing in more boards next year. I had a lot of people in asking for them. We sold a couple of used ones as a favor to some friends and word started getting out. I think I'd do a good snow-boarding business. The bike business is a bit too quiet in the winter. So I'm hoping it would be a complementary product line. There's good business in gear and clothing for snowboarders too."

While it would be nice for Jack to branch out, I thought he could use a quiet season to polish off his PhD. I knew better than to mention that.

"Jack. I need to talk to you."

"Shoot."

"It's about our time at St. Jude's."

"Sure." I noticed his eyes drifted toward the snowboard.

"You'll have to pay attention."

"Sorry."

Jack's three-*S* beginnings, "shoot, sure, and sorry," didn't bode well for the conversation. "I need you to help me here. And don't say 'swell.'"

To do him credit, he nodded and gave the impression of being fascinated.

"It's about all that bullying that went on with the girls."

He shrugged. "Like I said, except for that incident with Mona, I was only vaguely aware. Guys didn't pay much attention to girl politics, you know. For one thing, it seemed dangerous, and for another, it wasn't all that interesting. And for a third, I don't think we saw much. I think people like Serena and Jasmin and Tiffanee and Haley kept their machinations secret. The kind of thing they did to Mona would turn off any decent guy."

"I would hope so. I wonder why we misfits got off easy?"

"I suppose with me it was sports. I was good at basketball. It helped a lot. It's when you're perceived to be marginal that the hyenas cut you off from the pack. No one bothered you much either. Maybe because your mother was famous."

I made a face. "You think that was it?"

"You never seemed all that vulnerable. And you were kind of bossy then too. The kind of kid who might take legal action. I think it was that."

One of the reasons it's not a good idea to eat soup with Jack is that he almost always makes me laugh.

"I'm worried about Mona."

"Did you talk to Pepper?"

"Yeah. And she's telling me to butt out."

"Maybe you should butt out."

"But Mona isn't at work today. No one knows where she is. Her coworkers are worried. Her neighbors are worried. I'm worried."

"Does this remind you of the last time?"

"Of course it does, Jack. I have a sick feeling in the pit of my stomach."

"But, Charlotte, you have to leave it to the cops. They'll solve it. Let them have sick feelings in their stomachs. They get paid the big bucks for that."

"I'm not sure the bucks are that big and trust me, I'd love to be able to leave it to them. I am not trying to solve a crime. I just want to find Mona and help her. She told me she was going into hiding because someone is trying to implicate her in these hit-and-runs. And yet, the other day, I could have sworn she was mad enough to run down any of these women. She's acting very strange. I think she's having some kind of breakdown and she needs help. I should have done more when I was at school. Now I feel like crap that I didn't."

"You were always kind to her, Charlotte. You were nice to everyone."

"You just said I was bossy."

"That too. But in a kind way."

"She turned to me this time. I think her crazy talk is a cry for help. I can't refuse to get involved."

"Yeah, you can."

I didn't hang around to argue with Jack anymore. It was definitely a lose-lose situation. And I could see his point. I just couldn't get Mona and her problem out of my mind, and there wasn't a damn thing I could do about it.

Truffle decided to go back to the one real chair. Jack hopped out to make room for him. He didn't seem to mind. "I've got lots to do standing up. He's barky today, so I haven't had any worries about burglars. It's too bad he couldn't go with you. I think he might have been offended that you left him behind."

"He's a dog, Jack. He doesn't have human emotions. And even if they did let me take two dogs there, I don't think I could manage them. You have to make sure the dogs are comfortable and not stressed. And you have to talk to the residents and take care that everything's going all right. I'll just have to alternate them."

Jack said, "I could always come with you."

"What?"

"I could come with you. We could each have one and that would be a real party."

"But what about the shop?"

"I'm here six days a week, on Saturdays and plenty of evenings, even Sunday morning this week. Whatever your regular schedule is, I'll just open a bit later on that day. Do you want to ask Candy if that would be all right? I did go to the orientation sessions so that I could help you with the training, if you remember. It seems a shame to leave one of the little guys alone."

"I'll check with Candy. I'm sure she'd love it if you came along with Truffle. As you said, you were there for the sessions too. You'd have to join Woodbridge Therapy Dogs."

Of course, there are few dog-related organizations in Woodbridge that Jack is not a member of. I didn't see this as much of an impediment.

Jack said, "I'm up for it. I'll get one of my repair guys to cover the shop if I have to. Find out if we can do it."

Jack of course didn't worry about a thing. He didn't ask himself what could go wrong. He didn't worry and plan. He was always just ready to roll.

Five minutes later we had a date with Candy and Bella for the next morning. Our regular schedule to be determined. I raced home to try to catch up on the day's business.

— ✦ —

As I was getting ready to leave for my Monday course, Lilith called back to say she'd love to work on Hannah Yalden's kitchen.

"Are you kidding?" she said. "I've been dying to get inside one of those places. They look gorgeous. This is the only way I'm going to do it. I managed to rejig my schedule tomorrow and Thursday so we can go there early. Is that right? I love the kitchen cupboard cleanups. Maybe I'll score some of those utensils for the youth center. They always need cooking gear. Okay, gotta go. I'm seeing Seth tonight before the bedtime shift at Belleview."

Now that brought a smile to my face. Lilith was the opposite of the shy Seth, but their unlikely romance had blossomed during one of our organizing projects. It was a good news story.

I wasn't so lucky with Mona. She did not call back and say that she had been just overwrought and didn't feel murderous toward Serena and her friends or that she'd been mistaken about someone trying to implicate her or even that she had changed her mind about going into hiding. Luckily, I had that course to take my mind off Bethann's and Tiffanee's deaths and Mona's bizarre behavior. I knew I couldn't actually go searching for Mona. I still had Pepper's warning ringing in my ears. I settled the pooches comfortably on the sofa and made my way out to the winter wonderland.

—◆◆—

The Monday night session was Taking the Nightmare out of Your Mornings. I was expecting mostly moms of young children and teens, and that was what I got. I figured that the organized moms wouldn't be at my session. They wouldn't need to be. I glanced around the room and saw a number of tired and frazzled folks. I had tons of tips for them, mostly involving small changes to routines and habits, as well as for preparation the night before. I knew even without having children that if every child has a central place for school permission sheets, schedules, notes from the teacher, and any paper that might be needed, life might still not be perfect, but would be less stressful. For every parent who knew that, there seemed to be one who'd never thought of it. I was keen to pass on my own habits of preparing all but the last-minute bits of breakfast the night before, of setting the table and having lunches ready to go. Kids can do a lot of that on their own. I also recommended having every family member set out what they would wear—right down to the underwear. I said cheerfully, "If you watch television, use the ad time to knock off these little chores. Somehow four minutes the night before saves twenty in the morning. Don't ask me to explain why time behaves like that, but it does."

Not being a parent, I was naturally surprised by some of the situations people live with. Parents late for work, kids late for school, mismatched shoes, unbrushed teeth, temper tantrums, and missed meals. I know you have to pick your battles, but I also know lives can be better.

At the end, I handed everyone my top-five tips on small cards I'd had laminated. "If you adopt even one of these a month, you'll find life improves," I said at the end. "Any last questions?"

"Do you think these hit-and-runs are murder?" This came from the most frazzled woman in the room, the one whose child refused to get dressed in the morning and would only eat white food on white plates while standing up.

"The police are calling them hit-and-runs," I said. "And I know that they are investigating."

"People are saying you knew the victims," a small intense woman said.

"We went to the same school," I admitted, "but I didn't know Bethann then and I haven't seen her since. I do remember Tiffanee Dupont."

The very pregnant redhead in the last row said, "She was two years ahead of me at St. Jude's and she was very scary."

A beautiful gaunt woman wearing a periwinkle-blue sweater began to cry. "How can you say that? She was my yoga teacher. She was so wonderful. So kind and helpful. She helped me so much after my chemo."

"I don't know about that Bethann, but Tiffanee was a bitch. And I know that personally," the redhead said, resting her hand on her "bump" and sticking to her guns.

"People change." Tears rolled down the cheeks of Tiffanee's defender.

"If you say so, but I doubt it in this case." That redhead liked to have the last word.

I didn't want to get into this. "Please e-mail me or contact me on Facebook if you want to follow up on any of the tips and techniques from tonight. I'd love to hear from you.

We'll keep the group going to share successes and help each other overcome setbacks."

As they filed out of the room, the woman in the periwinkle sweater stayed behind. "I'm sorry for getting emotional. I just hated the idea of someone refusing to accept that Tiffanee was a wonderful person." She shot a poisonous glance at the retreating redhead.

This was a tricky situation. I'd had the same reaction as the redhead when I saw the tearful interviews on WINY. They didn't match up with the Tiffanee I'd known.

"It's hard to judge," I said. "People have their own experiences."

"And you don't think it was possible for her to change?"

I touched her arm and said, "I am glad you had a lovely experience with Tiffanee and that she helped you. That's good to hear."

I didn't see how the Tiffanee I remembered could have gone from the bully to the nurturing yoga teacher. But I saw no reason to ruin the memory for this kind person.

She sniffed. "Thank you. She mentioned once that she wasn't at all proud of her past. She'd had a lot of therapy, and it had helped her develop her spiritual side. She said she had some bad Karma to deal with."

<hr />

I didn't sleep well that night. I kept dreaming about Tiffanee, the beautiful, cruel girl I remembered and this new version, the kind, gentle yoga teacher. Bad Karma indeed. They were separate people in my dreams, one with the waist-length black hair and the other with the close-cropped do and the serene expression. Both Tiffanees were terrified of Mona. The dream started out with Mona weeping hysterically in a school locker, but for some reason when Jack opened it, she emerged dressed as a firefighter, only with stainless steel retractable claws; all very Wolfman. She was also about seven feet tall and very vengeful and very superhero-like. I woke up gasping as the stainless steel claws clicked out and slashed at the Tiffanees. And Mona shrieked, "You won't be the last two!"

I found myself wide-awake in a tangle of sheets. I knew I had to get up and shake those bad feelings out of my mind. I headed for the kitchen, warmed some milk in the microwave, and put a bit of vanilla in it. As Truffle and Sweet Marie joined me on the sofa for a reassuring cuddle, I sipped my warm milk slowly and thought about the situation. Could there have been enough therapy in the world to change Tiffanee? On the other hand, Haley had certainly changed; perhaps the hard time her family was going through helped her to be more empathetic. But what did I know about therapy and bullies? Nothing. Maybe it was time to learn. I made a note on my pristine To Do list: Check out therapists!

———— ✦ ————

Morning produced no more calls from Mona. I bundled Truffle and Sweet Marie into their warm sweaters, and after the quickest of outside visits—their hurry, not mine—I actually clicked on the WINY news to see if anything bad had happened to anyone else. The news was good in a way: no new fatalities. On the bad side, the police were still coming up empty on the two hit-and-runs. Todd Tyrell flashed a shot of Pepper whenever he brought the viewers' attention to the fact that the Woodbridge Police had no leads. He chose the clip where she looks like she's just left the hair salon. But never mind, no one else had died, even though an elderly couple had hit the guardrail on the top of Hemlock Hill and narrowly missed going over the thirty-foot embankment. They were lucky to have escaped with bruises and shock. The guardrail had been pretty much flattened. The day was off to a good start, even if I was groggy and yawning. Jack bounded up the stairs and greeted me with a grin. He wolfed down his breakfast and finished mine. I wasn't that hungry. I had a jam-packed day, starting with an eight o'clock appointment with Lilith at Hannah's.

———————

When I arrived at Hannah's place at five to eight, Lilith was already waiting for me in Rose Skipowski's ancient car, bins stashed in the backseat, and a good supply of plastic utensil drawers as well.

"I can't wait to see this place," she said, as we knocked on the glossy door right on the hour. It's best not to be even a minute early at that time of morning.

Lilith's hair was bubblegum pink this week. I wondered if it would glow in the dark. Hannah blinked, maybe at the hair, maybe at Lilith's nose ring and that parade of earrings. Alarm flitted across her face. It evaporated when I introduced Lilith in glowing terms. "Lilith is the best," I added to reinforce her confidence, once we'd shed our clumpy boots and headed for the kitchen.

"Amazing," Lilith said, glancing around. "This is the kitchen? Where is everything?"

"Hidden," I said. "Drawers below, no cabinets."

"No clutter." Lilith nodded. "It is gorgeous. Very elegant. Goes with the house." I could see her mentally calculating storage space. She turned to Hannah and said with a grin, "You'll always have to be vigilant if you want it to stay like this."

Hannah said, "We've already had a problem. That's why I called Charlotte." She smiled and added, "And you."

I glanced around at the gleaming empty counters. "How did the utensil reduction go?"

She shook her head. "I did find a bit of time to give it a try. I got rid of a lot of stuff. So now we seem to be down to four of everything. Not good, but I am sure we had *eight* potato mashers when we started."

"Uh-oh. You only have room for one potato masher. Only keep doubles when it's essential."

"We just couldn't do it. We're too worried about needing things. What if we throw them away and then have to buy them?"

I said, "Give them to charity. You'll get a tax receipt and if you have to buy one or two items, it won't be the end of the world. That happens. You'll still be way ahead."

Lilith piped up. "I volunteer at youth services and Charlotte's plugged into a women's shelter. You have no idea how welcome those donations would be."

"Oh. I hadn't thought of it that way. But I don't think my husband will agree. He gets very . . . attached to things. And anxious." Hannah was an elegant woman who ran her own business, but she was a bit unhinged by the kitchen. She fluttered around like a moth.

"Does that happen a lot?" I said. "Is he around? He should be part of this discussion."

"He's hiding. Took off at seven thirty, looking over his shoulder nervously. You'll never take him alive." At least she was starting to see the humor in it.

"Is he the person who wants the uncluttered minimal vibe?"

"We both do. But he's more, um, passionate about it."

"He can't have it both ways," I said. "Especially since he's not here. But we'll try to make it painless. Where are the remaining utensils?"

Hannah opened the first drawer. "Still there." That was true. The drawer was still jammed, as was the next one.

"No problem," I said. "Let's select the tools you have actually used in the past week or so and separate them."

Lilith positioned herself. I lifted a badly bent spatula from the first drawer and raised a questioning eyebrow.

Hannah. "Spatula. Sure."

I said, "Spatula, yes. But was it this spatula?"

She frowned. Lilith said with a grin, "We'll take that as a no and we'll just put this one over here."

Hannah winced.

"Don't worry," I said. "We're not throwing it out or giving it away. We'll deal with it later."

Next I lifted out a wooden spoon with a seriously burned handle. Hannah admitted defeat.

I was surprised to see that Hannah and her hidden hubby couldn't live without three melon ballers. "We do use them!" she protested. "Often. In the summer."

"I believe you. Which one do you use?"

She wavered before selecting the newest and flashiest of the batch.

I held up a zester. "Yes! We can't live without that. It was horribly expensive too."

"Horribly expensive doesn't cut it, but if you can't live without it, it stays."

It took the three of us a bit of time to go through all the utensils in the crammed drawers. We had a third pile for "once a year" items: In the end, the eighty-twenty rule prevailed. We had four times as many tools on the "didn't use" side than on the "did use." I wasn't surprised.

Hannah slumped against the glamorous black quartz counter. "I feel beat-up!"

"Here's my suggestion. Do you have a shelf in your garage with room for a bin?" I knew she did.

"Yes."

"We'll pack up these surplus-to-requirements items, label the container, and tuck it in the garage. Lilith will sort them, and separate them nicely in plastic utensil drawers, so you won't go crazy if you do need something. At the end of six months, whatever you haven't used, you don't need. You can give it to someone who does need it. How would that work?"

Hannah nodded slowly.

I added, "I'd be happy to explain it to your husband. I think he'll realize there's no downside."

Lilith said, "I'll check in after six months and I'll come and collect what you haven't taken back."

I knew from experience that would be everything in the box.

"You're on," Hannah said.

It was time to move on. As Lilith busied herself sorting out the 80 percent that was outward bound, I said, "So for homework for Thursday morning, I'd like you to think about what you do every day. There's lots of baking gear. Do you bake?"

Hannah laughed. "I do actually. I bake like a madwoman the first week of November and freeze it all for the holidays. After that, I'm too busy until January."

"But I see lots of baking supplies in prime spots. Make a list of what you do every day and what you do on the weekends and when you entertain. Think about how you work in the kitchen and how your husband does. When we come back we'll sort out the extra cookware as we did the utensils and we'll find a way to keep your daily tools at your fingertips."

"Fun," Lilith said.

"It will be." I'm not sure if Hannah was reassured, but I knew she'd do the homework and she was well on the way to solving her problem. Of course, by now I had to dash.

⸻ ◆◆ ⸻

Truffle and Sweet Marie were a bit surprised to be bundled into their coats for the second time that morning. They'd been dogs of leisure for a bit too long. Time to get to work. I tied on their therapy-dog scarves, collected Jack, and we spun off in a cloud of snow.

Once we were at Riverview Manor, Jack smiled and

shook hands with every resident he could. He bent over to make eye contact with them, repeated their names, and laughed at his own jokes, which seemed to go over well with everyone. He had Sweet Marie with him, although he didn't seem to need the cart. I used the cart for Truffle. Truffle was on his best behavior too and loved having his ears stroked. When I grow up, I sure hope I can be relaxed like Jack. He managed to have a chat with the chaplain and most of the staff, as well as a pair of round-faced and pleasant volunteers wearing large yellow smiley buttons. We each got a button too. Jack took time to make sure each resident could focus on Sweet Marie's face. I had to admit, Sweet Marie's glossy tan coat stood out next to Jack's Hawaiian shirt, the one with the red hibiscus against a yellow background. It was a bit harder for people to see Truffle's shiny black fur against my charcoal-gray cashmere sweater. I made a mental note to wear a contrasting sweater next visit. Or let Jack carry Truffle. Jack doesn't own any dark clothing.

As I paraded Truffle around to some new arrivals, Jack took a minute to chat with two of the visiting wives as well. I watched him bend down to engage with everyone he met. It takes more than blank stares and noncomprehension to stop Jack when he wants to interest you in a dog. As I know all too well, having resisted Truffle and Sweet Marie at first.

Wherever he went there followed smiles and even laughter. Sweet Marie was truly on her best behavior, letting her ears be stroked and her head be scratched. She was much more relaxed on this second visit. I was too. Truffle made me proud, managing to convey great dignity—which isn't all that easy when you're a wiener dog. He also seemed happy to meet everyone and be patted and stroked. I'm not funny like Jack, but people seemed happy enough to see me, and, what was more important, to share a happy moment with my cuddly little dog.

Bella and Candy were thrilled with the visit. Once we were back in the foyer, they shook our hands (well, mostly Jack's) and said how wonderful our visit had been and how this was going to work out beautifully.

Jack grinned his lopsided grin and said he was keen to keep coming. He was still wearing his yellow smiley-face volunteer button. Knowing Jack, he'd rustle up interest in volunteering back at CYCotics. His customers wouldn't know what hit them.

I didn't say much, but I knew he made the whole experience better. He helped me to relax and the dogs as well. I wasn't sure why I'd been so worried about this, but Jack had helped alleviate those worries. As usual.

As we exited, he said, "You know something weird?"

"No," I said. "What is weird?"

"You'll never guess who I saw there."

There's no point in trying to guess, especially as he'd said I never would, but also because Jack knew so many people in Woodbridge, but before I could say, "Just tell me," the dogs set off a storm of barking on spotting a Bernese mountain dog. We scuttled away hoping our new reputations hadn't been ruined by the little monsters showing their true colors. Once the beasties settled down in the Miata, we chatted about our visit and I forgot to ask who it was that I never would have guessed. I was more interested in discussing our new experience.

I said, "That was nice, seeing those couples together. It was beautiful. Even though the spouses were now in River-view and that must have been so hard on them, they are still so close and affectionate."

Jack turned and stared at me. "Isn't that the way it's supposed to be?"

"Not in my world. My mother had four husbands, remember? And we're not counting the many near misses. She couldn't make a go of it when all she had was love, glamour, and money, so I can't imagine her spending her days holding any of their hands in a dementia unit."

Jack shook his head, "Maybe that's the problem."

"What's the problem?"

"I think if my parents hadn't been killed, they would have always been there for each other no matter what life brought them."

Jack's roly-poly happy mom and dad flashed through my memory. It was such a tragedy that they had been killed in a head-on collision when Jack was in the first year of his PhD program. I said, "You're right. They would have been there for each other."

"That's the way it's supposed to be, Charlotte."

I said, "Mmm."

Jack was strangely silent for the rest of the drive.

———

I had plenty of ordinary business to take care of that day. I needed to check the evaluation forms from the session the night before to see if I needed to adjust my workshop in any way. I had some invoices to do up, a few bills to pay, and it was time to take stock of my own office supplies. Hours flew by. It was only when I dropped into CYCotics with Jack's afternoon coffee that I remembered to ask, "Who was it you saw at Riverview Manor, Jack?"

"What?"

I sighed. "The person you said I'd never guess. Who was it?"

"Right. That was a shocker."

"Quit teasing and just say it."

"It was that Serena."

My jaw dropped. "Serena Redding? The beauty queen of mean?"

"Yup."

"But that's awful. What was she doing there?"

"I don't know. I just caught a glimpse and I didn't see her with anyone else."

"Oh well, it probably wasn't even Serena."

"Pretty sure it was. And she was wearing a volunteer happy-face button and smiling her big lipsticky smile."

"Hard to imagine."

"Yup. That's why I mentioned it."

"But it's a bit troubling. The people in Riverview Manor are so very vulnerable and we know how cruel Serena was. I have to find out what's going on."

Eliminate the stress of hunting for keys at departure time.
Develop a routine to keep your keys on a hook or in a basket
by the door. This tiny change may take a couple of weeks to
become a habit, but it will start paying off soon.

9

Bella was more than happy to meet me during her coffee break in the small sunny cafeteria of Riverview Manor. She was waiting with coffee for both of us and a pair of yummy Danishes with apricot glaze. "We have an excellent bakery for the facility," she said as she waved me to my seat. "But you have to act fast or everything's gone in a flash."

We chatted casually while I used my ploy of finding out more about the patients and unit. I said I was worried about making the wrong kinds of comments. "Yesterday I asked someone if they remembered Sweet Marie. I felt foolish about that. I hope I am going to catch on."

"If anyone noticed at all, they'd just think you're being conversational. You're doing great," Bella said, squeezing my hand. "And your friend is also a natural."

I didn't want to get sidetracked onto a Jack conversation, because that happens very easily. "I noticed plenty of volunteers, but not many our age," I said.

"Most are retired, but we have everyone from high school kids to older seniors coming in here. We can use lots of different age groups. We want Riverview to feel like a regular community."

I'd been hoping she'd say that Serena Redding was a volunteer, but that didn't pan out.

"I thought I saw someone I went to high school with yesterday. Probably just a mistake on my part. People change so much."

"Oh. I wonder who that would be."

I said innocently, "I think her name is Serena."

"Of course, Serena Zeitz."

Jackpot. "Must be her married name. I knew her as Serena Redding."

"It is. She's married to Jerome Zeitz of InZeitz.com." She looked at me expectantly.

That took me by surprise. "The ethical investment guru?"

Bella lowered her voice. "The same. He made a huge fortune and retired young. He concentrates on good works now. Anyway, he's originally from this area and they just moved back to Woodbridge. Well, they live in this fabulous estate outside of town."

"Huh." How unfair was that?

"Yes. Jerome Zeitz is very passionate about helping the community. He endowed our new wing here. His grandmother died of Alzheimer's and it's something he cares deeply about."

I smiled and hoped she didn't read my mind. "So, Serena is now volunteering here?"

A shadow passed over Bella's face. "That's right."

Now I was in a situation. Could I say something to Bella about Serena? Should I? Was it worse to say something or not to? What if Serena had changed? Of course, from what I knew about her conversations with Mona and Haley, she could still create unhappiness and even panic. And I had no evidence that Serena was doing anything wrong at all. If Tiffanee could change, why couldn't Serena? I couldn't do anything about Mona, but I had to speak up about this. I guess I must have been biting my lip, because Bella touched my arm and said, "Is something wrong?"

I gave a guilty start. "No, no, no. I was just surprised to see her after—"

Bella said, "The harm she did as a teenager?"

"Oh. I was going to say—after all these years, but, yes, to tell the truth, that's what I meant. Did you know about the bullying?"

She nodded. "I did. I had a younger cousin who had a hard time with Serena and her gal pals. She had a breakdown and her parents took her out of St. Jude's as a result, so when Serena showed up here, I was vehemently opposed to having her volunteer. I took it up with the executive director."

I waited.

Bella hesitated and glanced around. She lowered her voice. "I shouldn't be telling you this. I know there are confidentiality issues, but I could tell by your face that you knew Serena's history."

"I sure did. I'm sorry. I was kind of mining you for information. I regret not standing up against her and the others at the time. The people here are terribly vulnerable. If Serena was up to her old—"

"She isn't. I am absolutely certain of that. This volunteer work is one of the ways she's chosen to make amends."

I couldn't stop myself from snorting. Bella said, "I know how you feel. It took me a long time to come around too. We had some pretty lively meetings about her being here. I even got in touch with my cousin about it."

"What did she say?"

"To my surprise, she'd forgiven Serena. Serena contacted her when she moved back here. She said she had to make amends. She expressed remorse and they talked it through. Maybe part of it is that my cousin did well at her new school, and her parents supported her and worked hard to help her get over it."

"Hmm. I am glad for your cousin's sake that she's worked past it, but what about your residents here? They're not in a position to work through anything. Or even explain what's happening to them. What do we know about Serena's motives?"

"I understand that Serena has a baby who almost died of meningitis last year. And when the child was at death's door, I guess she made a bargain with the Almighty. Changing herself in return for the child getting better and making amends to people she'd harmed."

"That might explain it, but I'm still suspicious."

"With good reason and so was I. And I think that having a husband who is committed to making the world a better place makes a difference. They haven't been married all that long, maybe three or four years. He is a wonderful man. He's done a lot to establish schools in Africa. He set up scholarship funds for underprivileged youth. He sponsors a big fund-raiser for the food cupboard. The hospital—"

"Oh fine," I said.

Bella met my eyes. "To reassure you, Serena is never alone with any of our people. There's always someone with her. And more to the point, everyone likes her. The patients and staff seem to light up when she shows up for her shift."

After a pause, I said, "You know, back at St. Jude's people always lit up when she was around, with the exception of the miserable kids she singled out for torment. She was so gorgeous and powerful. I don't know if lighting up at the sight of her is a good indication." I sat there wondering what Serena was up to. I stared at Bella's soft, kind face. "You keep an eye on her all the time?"

"We always will in a subtle way. On the off chance that I'm wrong. People do change, Charlotte, and I think we all deserve a second chance. Don't we all need that in some way?"

"I guess. But I hope you're right. Serena was so cruel and dangerous, I am surprised that they would take the risk."

"Her pastor came with her. She's been getting counseling for her . . . issues. He stands behind her and this is part of her work in the community to reclaim her goodness."

I barely stopped myself from snorting.

"Charlotte, don't you believe that people can change?"

"Sure, I think that lots of us can improve ourselves, learn to live better lives, but Serena? The things she did were horrible. I'm sorry; I'd like to believe it, but I just can't buy that."

Bella said, "I believe you're wrong. And I hope you come to realize it, Charlotte."

I didn't doubt her sincerity. I just hoped she was right, for everyone's sake.

On my way home, I took a slight detour down Spruce Street to Mona's place. I didn't plan on contacting her. I parked and sat there worrying. As I did, the garage door opened and a dark-blue sedan pulled out. From the window of number 18, Caroline waved to the driver. Must have been the other tenant There was still no small red car inside the garage and no lights showing from the small windows of Mona's basement apartment. Wherever Mona was, she still wasn't home. I confirmed that by tromping over to her door and knocking. I followed up by having a quick conversation with Caroline. She was worried too because there still hadn't been a word or a sound from Mona. She and Tony were taking good care of Mooch and Pooch, she assured me.

I knew that Pepper would probably haul me in if she knew I'd done that, but I was also well aware that Serena wasn't the only person who needed to make amends. I had to make a lot up to Mona for not standing up for her at St. Jude's. I didn't want to mess up this time, but it was hard to figure out what to do.

Next I drove by the police station. Pepper hadn't mentioned that I shouldn't do that. I found no red Aveo parked in the staff parking area.

So. Mona wasn't at home, wasn't at work. Where was she? And was she all right?

⁕

Jack chugged up the stairs before five. "The roads are crummy. I closed early. It's not bike-buying weather. Not even snowboard weather. I thought you were babysitting at Sally's tonight."

"I am, but not until six thirty. Her yoga class is at seven."

"Okay. Want to eat together?"

This was a ridiculous comment, as we eat together every night that we're home.

He said, "Shall I send out for Thai? Hey, your table's set."

"Don't pass out, but I actually have the makings of a stir-fry. I am just about to whip that up."

"Right. I forgot you owned a recipe. That would be good. Want me to chop?"

"I actually have two recipes, Jack. Don't minimize. And I have rice cooking, and I am not counting that as one of the recipes. But anyway, I already chopped red and yellow peppers, zucchini, celery, and garlic. We'll have to eat pizza for a week to get all these vitamins out of our systems."

As I heated the wok and dropped in some oil to sizzle, Jack entertained Truffle and Sweet Marie. He called out to me from the living room. "What got into you?"

I dropped some finely chopped garlic into the sizzling oil. "I was trying to get into a Zen mood after all this worry about Mona and Serena and who knows who else. It helped quite a bit." I watched the dogs frolicking with Jack as the veggies hopped in the hot wok. It was more fun than television. I tossed in a pile of shrimp and then some black-bean sauce to finish off.

Jack was suitably impressed. It doesn't take much and that's a good thing. The dogs were impressed too and hung around, full of hope. As I served up the fragrant results on my white square plates, Jack said, "Hey. I'll do the dishes."

"I was going to volunteer you. And by the way, you were right, Jack. You did see Serena and she actually is a volunteer at Riverview Manor."

Jack's fork paused midway to his mouth. "Now, that's scary. Those people are very vulnerable. What if Serena hasn't really changed her ways? Do the people in charge know about her history as a bully?"

I shrugged. "They do know. At least they've heard a version of her past, although maybe that's been sanitized. They think that she is trying to make up for the evil things she's done in her life, and they believe her. Bella didn't agree with taking her on as a volunteer, but apparently it's all working out."

"Did you mention that you'd trust her as far as you could throw a Buick?"

"I made my point, but Bella says it seems to be sincere. She says Serena is never alone anyway. I am not sure what to do about it. It's not like we have any standing at Riverview. Serena has them bamboozled for sure. Bella insists that she's keeping an eye on Serena just in case."

"That girl never did anything without an ulterior motive. So what would be her motive there? I don't get that."

"From what I can figure out she has a new husband. He's a wealthy philanthropist and a man who is into ethical behavior."

"Sounds like a guy who would be very disappointed to

learn about the kind of person Serena is. Maybe that's why she's trying to build bridges."

"She called a relative of Bella's to ask forgiveness for her actions as a teenager. She called Mona."

"I can't see anyone falling for that."

"Most people fell for it when we were at St. Jude's. Bella says the staff and residents like her a lot."

"Maybe she's trying to get at their money."

"The new husband is loaded. So I don't think that's it. Serena's always had money. I think she enjoyed power. That's her motivation. I wonder if that's why she called Mona."

"What do you mean?"

"Ostensibly to get forgiveness, but wanting to bring all those bad memories back to Mona. The girl's gone off the deep end. Perhaps Serena is enjoying the knowledge that she can cause a person to disintegrate. Especially a person like Mona who'd worked so hard to overcome that tough time, to build a life and make a contribution."

Jack scowled. "I guess we'd better try to find out what's going on."

For Christmas, I'd given Sally two hours of babysitting every Tuesday night so she could hurry off to the yoga class that was saving her sanity this extended winter. Her husband, Benjamin, was too busy with hospital activities, committees, and his medical practice to give her much time off. With four children under five, Sally crashed into bed by eight many nights. I'd actually found her asleep on the rug once. My babysitting was a big hit. Jack had given Sally the same gift on Friday afternoons. If you haven't gathered this already, he is crazy about small children and wild about babies. I love kids too, for about an hour and fifty-eight minutes.

'Nuff said.

I was armed with a stack of books and some wind-up toy frogs that seemed nicely unpredictable. On her way out, I'd asked Sally to subtly inquire about Tiffanee and find out what people in that yoga community were saying. As the door closed behind her, I took a deep breath, turned, and faced the darling rug rats.

--❦--

When she got home, Sally had the post-yoga boneless glow that people seem to get. She sank into her leather sofa and smiled dreamily at me.

I wasn't quite so glowing, although I did have peanut butter in my hair.

"How did it go?" she said, eying my hair and suppressing a smirk.

"Books were a hit. Frogs were so-so. Snack was a disaster."

She glanced past me into the kitchen. "I can see that."

Three preschoolers were out like lights under a blanket on the sofa. The baby was already asleep. Sally had given them their baths before I arrived. Bath times for Sally's kids have not been among my most glorious moments.

Sally said, "Thank you, thank you, thank you. I love them so much, but I need to get away from the little beasts from time to time."

"Hey, no need to explain to me."

She snorted. "Hey, come on. Peanut butter becomes you."

"Changing the subject. Did anyone at your yoga group talk about Tiffanee?"

"Sure. They all did."

"And?"

Sally yawned.

"Nope. Not boring," I said. "Murdered, you know. So what did they say?"

"She was a lovely, kind woman. A talented yoga instructor. A few people cried."

I scowled. "Not a bully?"

"Quite dramatically changed apparently."

"Do you think that can happen, Sal?"

She straightened up and thought for a minute. "Hard to imagine, but I suppose it might be possible. But I think you need to let it go, Charlotte. Stop obsessing about Serena and the rest of them."

"I need a favor from you."

"After my break tonight, I owe you. Have I told you I love you too? Not as much as I love Jack, because he gives me more hours, but quite a lot."

"You and Benjamin know lots of medical practitioners here. Have you come across anyone who specializes in bullying?"

"Not again with that, Charlotte. What did I just say? You need to keep your nose out of this."

"What I need is to help Mona. I should have done it as a teenager. I should have had the empathy and the guts. Now she's in crisis. I'm not going to get involved in any other way, but I'd like to talk to someone who is a capable professional with no ax to grind or guilty feelings like me. Is that so ridiculous?"

Sally's sigh was particularly dramatic, even by her standards.

I said, "Go ahead. Go for the Oscar, Sal. But it won't hurt anyone for me to talk to a shrink about this."

"A shrink may be just what you need."

"I don't understand why you are being like this," I said.

"Like what?"

"Obstructionistic. And mean."

"Mainly because I don't think you should get involved. Someone is killing people. You are always getting involved in murders and putting yourself in danger. And you put Jack in danger too because he'll do anything to help you."

"I understand your point of view. All that babysitting

time jeopardized if I'm six feet under. But I am trying to avoid exactly that by speaking to someone who is a professional. I'll find out what is the right thing to do. Didn't I just say that? And let me make the point again: If we had taken those bullies to task, Mona wouldn't have had to deal with all this by herself. We are partly responsible."

"Speak for yourself. Maybe they would have made her life even more hellish as soon as we turned around. Ours too."

I gave Sally's hand a quick squeeze. "We should have stood up for ourselves and each other too. And for everyone else who needed it. I feel ashamed that I didn't do that. And I want to make up for it."

Sally said, "Lucky for you I'm all mellowed out from yoga."

"You'll help?"

"Benjamin has a colleague, a psychologist who works with bullies and people who have been damaged by bullies."

"Will I like her?"

"Him."

"Same question."

"I think so. But you're not looking for a new friend. Just some expert advice. Right?"

She had me. "Good point. I just need information on the best way to deal with Mona. So that she's not damaged any more."

Sally said, "Unless Mona's actually behind these hit-and-runs. She must have been so damaged by all that horrible treatment. But if she is, then you'd better just stay out of her way."

"Pepper says Mona's in the clear for both of them. But Mona seemed to have gone off the deep end and I need to know she's not going to ruin her life or harm herself or someone else."

—◆—

On my way home that evening, I swung by Rose Skipowski's place halfway up the steep hill on North Hemlock, hoping it wasn't too late. I found Lilith knee-deep in an end-of-term assignment, but willing to stop for me. As for Rose, she was always up for an unexpected guest. She'd answered the door in an aqua and silver jogging suit with little heart-shaped rhinestones that added a bit of bling. Her running shoes were silver with matching rhinestone blingy bits. Really, you hardly noticed that portable oxygen machine.

"You're looking splendid," I said.

Rose twinkled. "I'm just back from my bridge club. Lilith's got me back into a lot of my old activities. I feel like a kid of seventy again. But the girl's a slave driver. A little snack for you, Charlotte?"

Rose had lemon sugar refrigerator cookies sliced and baking away within seconds of my arrival. I made the coffee, because while Rose makes the best cookies in town, she makes the worst coffee. I always have a plan.

"Sure thing," Lilith said when I filled her in about the Serena conundrum. "I've worked in a lot of the facilities in town. I bet I know someone who's employed at Riverview Manor. Or maybe someone who's done a co-op assignment there. It has a great reputation."

"Excellent. I need to have someone who might have observed Serena at work and who might be closer to the situation than the administrators, who might know what's going on. Bella Constantine is pretty plugged in. But I have a feeling that the personal-care workers might see things that she doesn't. And they wouldn't have a preconceived notion about Serena from the pastor and the rich husband."

"Let me snoop around and get back to you," Lilith said. "If she's up to no good, someone will have noticed something. I'm sure I'll have something by the time we meet at Hannah's on Thursday morning."

I enjoy sitting in Rose's seventies-style living room. It's like a time warp, right down to the ancient oversize answering machine. The first one in the world, possibly. While I was enjoying plotting with Lilith and stuffing my face with Rose's unbeatable lemon sugar cookies, Rose had been unusually quiet. Finally she said sadly, "I know it happens, but it's hard to believe that someone might hurt defenseless people."

I nodded. "And good people don't catch on in time."

Rose said, "I only wish I could help."

—◆◆—

Sally delivered as I knew she would. Jack had joined me on the sofa after I got back. He'd been busy on the phone and online setting up a silent auction to benefit WAG'D— that's Welcome All Good Dogs if I have failed to mention it. I knew I'd be asked to dig deep. And I would be making a good donation even if Jack didn't turn the pressure up. Which he would. The doggies, freshly walked and dried off, snuggled in between us and promptly went to sleep. "I couldn't find out anything about Serena and her change of personality," Jack said. "I did make a few calls about the auction and kind of sneaked it into the chat."

He polished off the lemon sugar cookies that Rose had sent home with me, leaving only the empty container. I cleaned it out and put it on the console to return to Rose. Now he was insisting on hearing all about the babysitting. "Not much to tell," I said. I felt mean when I saw his face, and made up for it by describing every mildly amusing thing the kids had done over the hour and a half until they'd keeled over.

"Sounds like fun," Jack said. "By the way, are you still hungry?"

I was debating whether to offer up the last container of B & J's New York Super Chunk Fudge. By rights, neither one of us should have been hungry. The phone rang and I put that thought on hold.

Sally said, "You want a shrink. You got a shrink. Sam Partridge and please don't make any of those 'for the birds' puns, because he's heard them all."

"I wasn't planning on making bad puns," I said, defending myself against something that hadn't crossed my mind. Although I did have a mental image of Dr. Sam Partridge, and I was certain this real one wouldn't run across a road in a random pattern when startled by a noise.

"He usually works out of his home office, but he has a clinic at the hospital tomorrow. He'll see you at noon, if you don't mind joining him while he has lunch. I was lucky that he picked up his phone when I called."

Sally is so gorgeous that I couldn't imagine any man who wouldn't pick up the phone. She doesn't like it when I say things like that, so I kept the thought to myself. "Join him? I'll buy lunch for him."

"Oh, that won't be necessary. Ten minutes, no more. He'll meet you in the cafeteria."

"How will I know what he looks like?"

"He'll recognize you."

I suppose that was the one advantage of finding myself on television so often, even if it was usually me getting hauled off to the hoosegow in frog pajamas and pink fluffy slippers.

"Now it's past my bedtime." Sally hung up in the middle of what sounded like a yawn.

10

Wednesday morning, I had three messages when I got back in from the first dog "walk." They like to be airlifted to do their business through most of the winter. Back home, dried off and rewarded with a tiny liver treat, they tilted their heads in interest, concluded there was no more food to be gained from listening, and headed back to Nap Central. They climbed back under their blanket to dream of spring and squirrels.

I replayed the first message. Mona was nearly impossible to understand. "I told you so! Why didn't you listen to me?" That was the most I could get out of it. I was still trying to make out the rest of the blubbered message before she abruptly hung up. I still hadn't learned where she was or what had triggered that particular call. Of course, that was cleared up by the second message. Pepper. "Well, bit of news for you. Not sure how you'll take it, but it's definitely serious. Give me a call."

Naturally, Pepper didn't pick up when I returned her call.

The third caller was Jack, phoning from the shop, where he'd been waiting for an early-morning delivery. "Holy crap. Something big has happened."

Why must absolutely everyone play games?

I called Jack back.

"Are you watching the news?" he said.

"No. I try to never—"

"Then I guess you don't know."

"That's right," I said with an edge to my voice. "I have a busy day, so please spit it out."

"Another hit-and-run. Turn on your television and call me later."

Click.

Dial tone. I was getting so sick of that.

I braced myself for Todd Tyrell's relentless cheer in the face of disaster. Snow swirled around his gelled head as he reported. I leaned forward to try to see where he was.

Tragedy struck again in Woodbridge for the third time in less than a week. A woman was killed while leaving an informal memorial for a friend, who was one of the two other victims. The victim's name has not been released, but WINY has learned that she was struck near her vehicle, which was parked behind the yoga studio where the private ceremony was being held.

The body was discovered by the yoga studio staff at about ten last night. It appeared that the victim had been dead for more than an hour at the time she was found. The gathering had been in memory of Tiffanee Dupont, a popular yoga teacher and mentor, whose funeral will be held later this week. WINY spoke early this morning to two friends of the dead woman.

A gorgeous brown-eyed blonde whose golden skin seemed out of place in the swirling snow filled the screen.

She flashed back an ultrawhite smile while tears trickled prettily down her velvety cheeks. Not everyone can do that. But of course, it came naturally to Serena Redding Zeitz.

I felt a chill run down my spine as she said, "Tiffanee was a *wonderful* woman, very *spiritual* and *evolved*. She was my lifelong friend. I can't *begin* to tell you how *devastated* we are. And now this . . . Things will *never* be the same." She broke off and dissolved into very attractive weeping. A distinguished silver-haired man—in what had to be a cashmere overcoat—led her away to comfort her. That revealed the woman behind her. Haley, mascara smeared, eyes swollen, shaking. As Todd thrust the mic into her ruined face, all she could manage was a strangled wail. Fortunately, Randy shambled up, got between Haley and Todd, and put his arms around his wife to keep her from collapsing. "They are very old friends. This has been very hard on everybody," he said, looking like he meant it. "Please leave us alone."

The camera lingered enough to catch Haley being sick in the fresh snowbank. While Haley was falling about, that beautiful witch Serena was no more grief stricken than my dogs were. I was 100 percent sure of that. I made a note to bring flowers or cookies to Haley though. She needed serious support.

I switched off Todd with a shudder. Now I understood the three messages. Mona didn't answer her phone. Pepper was probably in full investigation mode. Jack had no information.

Jasmin. It had to be Jasmin Lorenz who'd been killed.

I couldn't keep the thought out of my head: Two down. Two to go. And there was the one mistaken identity of course.

My appointment with Dr. Partridge wasn't until noon and that left me time to visit my favorite reference librarian.

"Don't have to," Ramona said. "I know half this stuff. So if you're asking me as a friend, I can just tell you. If you're asking me as a librarian, I'll give you documents and sources."

"Friend," I said.

"Okay, now I'm officially on my break, so I can say that Serena Redding is on her third marriage and—"

"What? She's my age!"

That outburst earned me the usual disapproving stares from the reference regulars.

"You want to know or not?"

"Keep spilling and I'll try to keep my voice down."

"Her former mother-in-law is a good friend of my aunt's. She says that Serena has actually made a profit on each marriage. Apparently this third one is on the rocks too."

"A profit?"

"Surely you know what a profit is, Charlotte."

"Very funny. But it doesn't seem very—"

"Modern?"

"Moral. Decent. Ethical."

"I hear you," Ramona agreed. "Of course, her ex-mother-in-law could be just the tiniest bit biased."

"I'm sure. But if anyone was going to use people that way, I guess it doesn't surprise me that it would be Serena."

"You and me both. I saw the results of her handiwork the summer I was working in parks. I saw what she did to Mona."

"Wait. We weren't even in high school then. I didn't realize when you were talking about Mona wearing the 'kick me' sign that it was Serena doing the kicking."

"She had help. It took me a long time to figure out that Serena was behind a lot of the cruel behavior of the other kids. She got to suck up to the counselors and come across like such a smart little angel, but she was not at all what she seemed. And if my aunt's friend is to be believed, nothing much has changed."

"She has a new persona; churchgoing, charitable, kind, giving. I'm trying to find out what she's up to."

"You don't want to get too close to her. This woman makes a nasty enemy."

"What's that they say? Keep your friends close and your enemies closer? Who said that?"

"Sun Tzu," Ramona said. "Way, way back in the day. Although I'll confirm the reference. I like to be sure about these things."

"That's okay. Can you keep me posted about what Serena's up to?"

"Sure thing, but it will be a hobby, not business. I'll troll around a bit too on my own time. Woodbridge is a pretty small town."

"Thank you. If you're in contact with Mona, tell her I said if she needs anything to get in touch. I'll be there for her. And I'll make a better job of it this time. She can even stay with me. She just needs to pick up her phone when I call."

—◆◆—

The cafeteria at Woodbridge General was a vast clatter of activity. Crowds of people in white coats accessorized with stethoscopes, or wearing scrubs and ID tags stood jostling and chatting, grabbing good-size servings of food they'd never let their patients get away with: pizza, fries, gravy. Fried cholesterol, supersize starch, sugared and salted snacks. As Jack would say, yowza. I glanced around. Staff tended to congregate at tables, laughing and socializing, a brief break from their demanding jobs.

Near the entrance a man was just taking a seat at a table for four near a window with a view over the park-like area in back of the hospital. Very serene. He carefully set out a lunch from a lunch bag that featured Homer Simpson.

As I approached, he glanced my way. He recognized me, no question about it. But Dr. Sam Partridge was not what I was expecting.

He waved and stood up. I smiled and waved back. I estimated he was five seven tops. A man I could have made eye contact with, if he wasn't wearing glasses with bottle-thick lenses. Behind the lenses, a pair of intelligent green eyes blinked back at me. The ceiling lights were reflected on his shiny head. His tidy fringe of gray hair could have worked on a medieval monk too. The hand-knit brown sweater was about as far from *GQ* as you could get, ditto the relaxed-fit jeans and the deck shoes. I put him in his midfifties. For an instant, I wished he was my father. Of course, my mother likes men with proper wardrobes.

I liked him before I even sat down. He wore a wedding ring. I thought he'd be a nice husband for someone to come home to. I imagined he was a good dad too, even if he could never have been mine.

He didn't want to shake my hand though. "I'm at the tail end of a bad cold and a bit of bronchitis. I think I'm past the contagious stage, but why take a chance. Picked it up here in the hospital. Make sure you use hand sanitizer while you're here," he said, pointing to his small sanitizer sitting next to a small blue container of medications and a mug of steaming coffee. He saw me check that out and said, "I'm doped up on cold meds to get through the day: antihistamines, decongestants, painkillers, you name it. Coffee too."

"I love those little dispensers," I said as I pulled my sanitizer out of my handbag. The last thing I needed was a cold.

"Sally said it was urgent." He had the kind of voice that could make you believe your fears and troubles would soon be fixed. If I hadn't had my own agenda, I think I might have leaned over and spilled every secret I'd ever had, just to be reassured by this man. I managed to hold back.

"I've been hoping it isn't urgent, but I fear that it is."

Behind the thick lenses, the green eyes twinkled. Or maybe they gleamed. Whichever, it was effective. "Let's hear it."

I watched as he opened three packets of sugar and sprinkled them slowly into his coffee.

"How about I give you the background while you eat. Then you can tell me what you think."

He smiled, stirred the coffee, and then started to unwrap a sandwich that had been carefully constructed and was obviously homemade. Someone cared deeply about this therapist. I imagined a small, round wife happily preparing celery, carrots, and a small container of hummus, then moving on to the sandwich, which was making my mouth water: I figured it was multigrain bread with smoked turkey and cheese, and some brilliant green, cheerful lettuce variety. I wondered if there were matching small, round children sitting at a table somewhere, each with the same lunch. I was going to have to deal with this mixing love and food fixation I seemed to be developing. Maybe the next time I saw Dr. Partridge, I'd be stretched out on the couch blabbing on about steaming bowls of soup and how I never got anything like that from my mother, although Jack's mom had made plenty. Now Jack was unlikely to get that from me. Not that he'd ever requested it. On the other hand, he didn't turn down the sandwiches I brought him from Ciao! Ciao! on a regular basis. These were modern times and I didn't have to be tied to a kitchen to have a happy life. Did I?

Dr. Partridge said, "Charlotte?"

"Oh, sorry. I got a bit distracted." I pulled myself together and started my long and bizarre story, trying not to leave out anything germane and giving what detail I could about the bullying incidents at St. Jude's and outside.

The green eyes watched my face carefully as I filled him in, without naming any names, on the rumored and known crimes of Serena and her ilk, Mona's reaction, Haley's guilt and regret, my own fears for Mona and my anger at myself for my inaction and at the bully who could still reach out after all that time to ruin lives.

"Sadly," he said, "this is not an uncommon story."

"What? You mean the hit-and-runs?"

He shook his head. "Of course, the hit-and-runs are unusual, although I wish they were nonexistent. I'm talking about the events at St. Jude's. The damage to your friend. And the fallout. For her and for you."

"Well, I like to fix things. And I need to know what to do."

He shook his head. "Not sure if you can fix this one. But I can give you some advice."

"I'll pay you for your time, of course."

"This bit will be on the house. There are often consequences to childhood bullying. A person can end up with diminished self-esteem, anger, depression. All that can happen. It's a horrible history for someone to carry around with them."

"Does treatment help?"

"I'm biased, of course, since that's what I do, but I believe it does, if the patient finds the right therapist to help them move past it. People need to work through the trauma. To see what was going on. And most important to understand and forgive their own helplessness. And see the bullies for what they were. Children, too. Adolescents in this case, but not adults. I hope your friend will get some professional help."

"So they get away with it? The bullies? The tormentors? They get forgiven by their victims and it's all la-la-la?"

"Not always. Many bullies get in trouble with the law, do jail time. That's another pattern."

"Well these bullies were beautiful, smart, successful, and respected, and in one case, rich and getting richer. They got away with it."

Dr. Partridge nodded. "Unfortunately, that's also a pattern. People in authority favor attractive, clever people. Research backs that up. Some of them will go on to bully as adults too. Others won't."

I couldn't hold back a rant. "Well, that explains why Serena Redding or Jasmin Lorenz or Haley McKee or Tiffanee Dupont never did jail time. They seemed to have had charmed lives. Well maybe not Haley, but the rest of them." It crossed my mind that being dead was worse than jail time for Tiffanee and Jasmin, but it didn't stop my tirade. "And Mona Pringle still lives with the nightmare. These people were getting away with murder."

Dr. Partridge had dropped his sandwich. Something flickered across his gentle, understanding face. Recognition. I was absolutely sure of that. And something else. Whatever it was, Dr. Partridge wasn't happy that I'd let those names slip. I could have sworn that he turned pale, but that must have been my imagination. I was way too emotionally involved in this whole business.

He picked up his sandwich, stared at it, and put it back in its little bag.

"What?" I said. "Do you know these people? Was one of them a patient?"

He regarded me sadly. "Charlotte, even if one of them had been my patient, you must know I can't tell you anything about that."

I did know that, of course, but I gave it my best shot anyway. "Was it Mona?"

Dr. Partridge let his disappointment show on his face. "Charlotte, please."

I blurted, "Because if it was Mona, she is in desperate shape. I am worried about her. She's strung out. If you can't tell me, can *you* contact her? You have to help. I mean, what *are* you permitted to do?"

He shook his head. "We're not like paramedics. We can't go racing after people with our sirens blaring, whether or not we have treated them. They have to come to us. If you see your friend, try to convince her to seek help. I would make myself available to any of these people, but we have our share of qualified practitioners in Woodbridge."

As I thanked Dr. Partridge and walked away, I noticed he seemed to have lost interest in his lovely lunch. On the plus side, he had given me a good idea.

—◆◆—

As I left the hospital, I saw Pepper hurrying in through the automatic doors.

"Everything all right?" I said.

"Routine follow-up. They do that with brain injuries. You?"

I hesitated, thinking that Pepper's brain injury had been almost a year ago and she was still dealing with it. "I just wanted to talk to someone about Mona. To try to find out whether she might be—"

"Charlotte. You can't get involved in this. I told you to leave Mona alone."

"I know. And I'm not investigating. I assure you I have no desire to. But I feel an obligation to help Mona. We all should. She's been missing work and she's leaving me hysterical messages and—"

"Good, as long as you're not involved. Oh, wait. You sound like you *are* involved. I told you not to go to her workplace or her home. What do you mean, talking to someone about her? Are you consulting medical personnel about Mona? What the hell is wrong with you? I'll haul you in and charge you. I mean it."

"I'd love not to be involved. I don't want anyone else to be hurt. Or killed. There are three people dead now. And Mona—"

She let that slide. "Let me remind you that we are investigating the three hit-and-runs. And I doubt if any one of them was in any way related to Mona."

"Are you serious? Two of them were her bullies."

"What makes you say that? We haven't released the name of the third victim yet."

"You don't have to be a big-shot detective to figure it out, Pepper. They interviewed Haley and Serena on WINY. Clearly it was Jasmin."

"Dammit, that Todd Tyrell does more harm."

"So it *was* her. Mona as good as told me. Can't you find her, Pepper? Before something else happens? I'm worried about Haley, and I don't even want that revolting Serena to be murdered."

Pepper snapped, "We're on it. I just told you that."

"But—"

"Do you have any real information for me, Charlotte?"

What now? I could hardly tell Pepper that I'd seen an odd expression on Dr. Partridge's face when I talked about Serena's nasty little cabal and their effect on Mona.

"I thought so. Go back to your closets, Charlotte. We don't need you getting killed too."

She disappeared down the long corridor. I noticed she was rubbing her temple as she went.

⸺◆⸺

Of course, I was starving by this time. I had ruined Dr. Partridge's lunch, but I hadn't taken my own. It was either pick up food or gnaw on the seats of the Miata. I headed to a new little take-out place that had a smoky bacon and lentil soup that was to die for—especially when you had garlicky croutons to drop in. A meal in a bowl; perfect for a wintry day. I got two servings for Mr. Jack "Hollow Legs" Reilly and one for me, and turboed over to CYCotics before the soup could cool. I was happy that I'd made the investment in snow tires. Jack was glad to get the soup, but not so glad to hear me obsessing about Mona.

"But where is she?" I said for the fourth time as we polished off our lunch.

"I don't want to rain on your parade. I know this is serious and I understand that you're worried, but you have to leave all this to the police. Pepper will deal with Mona. *She'll* find her. You can figure out another way to be a friend to Mona. She'll need you when they find her," Jack said.

"Did I tell you what Dr. Partridge said?"

"Several times."

"Well, it was revealing."

"I suppose in a useless way. If his expression was, as you interpreted it, that he treated someone who may have been a victim or a bully. Unless of course he didn't. Don't want to bring you down, Charlotte, but that's not going to get you too far. Not that you should be going far since you're not supposed to be investigating."

"Not investigating," I snapped, "just trying to find Mona before she loses her job or her mind. Or before someone else gets killed."

"Yes. And I don't want that to be you. This is already a dangerous situation. Don't forget that."

For sure it could have been dangerous, but not for me. I believed that Mona would not lash out at me, not harm me. Or Jack either for that matter. She had turned to me for help and I had helped her in the past, even if not enough. She was staying in touch even if her calls were alarming. I was worried that Mona had done something that could never be undone. I hoped like hell I was wrong.

"Jack. What do you think happened to those girls to turn them into monsters?"

"I don't know. I hardly knew them."

"You do know the kinds of things they did to people. You're the philosopher. Where's the justice in that?"

Jack stared at me. "Philosophy isn't about justice, Charlotte."

I sniffed. "Well, maybe it should be. Don't laugh at me."

"I'm glad you care about this whole situation. I'm glad you care about Mona and other people. And I agree with you. We should do whatever we can for Mona. I'll help you. But I hope you do know that you have a tendency to charge right in, no matter what the risks, and try to make everything right. You just have to learn to be cautious."

"We're just talking. I'm trying to get my head around what's happened with those hit-and-runs and what happened when we were all at St. Jude's. It's haunting me."

"That's the thing. Why is all this coming back to haunt you now?"

"Easy to answer. Because Serena Redding is back and now she's Mrs. Jerome Zeitz, so she has even more money and power than she did before. Oh wow, thanks, Jack. You've clarified it for me."

"Sarcasm?" He wrinkled his brow.

"Not at all, Jack." I picked up our lunch debris and tossed it in the recycle bin. I was smiling when I headed out the door. I had a flickering thought about Ramona's bit of intel on Serena's crumbling marriage. Her silver-haired husband had seemed truly caring in front of the television cameras. But I knew firsthand how the camera can deceive and distort.

—◆—

From a work point of view, the day had been a write-off so far. My third workshop was scheduled that night and was oddly enough entitled The Fine Art of Saying No. I knew that "no" was the biggest time-saver of all. And it could save a lot of regret. I thought back to my conversation at the library. Was Ramona, like me, filled with regret for failing to help Mona live a normal life as a kid?

I was deep in thought when the phone startled me.

"Mona! I am so glad to hear from you. Where are you? Let me—"

"Forget that, Charlotte. I'm not telling you where I am. We've been all through this."

"Sorry. Forgot myself. It's good to hear from you. I've been worried."

"That I'm a homicidal maniac?"

"I don't believe that for a minute." I didn't think that Mona could be systematically killing off people, partly because she sure didn't seem the type, but mainly because Pepper, who was, after all, a detective, insisted that Mona had airtight alibis.

She said, "Well I believe it."

"What?"

"Yeah. I'm pretty sure I have dissociative identity disorder."

"I'm sorry?"

"I've been researching that. You know, multiple personalities. They struggle to get control? Trauma can bring it on."

There was no doubt in my mind that Mona had suffered trauma, but this seemed extreme. "But, Mona—"

"Listen to me. I actually found a yoga mat that I think belongs—I should say *belonged*—to Tiffanee in my apartment. I don't own a yoga mat. I've never done yoga in my life. It wasn't here earlier. I didn't bring it in. And I found a silk scarf and a pair of green leather gloves here. They're not mine. So how did they get there? And where is my missing stuff?"

"Well, that's—" I was struggling to find answers to these questions. Was Mona getting more delusional?

"One or more of my other personalities is doing the killing. I have no memory of it, but that's what happens. The person has no memory of the alter-ego actions. But that would still be me. Underneath." I heard her voice crack.

"Mona, I am sure that's not the case. Let's talk to someone about it. I think you'll be very relieved if—"

"What if—?"

I waited.

And waited.

"What if what, Mona?"

"Three people are dead! Three! And one of them was completely innocent. What if I can't stop until I kill them all?" Her voice rose, cracked, and trailed off.

I decided I'd better get back to Dr. Partridge on this one. In the meantime, I wanted to keep Mona from freaking out. "You've been damaged by that pack of bullies and now you're reacting. You're not the bad guy here, Mona. We don't even know if anyone has been murdered."

"Glad someone thinks so."

"I'm not your only supporter, you know."

I heard a soft sniff. "That's news to me."

"It's the truth."

"Like who else is my supporter?"

"Pepper. She says she was with you when Tiffanee was killed. Even if your so-called alter egos were killing, you would have to be physically present for them to do it. Pepper says that's impossible."

"Don't you think my alters could find a way to fool the police? It's not like that's never been done before."

I thought about that. The 911 center was a busy place. I assumed that people must be coming and going, taking breaks, that kind of thing. Could we be absolutely certain that Mona hadn't managed to leave the area without anyone noticing? I had to follow up on this or make sure that Pepper did. I said, "And Ramona is another supporter. I saw her in the library today. She said if you need her, she'll be there for you and she'll do a better job this time. She wishes she had found a way to put an end to it when you were a kid at the playground."

Silence.

I blurted, "And I'm here for you too, Mona. I realize that I should have stood up for you. I should have found a way to make them stop."

While Mona was blowing her nose, I kept talking. "Jack Reilly too. He said he'd be willing to help."

"That's weird, Charlotte," Mona said with a bizarre high-pitched laugh.

"Why?"

"Because you and Ramona and Jack were practically the only people who ever did try to help me. I never forgot that. You're not the problem."

"Margaret and Sally helped you," I said. "Pepper too."

"And I appreciated that then and now. But Pepper's a cop. If she has to arrest me, she will. Maybe that's the best thing. Do you know who the first victim was?"

I hesitated. "Bethann Reynolds."

"Exactly. She was another victim of bullying. She also managed to get her life together and recently started to fight back about injustice. It's ironic that I would have killed her by mistake, thinking she was Serena."

I said, "But—"

"But nothing. She looked a bit like Serena, same height, blond hair, not as classy a hairdo, but she was bundled up with a scarf because of the blowing wind. There was that yellow Hummer parked on the street and she was crossing right by it. That's all it took for me to kill her. I think the best thing would be for Pepper to stop me before I kill again."

"Let me repeat: Pepper says you couldn't have killed Bethann."

"Right, like no one's ever been mistaken about the time of a death. It doesn't take long to hit somebody with a car."

"Oh."

Could Pepper have been mistaken about the time? And what if this wacky idea was true? I sure didn't want Mona out there killing anyone else.

"Let us help. Tell me where you are. Or at least meet up with me and talk things through."

"Not happening. It's too late for me, Charlotte. Way too late. You won't find me."

"Mona! Wait!" I stood staring at the receiver and listening to the dial tone.

I left a message for Pepper, knowing she wouldn't call me back.

——••——

I popped into Kristee's Kandees immediately after that. I felt the need for some extra black-and-white fudge. Some for bribes, peace offerings, whatever. One for a thank-you to Ramona. She had done a lot to help set up and promote my workshops.

Some of the fudge was for me. It felt quite urgent, getting my mitts on it.

Kristee wasn't faking any sorrow over the latest death. Once again, she was practically gleeful. "Jasmin?" she said. "I suppose she'll rot in hell with the others. How about I toss in an extra piece to celebrate, Charlotte?"

Of course, I didn't want to turn down an extra piece. I said, "Not everyone feels that way, Kristee. Mona Pringle was probably the person most victimized and yet she's practically distraught."

"I find that hard to believe. Does she think she's killing them in her sleep or something? Whoa. You should see your face. She does?"

"Of course she doesn't." I backpedaled at some speed.

"But she is upset, and she has been since Serena came back."

"Not surprised. That Serena's all 'oh, can we be friends? I truly regret. I want to make amends, reconnect.' Blah-blah-blah. My fat fanny she wants to make amends. She's up to something. She's all about herself. Too bad no one's bumped her off yet."

"She called you too?"

"Yeah and I told her where she could shove her so-called amends. You want these gift wrapped, Charlotte?"

Minutes later, after another tirade or two, I fled Kristee's. I opened one of the gift-wrapped boxes and ate three pieces at the first red light.

—••—

Luck seemed to be with me and after a few extremely deceitful phone calls to find out when he left the hospital, I tracked Dr. Partridge to the parking lot of Woodbridge General. I'd headed out there, as he hadn't returned my calls asking about dissociative identity disorder. That bit of luck didn't last long, as Dr. Partridge spotted me and actually sprinted to his vehicle, a sensible black Subaru. As I stood there, openmouthed, he got into the car and accelerated out of the lot.

"Yeah, sure, Dr. Partridge, thanks a lot," I muttered as I drove away from the hospital with his elegantly wrapped package of black-and-white fudge still on the seat. The police (aka Pepper) had also failed to return my calls. Something bizarre was going on. It obviously had to do with all the bullying that Serena and her coven had done as teenagers. Three people had died and they were all connected. Bethann looked like Serena, but she'd also been bullied. There seemed to me to be a limited cast of characters. So, moving on: Either the deaths were random or they weren't. There wasn't much chance they were random. So, the hit-and-run driver was either Mona or it wasn't. If it was Mona, it was either her normal self or one of her alters. Whatever the situation, I needed to find her and keep her (or them) from hurting anyone else. If it wasn't Mona, I had to discover who *was* behind these crimes and stop them before someone else was killed. So, by process of elimination: If it wasn't Mona, it must have been Serena. If it was Serena, what the hell was she up to? She had contacted Mona and Kristee and even Bella's cousin. Had that contact been intended to upset them? Control them? Kristee was furious. Mona seemed beyond distraught and into the deranged zone. Not good in any case. Who knew what Tiffanee's or Jasmin's state of mind had been or even if Serena had been in touch with them. We'd never been friends or even friendly. I hadn't seen them since I'd returned to Woodbridge. It wasn't like I could just walk into one of their homes and ask the grieving families the tough questions. As for Bethann, I hadn't known her at all. Couldn't just walk in there either. No. I needed a plan. Well. Two plans.

*You don't have to be connected all the time.
Our electronic time-savers can waste as much time as they
save and distract you from your priorities. Learn when to
unplug for better concentration, relaxation, or efficiency.*

11

The phone was ringing when I opened my door. Lilith's voice greeted me. "Guess you were wrong," she said cheerfully. "I am happy to say that, because I hated the idea of someone being cruel to the residents at Riverview or any vulnerable people. I felt murderous."

I shivered as she spoke. Several times in the past couple of days, I had felt murderous toward Serena too, not a feeling I liked living with. My second line started beeping as Lilith talked. BLOCKED NUMBER. It was probably Mona, but I let it go to message. I needed to know what Lilith had learned about Serena. I was pretty sure Mona would call back.

She continued, "I talked to everyone I knew. Made up a story about Serena doing something at our college and wanting to know what kind of person she was. The weird thing was that everyone likes her. She is kind and considerate and, anyway, she's never alone with a resident."

"So far," I muttered.

"Never. It's their policy. No volunteers are ever alone with the residents. It's to protect everyone. All I can say is if she wanted to make some poor soul miserable, she picked the wrong place."

"What about staff? They can be vulnerable too. To blackmail or rumors. Whispering campaigns. False accusations. That's her style."

"No sign of it. Honestly, Charlotte. Maybe she did change."

"My mother likes to say 'and maybe pigs can fly.'"

"I don't know what else to tell you." Even Lilith was having trouble staying loyal to me on this one. Such was the power of Serena. At last she added, "I'll keep an open mind. I know people aren't always what they seem. Gotta go. I have a bunch of papers due and I have to call Seth after that. I'll see you tomorrow at Hannah's. That's a quick and fun project. Good luck with your workshop tonight."

"Mmm," I said absently. I had an idea of who might know what I should do about the Serena situation, and there was possibly a way I could ask that wouldn't compromise his ethics.

◆◆

The evening workshop on "just say no" went quite well considering my state of mind. I kept hearing a small voice in my head, trilling, "Just say no to murder." And, of course, I couldn't get Mona out of my mind.

The group was divided neatly into harried moms and women who could probably scale Mount Everest on a weekend and create the corporate five-year plan on the Monday after. There were two men, one in his twenties, and one in that uncharted territory between sixty and seventy.

Almost everyone raised their hands when I asked who felt guilty saying no. The younger man just shrugged. I suggested that people were better off feeling guilty than carrying a lifetime of regret. We all shared stories of the things we'd said yes to and regretted.

The class favorite was the wife whose mother-in-law insisted on having a key to her daughter-in-law's home and who let herself in without warning any time of the day or evening. On one excursion, she reorganized the daughter-in-law's lingerie drawer. We all gasped at that.

"What can I do? I tell her no and she just doesn't listen."

Of course, this was much more of a boundary issue than a time-management one, but we were all in agreement. A line needed to be drawn in the sand. Most people were in favor of changing the locks.

"Easy for them," the young wife said. "You can't say no to your kids or your bosses or your dogs, but you think I can just do that? This woman is a family member."

We role-played that one. The younger man enjoyed playing the part of the mother-in-law. At the end of a number of scenarios, we'd reached a plan that would allow the mother-in-law from hell to save face, and for privacy to be restored. I sure hoped that husband would be on board. Of course, the doors would be rekeyed after an expression of thanks for all the help, and the request to knock and not use the key. Time would tell.

"Let me know," I said, as we moved on to the neighbor who borrowed and never returned, the school committee's endless request for baked goods, and the boss who didn't believe in weekends.

By the end, everyone had a couple of practiced comments and strategies to avoid yes. "I'll think about it and get back to you." "I'd love to but I have no time left." And just plain no.

Everyone said that they'd let me know how it worked out. In the case of the boss from hell, there were three offers of help with a job search to find a better place to work.

"I'm living proof that you can ditch a lucrative career

and find happiness being your own boss. Less money, more happiness. That frequently comes from saying no."

This group apparently hadn't seen my multiple arrests on television, so they took me seriously. I was glad they hadn't managed their time well enough to catch the local news on a regular basis.

After we all departed from the library, most of us still chuckling, I tried Pepper's cell and home phones with no luck. Mona's dissociative identity disorder was the subject. Of course, they weren't the first messages I'd left Pepper on that subject.

I thought it might be worth trying Haley again, just to warn her. Of course, there was no answer at her home either. I had no idea how to track her down. With an office cleaning business, she and Randy could be anywhere. As it was after hours, they'd be out somewhere working hard. The question was, were they in danger from Mona? I didn't want to believe it, but I had to consider that it could be the truth. I had no choice but to take action. And I didn't have much choice about what.

What the hell. I tried dialing 911 once again. I figured Mona wasn't there. I hoped for her friend Brian.

A male voice answered.

"Brian?" I said.

"Nine-one-one," he repeated. "We don't do first names here."

"Mona always did. Is that you, Brian? Because if it is I need to talk to you about her."

"This line is for emergencies."

"Come on, Brian. It *is* an emergency, for Mona. I think you must have figured that out."

He gasped. "Have you seen her?"

"No and I need to find her. Can I meet with you?"

"I'm off at eleven."

"Sure. Where can we connect?"

"Not much is open at that time around here, but there's Al's All Night. Right by the station. I'll be there by ten after."

"That sounds fine. I'll see you at Al's then. I'm buying."

——

I trotted the reluctant pooches out for their walk, trotted them back in again, and hit the computer. I spent the time well doing as much research as I could into dissociative identity disorder. It's a controversial diagnosis at best, but, if you bought into it, could result from trauma. Mona was right, if she did have more than one personality vying for her head space, she would have no memories of that person's activities.

Jack was snoring softly on the sofa. Even Mona's tale of her multiple personalities hadn't kept him awake. I left the sleeping dogs and Jack and headed out into the blustery night. I wanted to be curled up on the sofa with Jack, wearing my frog pajamas and pink fluffy slippers. I sure hoped that my meeting with Brian would pay off. I drove down Long March Road toward downtown and the police station. Al's All Night was the only pink neon-lit spark in the gloomy swirl of snow. I pushed open the door and inhaled the aroma of coffee and fries and hamburgers. Two uniformed police officers who must have just finished a shift were starting on coffees. One of them spotted me and gave the other one an elbow in the ribs. His friend turned and I recognized that smart young cop Dean Oliver. He nodded and gave me the slightest of grins. What can I say? We have a complicated relationship. I waved back and hesitated. Dean owed me. Could I fill him in on this situation with Mona? Would that be a betrayal of Pepper? Or an unfair and useless burden on him? I am not at my best at this time of night, so I found myself dithering. Before I could make up my mind about the right thing to do, the door opened and Brian blew in along with a gust of wind and a puff of snow.

I waved again to Dean—whose eyebrows rose—and joined Brian in one of the battered booths. He signaled the waitress, who arrived on the double. Brian went for Sleepytime herbal tea and apple pie à la mode. I know a winning combination when I hear one and ordered the same.

"Thanks for seeing me, Brian."

"Anything for pie," he said.

Up close I could see the circles under his eyes. I imagined an extra 911 shift, even in sleepy Woodbridge, could leave you exhausted.

I smiled. "I am hoping you can help me with Mona."

"Mona is my friend," he said, a hint of warning in his voice.

"Mine too, although I know you are much closer. I want to help her and I think she's in big trouble."

A guarded look crept over his face.

I kept talking. "Mona believes she might have dissociative identity disorder and maybe one of her other personalities is behind these hit-and-runs."

"That's crazy, but in a totally different way."

"Exactly. I doubt if that's the case, especially as the police believe she is covered for the murders, but the point is that she thinks it is and that's causing her to behave in bizarre ways."

He lowered his eyes, not sure of how to deal with me, I figured.

"Here's what I know," I said. "Mona was bullied, brutally, by this cabal of girls who were in high school at the same time Mona and I were. The ringleader is back, and that seems to have set Mona off."

"That would be Serena."

"Right. I see that you know about her."

"Mona talked about her returning. Talked about hating

her and how she was back and it was causing her a lot of stress."

"I know. In case you think she was overreacting, I do want to say that this bullying was cruel and unrelenting for years, I guess."

Brian's eyes flashed. "I don't think she was overreacting. I'm a gay man from a small town. Do you think I didn't get bullied in school? Do you think I wouldn't recognize how she felt? It's taken me ten years of therapy to just start to get over it."

"I'm sorry. I didn't mean that. I didn't realize at the time how bad it was. I let her down when we were in school and I don't want to let her down this time."

"Okay. I get that."

"Good. She called me and said she was fantasizing about running Serena over and seeing her splatter all over the windshield. Her words. Then the same night, Bethann Reynolds was killed."

"Oh boy."

Our Sleepytime tea and apple pie arrived just at that moment. I waited to finish talking until our waitress sauntered past the two police officers, swaying her hips. Dean turned back and gave me a look. I had no idea what that look meant.

"I'm asking myself what triggered all this emotion. Do you know exactly what happened when Serena got in touch with her?"

He took a long sip of his tea and then seemed to make a decision. "I guess it's okay to tell you."

"Tell me what?"

"She came in to work the other day and she was in total distress. Her face was beet red and she was sputtering. I mean totally enraged. She wasn't in any shape to go on the phones."

I nodded. "What was she so upset about?"

"Seems this Serena had called her to tell her she was back. Made a big deal about the good old days and how she wanted to see Mona again. She was trying to set up friend dates."

"I can see where Mona would be upset about that."

"An understatement. I had to cover for her when she was freaking out in the ladies' room. She wore her sunglasses for the rest of the morning and, so help me, her hands were shaking. I told her to go home, but she said work was the only place she could feel safe now."

"Wow. That's awful. So Serena actually got her all riled up again."

Brian said, "Yup. Nasty lady."

"Or stupid perhaps. Maybe she didn't even realize the impact she'd have."

Brian's face hardened. "I bet she couldn't wait to start playing those same old head games again. What?"

I shook my head. "Nothing. Just reacting to the whole horrible scenario." But I was also asking myself if Mona, Kristee, and Bella's cousin were the only former victims that Serena had contacted. Probably not.

"It is horrible. Serena's the one who should have gotten hit. The other two bitches got killed. Tiffanee and Jasmin. They probably deserved it too."

I didn't make any comments about remarks unbecoming to a 911 operater. "Bethann Reynolds didn't deserve it though. She was just an innocent person crossing the street, searching for her cat. And she'd been bullied too. She was quite reclusive as a result. It's all very unfair."

His shoulders slumped. "As horrible as Serena was and even though I know she had an alibi, I can't believe that Mona would ever run over Serena and the others."

I said, "I agree. In fact, the only person who seems to believe that Mona could have done it is Mona herself." I didn't let on that I'd actually worried a lot about that. "She *suspects* that she has alter egos who may have done it."

He said, "I've been working with Mona since she joined 911 ten years ago. We've stuck together. We've been friends, colleagues. We're tight. Mona's always the same. I don't see how it's possible for her to have alternate personalities with no sign of that over ten years."

I nodded. "Good point and I'm glad to hear that."

He frowned. "But?"

He must have read my mind. I hesitated. "I've read that dissociative identity disorder can be triggered by a traumatic event. And retriggered as well."

"You mean the phone call from Serena might have sent her over the edge?"

"Yes. I can't imagine how awful it would have been for Mona to pick up the phone and hear her tormentor's voice after all these years."

"She worked hard to get over her teenaged trauma and have a normal life. It's not fair. I think if I'd seen that Serena, I might have run over her myself."

"Except, it wasn't Serena. It was another victim. We have to keep that in mind."

"I don't buy into this multiple personality crap, but I understand that we do have to help her."

"I agree. She needs help. But first we have to find her. She's not at home. Do you have any idea where she could go?"

He shook his head and his sandy hair flopped over his eyes. "She never went anywhere. Home. Work. Here sometimes after work with me. To the movies. The grocery store. The drugstore. The vet with her cat or dog. She could hardly be hiding out at any of those places. Right?"

"Family?"

"Her parents retired and moved somewhere south, Georgia maybe."

"Could she have gone to see them?"

"I don't think so. She didn't get on well with them. Held

them responsible for not standing up for her. I don't think she's seen her parents in five or six years. So she probably wouldn't turn up on their doorstep to ask them to let her hide out because her alter egos were running people down."

"Good point."

He shook his head vigorously. "I'm sure she wouldn't go to them. They never made her feel safe."

"And she wants to feel safe now. Needs to. But where?"

"Search me."

"I'm going to give you my cell phone number and I want yours too. Call me if you think of anyplace else that she might have mentioned. Or if she calls you, listen for background noises."

"I guess I can do that, but we're grasping at straws."

"For sure, but it's better than nothing. You mentioned the movies. Do you think she might be hiding out in a movie theater?"

Brian blinked. "It's possible, I suppose. There's not that many around Woodbridge. I could check them out tomorrow. I think they'll all be closed up now for the night. Although that's kind of weird and creepy and Mona's not a creepy person. Eccentric, yes, but not creepy."

"You do that. I'm going to talk to someone else who might shed light on this."

"Good luck. No one knows her better than I do."

"I'm thinking of a mental health professional who deals with these issues."

"You won't tell him about the alter egos, will you?"

"Of course I will. I already have. I left a message. We need to know what to do. Even if it's not true, Mona thinks it is and what does that mean for her behavior?"

I was glad to have met Brian. I liked the way he cared about Mona and believed in her. We each had the other's home and cell phone numbers. We agreed to touch base the

next day and to stay in contact with ideas. I felt depressed
as I headed out into the stinging snow and home.

Pepper still hadn't called me back. Something else was
bothering me. In the back of my mind, a thought flickered.
Amsterdam Avenue was less than a half mile from the police station. Was that close enough? Brian had admitted
that he'd covered for Mona when she was distraught. Had
he also covered for her during the murders without being
aware of what he was doing?

—❧—

Thursday morning at Hannah's, I had trouble concentrat-
ing. I'd had no response from Pepper and no more calls
from Mona. Fortunately Lilith was there and managed a
steady stream of pleasant chat as we set up the baking storage and the food prep storage. We walked through the typical meal prep with Hannah and set up the most frequently
used utensils and cookware close at hand. We settled on a
small number of cleaning products, near the sink. All common sense, but that can desert a person when households
merge. At the end of our session, the kitchen was trimmed
and workable. The charity box was brimming and Lilith
was happy to take the lot to her youth services organiza-
tion. As we opened each cupboard, Hannah was able to
smile happily. At least something had gone well.

"I feel like such an idiot," she said. "This was such a
simple process."

"Hey, don't worry about it. You were suffering from
TMS," Lilith said.

Hannah's eyebrows rose. "What's that?"

"Too much stuff," Lilith and I said in unison.

"Never again," Hannah said. "And I will give your name
to everyone I know. Both of you!"

We left with a check and a promise I'd check in a few
months to see what might have sneaked back into the gor-

geous kitchen. I entered it in my agenda on the spot. I was willing to bet that Hannah would make sure the kitchen stayed the way it was.

Even so, I couldn't wait to get out of there.

— ❦ —

I was desperate to speak to Dr. Partridge. Lucky for me, his office address was listed in the phone book. I remembered Sally mentioning his office was at home, so that address was my first stop. The luck ended there.

The woman who answered the door of the white Cape Cod–style home had a silver bun and eyes rimmed with red. Her nose matched the eyes. She was somewhere in her early sixties and still attractive despite the fact she'd obviously been crying for hours. Dr. Partridge's mother perhaps? I decided she was a bit too youthful to have a son who was in his fifties and I wondered for a second if she was a patient whose appointment had at long last dealt with some deep-seated issues.

"Charlotte Adams," I said firmly. "I am here to see Dr. Partridge." I didn't say he was expecting me, as he wasn't. I was there to see him though.

She gasped and covered her hand with her mouth. Her entire body quivered. Was everyone in Woodbridge planning to spend the day in tears? What the hell was going on? Maybe a full moon with a holdover to the day?

"What is it? What's wrong?" I blurted. "Can I do anything to help?"

"I need to sit down," she said, so weakly I could hardly hear her. I followed her as she staggered into the house and collapsed into a chair in the living room. I sat in the next chair and stared as she wiped her eyes with her flowered apron. Was she his housekeeper? Had he just given her notice? What could I do? What should I do? "Can I get you something? A drink of water?" That was lame, but I felt quite useless.

"Is Dr. Partridge here?" I said eventually.

That started another torrent of tears, but I waited it out. Eventually she was able to shake her head.

"Do you know where I can find him?" I waited.

"They took him away." She shuddered.

"What? Who did?" I kept my voice gentle despite that shock. I had a vision of the police frog-marching the psychologist out the door into the snow.

Another deep shudder and she seemed to regain a bit of composure. One more sniff and she was able to say, "The paramedics."

"Paramedics! What happened?"

"I don't know. They came and took away all his medications. He was . . . Who did you say you were again?"

"Charlotte Adams. I've been meeting with Dr. Partridge to discuss some bullying issues and I was hoping to catch him this morning."

I waited again, and then asked softly, "Are you a relative?"

"What? No. I'm Lydia Johnson, the housekeeper. Dr. Partridge is a widower. I've been caring for him for years."

I blurted out, "Oh, I wondered who made those lunches."

She looked at me strangely. "He makes those himself. I just sort of manage the place, arrange to keep it up; it's just a few hours a week because he's such an orderly person, but he works so hard and he likes everything under control and now . . ."

I gave her a chance to get a grip. Finally, she squared her shoulders and stared at me with heartbreak on her face. "He's the kindest man I ever met. He hadn't been sleeping well. How could I let this happen?"

"What did happen?"

"He was unconscious when I found him this morning. I think he may die."

*Once a year, buy all your birthday cards. It will only take
a couple of minutes to list family, friends, and colleagues.
Pick up a couple of lovely cards without text for sympathy,
celebration—whatever. You'll be ready for almost anything.*

12

Sally was still my go-to gal for anything to do with the
medical community in Woodbridge. She had already heard
the news when I reached her by phone.

"Benjamin called me. Everyone at Woodbridge General
is reeling. Sam Partridge is the most even, sensible man
you could ever meet."

"I know. I met him, thanks to you. But what—?"

"He'd had a horrible cold and a bit of bronchitis and he
hadn't been sleeping. It seems he got up in the middle of the
night and took a bunch of medications and probably got mixed
up. Maybe he was groggy and doubled or tripled his dose of
things that shouldn't be taken together. They think he fell and
hit his head after that. Benjamin says that a lot of people are
injured in falls after they've messed up their meds."

I thought back to our meeting in the hospital cafeteria.
"He mentioned that he had a cold. He had a pill dispenser
with him at the hospital, and he said he was taking a lot of
stuff."

"That fits, I guess," Sally said with a sigh. "You'd think a medical professional would be more cautious, but I know that Benjamin often isn't careful about himself."

"Is he going to be all right?"

"Touch and go." She paused to clear her throat. "They don't know yet."

I thought about Dr. Partridge. Sally was right. He was a sensible man. That had been obvious from his lunches, the way they were organized, packed, and even eaten. What were the chances that such an orderly, intelligent person would mix up his meds? If Dr. Partridge could make a mistake like that, anyone could. But I remembered that he had them in a small blue pill container. If memory served, most of the compartments had been full. Something was very wrong here.

"Did they find his pill container, Sally?"

"What?"

"He had one of those little blue—"

"How would I know? And why on earth would you even ask that?"

"It's odd that something should happen to him when he had all his meds organized *and* he had treated at least one of the people involved in this bullying thing."

"Who?"

"I can't tell you, Sal."

"Don't go getting like that, Charlotte Adams."

"I mean I can't tell you because I don't know. I could tell by his reaction when I asked him that he had treated one of them. He talked about confidentiality. He didn't say he hadn't or that he didn't know what I was talking about. He didn't want to talk to me about it. He raced out of the parking lot to avoid me yesterday afternoon. So I am convinced he did treat someone, but I have no idea who. Could have been Mona. Could have been one of the cabal. But he knew exactly what I was talking about. And it had an impact on him. I wonder if he actually got in touch with one of them, even though he said that a therapist wouldn't do that."

Sally said, "Then I'm responsible if he dies."

"Of course you're not. Why would you say something like that?"

"Because I set you up to meet with him."

"Sally, we have to consider that the person who was under his care might have done this to keep him quiet. It's not your fault or mine." While I said that, deep down I felt a horrible grinding guilt. Whom had I told about Dr. Partridge? It definitely wasn't Sally's fault, but there was a good chance that it was mine. Had I let it slip to Mona? I didn't think I had, but if so, I was too stupid to live. I could hear Sally crying softly on her end of the phone.

"Sally, you have to tell Benjamin what I said. Tell him to let the police know. I don't get the best response. Pepper just blows me off whenever I try to talk to her about this. And she's not even returning my calls. But the point is that Dr. Partridge is still alive and someone wants him dead."

———❖———

I needed to think about Mona. I called Brian and got him on his cell phone. He was continuing to try to reach Mona without any luck either. At least the police hadn't told him to mind his own business. Finally, I decided I could do something to help her when she did show up or get in touch.

First I headed home and borrowed Jack's brown Mini. I changed into a green winter jacket and a white wool hat that covered my hair. I drove the short distance to Amsterdam Avenue and pulled in. I could have walked easily, but I wanted to be able to depart quickly if I had to.

A dark sedan was parked in Bethann's driveway. I took a deep breath, picked up the package of black-and-white fudge I'd intended for Dr. Partridge, and headed over.

I found a middle-aged man with a gray brush cut and bags under his eyes. He was just leaving.

"Hello," I said. "I was at school with Bethann and I just heard the news. I wanted to offer my condolences to the family."

He nodded, sadly. "I'm her brother-in-law. No one else is here."

I handed him the package of fudge and said, "I am sorry for your loss. It was a shock."

"Yes."

I added, "It's very strange. People from our high school class appear to be getting phone calls and reconnecting after all those years. Some of the reconnections are quite upsetting. But more importantly, the people who have been killed were all linked to St. Jude's and the person who's been calling around to reconnect. I'd been going to ask if Bethann also had any of those calls."

He stared at me blankly. "I don't know. My wife might."

"Would you mind asking your wife if she knows of any upsetting calls that Bethann had? I don't want to bring any more grief to your family, but there may be things that the police should be informed about." I passed him my card and said, "Please give me a call if there was anything odd that happened to Bethann in the last couple of weeks. Or if she heard from or met with someone from her high school days."

I left him staring at it and hightailed it out of there before I ran into one of Woodbridge's finest.

———◆◆———

I returned the Mini, collected the Miata, and drove to the uptown end of Long March Road, where I trudged through the endless snow to the old arcade. Margaret Tang's new law office was on the second floor over my favorite kids' store,

Cuddleship. I thumped up the stairs and opened the door. She still hadn't added D'Angelo to her name on the door although she used it in her private life. Maybe she didn't want her clients to know about the police connection.

Margaret always seemed to have an intermediary guarding her privacy. For years, I'd been trying to get past her mother. Her new husband didn't necessarily pass on messages. In this case it was her equally new legal assistant who seemed ridiculously young even to me.

"I'm sorry. Do you have an appointment?" she said, shaking her dark hair as she said it.

Margaret's voice carried the day. "It's okay, Alison. This is my friend Charlotte Adams."

I thought Alison muttered, "Everyone in town knows who she is." But that could have been my imagination.

Everything in the office was like Margaret, reserved, practical, muted, and solid. Well thought out too. You could count on this furniture, the same way you could count on Margaret. I sure hoped that Mona could count on her too. She was going to need one hell of a lawyer. These days, Margaret wanted a life. She did mostly real estate, business contracts, and wills. But she was the smartest person I knew. If she hadn't come back to Woodbridge to be near her parents, she would have had a meteoric career somewhere.

I launched into my long story about Mona's calls and her latest claims that she had dissociative identity disorder and one of her alters was killing people. Margaret listened with her usual sangfroid. She did not roll her eyes, which must have been difficult.

"She could use some legal advice, even if the police don't think she could have done it. That could change. I know that the hard way," I said.

"She's better off with representation, for sure."

"Will you do it? After all, we were there when she was

being traumatized by Serena. I don't know what she can afford, but I can pay."

Margaret exhaled. That's a huge emotional reaction for her. "I'll do it pro bono, but MPD, I'm not so sure that multiple personality disorder or dissociative identity disorder, whatever term, will fly in court. It's been known to blow up in the defendant's face."

"But it shouldn't get to court, if she's not guilty of anything. I find it hard to believe and it does fly in the face of evidence."

"If she keeps saying she's guilty, there's bound to be trouble. For instance, if someone else is tried for those hit-and-runs, Mona's ravings will be good news for that defense."

"But we don't believe it."

Margaret said, "However, she has a *theory* that she's guilty. Let's make sure no one else hears that until they need to."

"Right." Oh crap. Who had I told? "I mentioned it to Jack. And Sally. Her 911 colleague Brian. I left a message for Dr. Partridge. And a few for Pepper. I think that's it."

"Who's Dr. Partridge?"

"He's a psychologist who I believe treated one or more of the bullies. And at this moment, he's in the hospital fighting for his life."

"Are you serious? Another hit-and-run?"

"Sally said that Benjamin thought Dr. Partridge might have taken a double or even triple dose of decongestants and antihistamines and painkillers all at the same time. Apparently he fell and hit his head. Between the overdose and the head injury, he's in a bad way."

"So . . . an accident?"

"I don't believe it was. I suspect someone knew I was talking to him about the bullies and they wanted to silence him before he revealed a name. It's all very upsetting. I am sure that Serena is behind that and the other deaths. It was easy to find where he lived. He saw clients at home and someone with a dangerous agenda could have dropped in and slipped a little something into his coffee if he left the room. He liked his coffee very sweet and might not have noticed. That's speculation, of course. And I haven't worked out all the details yet. But we shouldn't overlook the possibility that Mona could be involved. Or one of her so-called alters."

"No argument." Margaret handed me her business card. She wrote her home and cell numbers on it. "Make sure she gets this somehow. Tell her I'll be there for her."

I found myself overcome with emotion. When I could speak, I said, "We all have to be, even in the unlikely event she's guilty."

Margaret nodded. "We'll pull together. Don't worry. I'll be kind of glad to have something interesting to work on."

I added, "But first we have to stop the killing."

"We don't. Say no to that, Charlotte. Give Mona the card. Leave the rest to the police. Take that advice to heart. Otherwise, one of these days you could be the person who gets killed."

———— ✦ ————

I called Woodbridge Police. For some reason, I knew their number as well as 911. I was trying for Dean Oliver. Of course, he wasn't on that day. I should have realized that, as I had seen him at the end of his shift the night before. I tried all the Olivers in the Woodbridge phone listings until I recognized his voice when he picked up.

He said, "I'm glad to talk to you. I've been studying hard to make sergeant and the exam is coming up. You will be a nice change of pace."

"Great. What's your favorite lunch place? On me."

"Sorry. I can't do lunch."

Damn. Another cop who didn't want to give me the time of day. I didn't want to give up though. "Do you have time for coffee?"

"How about dinner?"

That was better. "I'm way behind this week. But if you don't mind casual and early, I'd like that."

"Name the place."

I said, "What about Jalapeño? It's very relaxed, downtown, and there should be good parking on a snowy night."

"Hey, every night's a snowy night. Say six?"

It was a deal.

———✦———

The wind was swirling surplus snow as I trotted up the walkway to Dr. Partridge's house the second time. It was yet another trip out in the bone-chilling winter that just wouldn't quit. I was hoping that Lydia Johnson was still there. The walkway had been shoveled since my earlier visit and the downstairs lights were glowing warmly.

She answered the door and looked surprised. I took the initiative. I handed her the gift of Kristee's black-and-white fudge, in its distinctive black box with the shiny sheer white ribbon. "I know you are having a tough time, but can you help me, Lydia?"

I had correctly gauged that this was a woman who loved to be helpful. "Of course, come in. I'm glad of the company. I've been going crazy waiting for word and I've been trying to keep busy." Her eyes were still rimmed in pink, but keeping busy had obviously helped.

I stepped into the hallway. Something delicious was cooking, stew perhaps, and there was a faint whiff of fresh bread.

"I'm keeping busy," she said again. "I've decided to be optimistic and make his favorite meals and fill up the freezer. It's . . ."

"A good idea," I said. "This won't take long."

"Take all the time you want. Do you like living room or kitchen? I have to check my soup."

"I like kitchens. Especially if someone has been cooking in them."

That earned me a weak smile and soon I was sitting in the bright kitchen and inhaling the aromas of soup and what turned out to be rolls.

She bustled about and produced some hot tea and a plate of rolls with butter and a choice of cheddar, or strawberry jam. "I'm not sure how I can help you, but I'm glad you dropped in."

The truth is the best option. I gave it a shot. "There have been some incidents in town that appear to be connected with bullying incidents that took place at St. Jude's High School about fourteen years ago."

"Fourteen years ago? Sam had just finished setting up his practice in Woodbridge not long before that. He came here because of his wife, you know."

"I didn't know."

"She was a physician, doing a residency at Woodbridge General. He followed her, but he had to start all over building up clients."

"Sometimes it's good to start over," I said. "It certainly was for me."

"And it would have been for him too, if Janelle had lived. They bought this house together. She hired me first so they could have some of the comforts of home even though they were both slogging away long hours. She was a very thoughtful person and the love of his life. I think that's why he stays here, rattling around in this place. He can never leave it. It's a long time for a man to be alone."

This was a fascinating glimpse into Dr. Partridge's life, but it was off topic for me. "I was hoping he could tell me about the bullies and the outlook for them."

She straightened up and pursed her lips. "He'd never talk about his patients."

"I know that. And rightly so, but I wanted more general information. I need to know if a bully can ever truly change. One of the—I guess I could say guilty parties—is now volunteering with very vulnerable people and I'm very worried about that. Also one of the bully's earlier victims seems to be falling apart. I was hoping for advice on how to help her. So I urgently needed to talk to Dr. Partridge."

"I am sure he would have helped."

"This accident of his troubles me."

"Of course, it's tragic. Beyond tragic."

"And it could be convenient for someone."

Her teacup crashed onto the saucer. "What? Who could find something like that convenient?"

"Perhaps one of those bullies he treated." I didn't say perhaps the victim. I hated the idea of Mona being guilty, but while I had to face up to it, I could keep it to myself in this case.

"But why?"

"Because people are dying. There have been several hit-and-runs in Woodbridge, resulting in three deaths. You must have heard about them."

She turned even paler.

I pressed my point. "The people involved are connected with this bullying business. I don't believe these are accidents, although the police seem to. I am sure Dr. Partridge would figure that out. I don't know if the guilty party might have wanted to make sure he was— Lydia? Are you all right?"

She was swaying in her chair, her face now white as the porcelain cup, her eyes staring.

"What is it?" I said. "Do you know something about this?"

She shuddered as she spoke. "Hit-and-run deaths?"

"Yes. That's right."

"Oh my God."

"What is it? The hit-and-runs?"

"Janelle."

"His wife?" I was desperate to stay on topic and didn't want to digress to discuss the tragedy of the long-dead wife.

She nodded. "Didn't you know?"

"Know what?"

"That's how she died." Her hands shook. "This is so shocking."

I couldn't believe my ears. "He never mentioned it."

"He wouldn't. He still finds it hard to talk about it. She got home late from the hospital one night and was hit just as she got out of the car. The driveway was being repaired and she had to park the car across the street. It was a dark night, raining, but the driver must have known he'd hit her. How could he not have? Sam found her body hours later when he went out searching for her. That was the end of their storybook marriage."

I shivered.

Lydia sputtered. "That driver left her for dead on the road. I am still so angry about that."

I actually felt a pounding in my ears. This explained Dr. Partridge's odd reaction to my questions. "Hit-and-run" would have triggered powerful emotions in him.

Thinking about Dr. Partridge, I'd tuned out Lydia, who was still sounding off. "He should have been caught and put on trial. But the police were quite useless."

"Tell me about it. I can't get them to listen to me at all. Do you mean they never found the person who killed Mrs. Partridge?"

"She was also Dr. Partridge."

"Sorry, of course."

"That doesn't matter. I don't know why I snapped at you. It's just so upsetting, that's all. And no. They never found the man who did it. He's probably having a happy comfortable life while Janelle lies cold and dead for fourteen years and Sam has had his life ruined."

"There's something—"

She cut me off, taking my hand. Tears were welling in her eyes again. "Talking about these hit-and-runs triggers all these memories and feelings. I can't believe it. Is he doing it on purpose? Could it be the same man? I suppose it couldn't be."

I took a deep breath. "You keep saying 'he' for the driver. Is there any reason to think it was a man?"

She shuddered. After a long pause she said, "It never entered my mind that a woman could do something like that. Do you think it's possible for a woman to deliberately smash into someone with a vehicle? Such violence."

I understood her feelings. It would have to be someone who enjoyed inflicting pain and misery for the victims and the families. "I do. Horrible, but possible. I believe it is a woman who's committing these hit-and-runs. And I am beginning to wonder if it was a *girl* who ran down Dr. Janelle Partridge all those years ago."

She turned pale. "A girl? But why?"

"I don't know for sure, but Dr. Partridge saw at least one person who was involved in the bullying episodes."

"That might make sense. You know, something strange. The night Janelle died, she was driving Sam's car. It was a snowy night and his tires were better than hers. She was bundled up. Perhaps someone thought they were getting rid of him."

"That makes sense. And that's why I am here. I didn't even know how his wife died, but I was pretty sure that Dr. Partridge was not the type of person to mix up his medications. Do you disagree with that?"

Her mouth hung open. She closed it and shook her head violently. "No. No, he wasn't the type to do that. He was very methodical. Are you suggesting that someone . . . ? I don't even know how anyone else could have done that."

"I don't know how. But I am convinced that someone did. I also know that the police won't believe me. So I am hoping for help from you."

"Anything I can do. It's horrifying to consider that someone would do that to Sam, but it makes more sense. I don't believe he made that mistake himself."

"Exactly."

"But I would have known if someone was in the house last night. There was no sign of anyone breaking in and we are the only two people with a key."

"I have a glimmer of an idea. The medications didn't have to be mixed up. Someone just needed to ensure that he had an overdose."

She blinked. "But how could someone do that?"

"Could someone have come by here?"

"I don't know. I was out at my bridge club. Sam was already in bed when I came home at about ten."

"Do you live here?"

"Yes. I get my accommodation and Sam gets a bit of TLC. I have a separate entrance and we both guard our privacy, but it's nice to have a bit of company. At any rate, ten was a bit early even for him, although he gets up at dawn. The lights were all out except the hall light, which he always leaves on for me."

"Is there any way for you to know if he had clients last night?"

She shrugged. "He rarely sees them in the night, but he has an appointment book. It's in his office." She stood up, resolute. "Let's go."

I followed her down the hall and into a large office that would have originally been a dining room. The cool blue walls were lined with books, neatly organized. The large teak desk was as I might have expected; neat with a small in-basket and a twin out-basket. The in-basket was empty, I noticed admiringly. The out-basket held a few documents.

Lydia said, "It should be right there."

"Where?"

"On his desk. He leaves it right there every day. Where is it?" She checked the out-basket, then whirled around as if expecting to find it on one of the two comfortable chairs or lying on the plush oriental carpet. "That is very strange. Someone must have taken it. Unless it's upstairs in his bedroom." She hesitated and then made straight for the staircase and upstairs in good time. I followed her, hoping to get away with it.

At the door, she said, "I haven't let myself come back in here. I suppose I'll have to face it sooner or later."

In the bedroom, the bed was still made but rumpled, as if someone had slept on top of the covers. A glass of water had been knocked from the bedside table onto the floor. A jumble of clothing lay on the floor—pants, shirt, hand-knit brown sweater, socks, and underwear. Nothing else was out of order to my mind. There was no sign of an appointment book.

"But understandable," I said. "My guess is that somebody didn't want anyone to find out that she had been to see him."

"That would explain it," she said, frowning, as she bent to pick up a pair of pants and a shirt. "Now, that's odd."

"Let me guess. He always hangs everything up before he goes to bed."

"And his laundry's in the hamper. I don't think Sam's clothes would have ever touched the floor before this. I've never had to pick them up. What does it mean?"

I could feel the answer explode in my head. I knew what it would mean for me. "It means that he was drugged before he went upstairs. Someone slipped him an extra dose of whatever medications he was taking."

"But how?"

"Perhaps they slipped something into his coffee or tea."

"Oh, coffee. He was always drinking coffee."

"And he took it very sweet."

She smiled. "Three sugars in each one."

"So perhaps he wouldn't notice the taste. Did you find a cup or a mug?"

"Mug. He always used a mug. Oh my heavens. I washed them up when I saw them."

"Them?"

"Yes. There were two in the living room. If there was something in one of them, that would be gone now."

"You had no way of knowing. He would have been extremely groggy by the time he got up here and that might explain the clothes on the floor. It would have been all he could have done to get on the bed. He must have knocked over the glass of water then and fell and hit his head trying to get it. Or maybe he had been reaching for the phone to call for help and lost consciousness."

"Who could have done such a terrible thing?"

"Like I said before, it's someone with a lot to lose, perhaps. I'm guessing it was a bully-turned-murderer who was afraid that Dr. Partridge would reveal her secret."

A small voice in the back of my head said, Don't forget Mona.

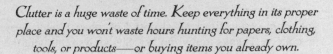

Clutter is a huge waste of time. Keep everything in its proper place and you won't waste hours hunting for papers, clothing, tools, or products—or buying items you already own.

13

You would think with all the social networks in our lives that it would have been easy to find photos of Serena and her nasty little clique. But you would be wrong. I tried Google Images. I stuck my nose into Facebook. Serena was represented by a large golden retriever. Haley wasn't even on Facebook. Tiffanee was represented by a yoga symbol and Jasmin by a bouquet of flowers. I called the library and asked Ramona to see what she could turn up. An hour later, Ramona called back and said, "No luck."

I struck out with my next tactic, even though I'd been counting on Sally.

"High school yearbooks? You must be kidding. That wasn't a good time for me and, except for you and Margaret and Jack, I hoped never to be reminded of it."

"So, long gone then?"

"Right. Don't you have yours?" Sally was teasing. "Or did you declutter it?"

"It would have been worth keeping actually, but every

memento of my life was disposed of when I went away to college. Thanks to my mother. She views sentiment the way some mothers view germs."

Sally chuckled. "Try Margaret."

"I did. No luck. She felt the same way you did."

"Jack?"

"He did have it, but he has no idea where it is now. Probably in storage with his parents' things. Jack just stashed everything they owned in the other two bedrooms on my level and left it at that. Their whole lives are in there. I don't even like to think about what that space is like."

"Would you ever ask Pepper?"

"Not in this case."

"I guess you're out of luck," Sally said.

"Maybe not. You just gave me an idea. Thanks."

Sally said, "Oh no. Not Nick."

———

I pulled up at the house on Old Pine Street and was happy to see "Nick the Stick" Monahan's shiny truck in the driveway. I was even happier to note that Pepper's vehicle was not there. Nick was ridiculously glad to see me. So was Little Nick. Both appeared to have been playing with an astonishing selection of toy cars and trucks in the living room.

"What can I do you for, Charley?" Nick said.

"I need a big favor."

"Anything for you." I swear he licked his lips.

"I need to borrow your high school yearbook." I didn't bother to ask if he still had it. Of course he did. He'd been a big man in high school, a football star if not too twinkly in academic terms. Nick would never let go of that.

"What for?" I thought that brought on a nervous twitch.

"I need a photo."

"Of me?"

"Afraid not, Nick. Serena Redding and her friends."

"Oh. Why?"

"It's a long story."

"You can tell me. I can keep a secret."

Nick could no more keep a secret than he could build a nuclear reactor, but it seemed rude to mention that, especially as I needed this favor. "It's sort of a reunion thing. I want to do some Photoshopping for fun."

"Why didn't you say so? I won't mention it to anyone."

"Especially not Pepper."

"I won't tell her you were here. She might get—you know. I don't have my yearbook anymore because she destroyed it one night after a fight. She thought I might have been eying this one girl. I mean, it was what, fourteen years ago, and I see girls every day, but try talking to her about that. Actually, don't, Charley."

"Rats."

"But I have some pictures and she doesn't know about them. They're in my workshop with my tool manuals. You know I can't use my closet anymore."

Nick trotted downstairs to the basement and returned in no time with some prints.

I sat on the sofa and checked through them quickly. Sure enough, there was one of the Cheerleaders' Club. There they were: Serena, Tiffanee, Haley, and Jasmin. The gorgeous big smiles, the luminous perfect skin, the fashionable (for the time) hair, the trim yet curvy figures. They radiated confidence and wholesome sexiness. Hard to believe that appearances could be so deceiving. All four had written cute, provocative notes to Nick.

"I've got a copy of the class photo," he said. Of course he would. Nick managed to make all the other guys seem lackluster. More than one girl was beaming at him.

In fact, Nick also had individual photos of most of the girls in our graduating class.

"Can I borrow these?"

Nick blanched. "What? Borrow them? Why? They're my only copies. What if something happens to them?"

"Nothing's going to happen. They're in much more danger from Pepper in your house."

"But what if something does? Everyone wrote captions for me. You couldn't ever replace that."

I was short of time so I played the guilt card. "You owe me, Nick."

"Aw, come on, Charley. Don't be like that."

"Just sayin', your life and Little Nick's too. I'll bring these back tomorrow morning."

Nick acquiesced sadly. "Just don't tell Pepper."

"Don't worry about that." I had no intention of telling Pepper anything until I had a bit more information. Even then I didn't think that Nick's photos had to be part of any discussion. I got the hell out of there, before Nick got either amorous or sentimental or depressed or any of the other Nick emotions I didn't care for.

—⧓—

I took a few minutes to swing by my apartment and pop the dogs out briefly. They were anything but grateful. Left to their own, they would have slept until spring, if it ever came. I wondered if they would enjoy coming along with me on my errands that afternoon. They love the car, but there seemed no appetite for that. After I dried their little paws and sent them back to their blanket, I headed for my office and the combination printer/fax/photocopier. I copied the photos of the bullies and the class photo. I glanced around the small, usually tidy office. All my administrative plans for the week's work had been derailed. I was now behind on my invoicing, planning for the downsizing clients, marketing plans, and more. But what choice did I have? I know what I would have told a client. But then, most of my clients weren't trying to solve a trio of murders.

----••----

The third time I arrived at Dr. Partridge's home, I followed fresh footsteps in an inch of snow right up to the front door. I shivered and stamped my feet. It had stopped snowing, but the bitter cold chilled right to the bone.

Lydia let me in with a grim smile. She seemed glad to see me, but worried about what I might have to say this time. She had a merry blaze going in the living room fireplace and I was glad to join her in front of it. "I just got back from the hospital twenty minutes ago. It felt so cold here that I felt I had to make a fire. Hot tea is made too," she said. "It's the one thing I can manage to do consistently."

"How is Dr. Partridge doing?"

"There's not much change. It's very disheartening to—" She turned away, shoulders slumping. I knew that Sam Partridge was the only important person in Lydia's life. I could only imagine how upset she must feel. I reached over and gave her a hug. I felt her shudder. "Thank you, Charlotte. I'll get the tea now."

In no time at all, she was back with a tray, a teapot, and pretty cups, different ones this time. She seemed composed, but her eyes were rimmed with red once again.

As we sipped tea and munched on shortbread cookies, I said, "I'd like to show you some pictures."

"What kind of pictures?"

"Just pictures I had copied."

"What am I looking for?"

"I'm not sure. Let's see if anyone strikes you as familiar."

I didn't want to prejudice her answers, so I started with the large shot of the entire graduating class. She chuckled and pointed to me. "You haven't changed that much."

I wasn't sure how to take that. "Anyone else?"

"Hard to say. She followed each student with her finger, starting with the first row and pausing from time to time. She stopped at Sally. "I know her. Her husband's a physician at the hospital, a colleague of Sam's." Her face was serious, intent. Her finger paused by Serena. She frowned and moved on. She slowed by Tiffanee and Haley too, as well as a few others. Of course, each figure was so tiny and the photo had been taken years earlier. Also, there were quite a few attractive blondes and brunettes. "They're all the same type, aren't they? I can't be sure. Although, she's familiar. And so is this girl." She pointed to Tiffanee and then Jasmin.

Her finger came to a stop at the end of the third row; a slight diffident figure, sloping shoulders. Lydia tapped at the face.

"She's different. And familiar."

I blurted, "Can you really see her face? It almost could be anyone."

Lydia shot me a startled glance. "Of course I'm sure. I recognize that girl. For sure. She's quite distinctive. I think she came here to see Sam when she was a girl. She seemed to be very jumpy and easily upset. Her skin was broken out and she bit her nails. I've seen her more recently. She's older and more presentable, I suppose you'd say, but I've seen her right here in the neighborhood."

Oh no. Mona.

"Visiting?"

"No, just driving by. It took me a while to place her, but as I said, she is distinctive."

Mona, Mona. What have you done? Were you stalking Dr. Partridge? I'd been hoping that the cabal would get fingered, and instead, here was something that just made things worse for Mona. I felt sick to my stomach. Even though I knew it was wrong, I could understand Mona wanting revenge on the people who had harmed her. But nothing would explain harming Dr. Partridge.

"I suppose," I said with great reluctance. "Here, I'd like to show you one other picture." I flipped through the photocopies to where the cheerleaders were featured. Serena, Tiffanee, Jasmin, and Haley were all there, white smiles gleaming, hair poufy, perfect lips glossy, and lots of leg showing. The photo was larger and each face clearly recognizable.

"Do any of these girls appear familiar?" I said. I tried not to emphasize Serena in this. As much as I wanted her to be implicated, I wanted the truth and to be sure of the truth more.

Lydia stared at the picture and then back to me. "They all do."

"They came as clients?"

"One of them did. I think the others used to pick her up. If I remember correctly, she was only seeing Sam because her parents insisted. I don't remember which girl was which. They were such a collective, except for the girl with the long black hair. Those big smiles, but I always felt they were ready to sneer. You don't think it was one of them?"

"I don't know."

"What about the other one?"

I knew she meant Mona. "I hope not."

"In that case, I hope not too. It is odd isn't it, to see them again recently."

"What?"

"Some of them—" She stopped as the phone rang. She held her hand over her heart as she answered it. I realized that I was holding my breath.

Her hands were shaking. "They want me back at the hospital. Sam's brother, Will, has flown in. He is coming for me any minute."

In the rush as she got ready—hat, coats, boots, gloves—I waited for my chance. Once she was ready, standing, white-faced, by the front door, I said, "You said you saw some of them recently. Which—"

She turned to me, agony written on her face. "Please, Charlotte. I am unable to think about anything but Sam today. Oh, there's Will pulling up outside now. You'll have to excuse me. I can't keep him waiting. I am sorry to leave like this."

"Please let me know what happens. I hope he is all right. I'll call you."

She shuddered and opened the door. We both emerged from the warm and friendly house into the bitter wind and eternally swirling snow.

—◆◆—

I stood there for a while, watching the car drive out of sight. Then I climbed into my frigid little car and drove off slowly. Where was Mona? What had she done? And worse, what would she do? I wanted to believe that one of the others was responsible, but I had nothing at all to go on. Mona was the one that Lydia was sure had been in the neighborhood. The point was, had she been in the house too? And which of the cabal had been by, perhaps to see Dr. Partridge when he was alone in the house? With Lydia gone, there was no way to know. Or was there?

I circled by again and stared at the buildings across the street. The late afternoon was gloomy because of the end- less snow, and lights gleamed from the front windows of three of the houses. Some people were home during the day. Maybe they looked out those windows.

—◆◆—

The first neighbor refused to open her door to me. The sec- ond one didn't even come to answer it. I could sense the presence of someone hiding in the back of the house to avoid me, whoever I was. I was chilled and stiff by the time I pounded on the third door.

A small, round Hispanic woman, with a moon face and

black hair in an updo, answered. She flinched at the snow. "Is it ever going to end?" she said.

"Hello," I said, my teeth chattering. "My name is Charlotte Adams and I wanted to ask you some questions about what happened to Dr. Partridge." I turned and pointed to the white Cape Cod across the street.

"Oh! I recognize you from the television," she said.

Was that going to be a bad or a good thing?

Turned out to be good. Her name was Maria and soon I was in her very warm living room, being served steaming hot chocolate and empanadas. I couldn't believe my luck, although my waistband was already beginning to feel tight.

"I will never get used to this country," she said. "I dream of Venezuela all through the winter, but it's not enough, is it? I stay inside all day."

I shook my head. "I have some photos. I'd like to know if you recognize any of these people."

She took her time, staring at the photos, much as Lydia had done. Nodding to herself and uttering soft Spanish comments.

"These are old photos."

"Yes, but I think most of them are still recognizable."

"This one," she said, pointing. "She has been here yesterday."

"Yesterday?"

"Last night."

"I knew it! Serena."

That said it all. I was going straight to the police.

"And this one," she said, fingering Mona. "I saw her, but not at the house. She seemed to be behind the other one, watching from the car."

"Could you tell that from the window?"

"My husband noticed. We were coming home from Hannaford's and he noticed the car was still there after all the time we were gone. The windows were clear of snow.

It struck him funny." She offered me another empanada. They were spectacular. Who could refuse?

"What kind of car?" I asked.

"A small red one. So much tragedy in that man's life. Losing his wife so young. Now this other terrible accident."

"The other woman," I started to say.

"The beautiful one?"

"Yes." It bugged me to say it. "Was she in the house long?"

"I would say at least forty-five minutes. She seemed upset when she left."

"You could tell that?"

"She came out just as we arrived back. My husband noticed the little red car. I noticed the woman. She'd been crying. She got into her car."

"What kind of car?"

"A big yellow one. You know the ones like some kind of army machine. A zinger?"

"Hummer, maybe?"

"Yes. My husband loves them. I think they are horrible."

"And she drove away?"

"Yes. Very fast, right down the middle of the road. And the little red car followed her."

Everyone needs to take time to unwind and get enough sleep.
If you fail to make this investment in your rest and recovery,
you'll be far less efficient, plus prone to burnout.

14

My tactic of letting Pepper know met with the usually deafening silence. I'd given up hope that she'd call me back. I added Mona to the hopeless list too. No one answered at Haley's. That worried me. As one of the remaining bullies, Haley was unlikely to be killed by a car if she stayed inside her cozy cabin, but what if she'd ignored my warnings and headed out on errands? She was high-strung and jumpy, not overly logical, and she'd be an easy target on those lonely country roads.

It was late afternoon when I decided to head out to check on Haley. I found myself yawning. I hadn't had much downtime this week and it was starting to catch up to me. The Miata was bumping and grinding along the packed snow on the backcountry road to Haley's home in the woods. I pulled up in front of the house and sniffed the wood smoke. The van was there. I was glad I caught them before they left for work.

Randy arrived at the door, yawning. He seemed surprised to see me. I figured Haley didn't get a lot of friends dropping in. He opened the door and gestured for me to come in. "I'll get her," he said. "She's doing laundry. That coffee's nice and fresh if you'd like some. I just put it on for her."

The coffee smelled heavenly. If it tasted half as good, it would be wonderful.

I accepted a nice full mug. The coffee didn't disappoint. Randy was apparently much better at making it than Haley.

Randy called, "Honey, you got company again. Leave everything and have your coffee with your friend."

A full three minutes passed before Haley appeared at the top of the basement stairs, her face even paler than usual. Relief washed over her features when she saw me. Randy noticed it too.

"Who'd you think it was, honey? The IRS?"

She rolled her eyes. "Charlotte. This is a surprise."

"Sorry to keep dropping in uninvited, Haley. This won't take long."

She watched me, her watery eyes worried. "What is it?"

"I wondered how you found out that Serena was back."

Her mouth tightened. She glanced at Randy, then back at me. "Didn't I tell you? She called me. I guess I'm not that hard to find."

"What did she say?"

"Just that she was coming back and she'd been looking forward to seeing me and how my life turned out. She wanted us to get together again. Get our groove back. All that. It was awful. I didn't want to go back to that relationship, like I said."

She was being vague and all of a sudden it hit me. Except for the incident with Mona, Jack had been pretty much unaware of the mean girls' cruelty. What if Randy had no idea what a bitch his wife had been? Haley wouldn't want him to know. She was very much ashamed of herself. I imagined she wouldn't want her daughter to find out either. I sure wouldn't have if I'd been in her shoes. Even so, I thought she would be better off coming clean with both of them. Otherwise Serena would continue to have power over her.

"She called Mona Pringle too."

"Oh, poor Mona."

"What's going on, honey?"

"Nothing. I'll explain later. Can you let me talk with Charlotte in private, please?"

"Sure thing. Time for me to get dressed anyway." I thought Randy seemed offended as he shuffled up the stairs and disappeared. A door closed softly.

I said, "And she called Kristee too."

Haley gasped. "But why?"

I shrugged. "I don't know."

"She made Kristee's life hell too. We all did. A fat girl like that. Serena found it irresistible. I am too ashamed to ever go near her candy shop just knowing the things we did to her. The cruel things we said. I could shrivel up and die. I guess she's calling all the people she made suffer."

"I wonder who else she called. Do you think she truly wanted to make amends?"

"Amends?" Haley barked with laughter, although there was no humor in that laugh. "You must be kidding. She just wants to wield that old power again, to watch people squirm, to know they probably won't sleep well just knowing she's back. They'll be looking behind them, jumping when the phone rings. Tossing and turning in bed. She's getting high on that. I told her I have a new life now and I'm busy with my family and I don't have any spare time. She told me what she thought of my 'pathetic little life.' But you know what? I got off lightly. I might be feeling nervous and jumpy, but those other girls will be panicked. I realize that's what's happening with me and I wasn't even one of her victims. I was one of the bullies. When I think that I actually locked Mona in that locker intending to leave her there all weekend, I can't—"

A small noise from the second floor caught our attention. We both glanced up at the source. Near the top of the staircase, a plump teenager stared down at Haley and me.

Haley said, "Brie!"

With her dark hair and broad face, Brie took after her father, Randy, not Haley. She stared openmouthed for a minute before turning and rushing back to her room. The door slammed behind her, the sound reverberating. What had the expression been on her face? Horror, mixed with contempt?

Randy stepped out of the next doorway, a sweatshirt in his hands. He stared down the hall in the direction I took to be his daughter's room. Then he turned to regard his wife, the first of many questions starting to rise on his lips.

Haley couldn't hold back the tears. "It's starting. Everything's starting to go wrong. Serena won't rest until she ruins everyone's life again. I wouldn't have thought she could cause problems in my own family, but now—"

I waited until she pulled herself together. I said in a low voice, "Perhaps you have to level with them, if they don't know."

Her voice wobbled. "I don't want them to know what I did, what I was. What I did to—"

I knew she was thinking about what she had done to kids like Brie.

Haley said, "I did terrible things. I am sorry for my actions, but I can't undo them."

"Maybe you can make a start," I said. "You can't undo those terrible things, but you could do some good."

At the sound of Randy's heavy footsteps heading downstairs, Haley began to sob. "Stay with me," she said, reaching over and grabbing my sleeve.

"What the hell are you doing to her?" Randy bellowed.

Haley turned her tear-streaked face to him. "She didn't do anything. I have to tell you something. Something that's been bothering me a lot."

"I knew something was wrong. You've been so mopey lately."

She nodded and took a deep, ragged breath. "I am not the person you think I am, Randy."

"'Course, you are, honey. Who else would you be?"

She shook her head and the stringy curls swayed. "Not who you think, for sure. Not that person."

"I've known you all my life. We went to school together. I love you, honey. You are my beautiful girl. My prom princess. Why are you so upset?"

I was conscious of a scuffling on the stairs. I turned to see Brie had returned and was now crouched near the bottom stair, listening intently to her mother.

"I did terrible things to people. You have no idea. Cruel things."

"No, you didn't, honey."

Haley wailed. "Yes! I did! I am so sorry. I hurt people. I humiliated them. People who didn't deserve it. I was under Serena's thumb and I would have done anything she told me to do. I never thought about how much it would have hurt . . ."

"Mona," I said. "It hurt Mona."

"Who's Mona?"

"Now she's a 911 operator. Then she was a skinny awkward kid who was put through hell."

"Honey, it's a long time ago. People get over stupid kids games. It's one person and she must have turned out all right to be a 911 operator."

"She's pretty messed up over this," I said. "She was holding it together until Serena called her."

"But that's Serena, not you. Even I knew she had a mean streak."

"It wasn't just one person," Haley hiccupped. "And I was just as involved as Serena."

"Not just Mona. Kristee too," I said.

"What did you girls do to them?"

"Not Charlotte. She wasn't part of it."

I said, "I didn't step forward to help Mona or Kristee when they needed me. That's why I need to do something now."

"Kristee? She that gal with the chocolate shop? Kind of . . ." His voice trailed off and his eyes darted to his daughter's round face.

"Fat?" Brie said from her place on the stairs. "Was she fat, Mom?"

"Not very, I suppose, but we tormented her."

"She's another one doing okay now though," Randy said. "People have to rise above these things."

I didn't want to say what had happened to Kristee, the pig nose, the food dumps, the other torments. There was no point in rubbing it in about Brie's mother's crimes. But I was pretty sure Brie knew firsthand what Kristee had gone through.

"I didn't realize," Haley sobbed, "but now I do. I want to make it up to people. I am so afraid of what Serena will do."

"What could she do?" Randy and I said practically in unison.

"Randy's right," I said. "She doesn't have any power over you now. Just don't associate with her. You asked me for forgiveness and you did far less damage to me. Maybe you can make amends to Mona and Kristee."

"They'd never forgive me."

"Maybe not. I don't know. It's too late for Bethann Reynolds, but you can do the right thing for Kristee and Mona. Talk to them. Tell them you truly regret what you were part of and why. Even if they don't forgive you, that can help you break free from Serena and let you move on."

"That makes sense to me, honey," Randy said.

A soft voice broke in from the stairs. "They'll never forgive you. Never, and there's no reason why they should. Why should you end up happy with a family when their lives were practically ruined? I know what it's like to be one of *them*. I hate you. I wish you weren't my mother." Brie turned and stumbled up the stairs.

"Brie, baby," Randy lumbered after her. "You don't mean that."

"The hell I don't."

It took a couple more minutes for Haley to stop weeping. "I never wanted my family to know what I did. Randy will forgive me anything, but Brie will never trust me again."

"If you do the right thing now, Brie will come around in time. It sounds to me like she's had her share of bullying to deal with."

"She has such a pretty face and she hardly eats a thing, but she's like Randy's mom and sister—they're just round people. She's artistic. She doesn't have many friends outside of her books. I should have been on the lookout. No wonder she's so angry at me."

"Maybe you can get some counseling for her, and for yourself."

"Thanks, Charlotte, but I can't even afford that."

"There are some community resources that could help you both. I'll check into that. But I don't know if you should thank me. I think I made things worse. I was just trying to figure out who else she would have contacted to make amends. She got Mona and Kristee both into a state. Mona's panicked and Kristee's mad as hell. Could there be anyone else?"

Haley bit her lip. "I wonder if she called Bethann too. She was also a target, as well as Mona and Kristee."

"Do you think she might have?" This reminded me that I hadn't heard back from Bethann's brother-in-law. I could hardly pressure the grieving family, but I was still hoping he'd find out something for me.

Haley said, "Sure. Bethann was such a little rabbit. She'd cry as soon as Serena walked by her. She'd panic and run away. I bet Serena missed having all that impact on people, even though she's pretending to be so nice. She always loved it when someone was suffering. It was probably fun for her to revive all that, to make them miserable again."

I thought about it. "Bethann's dead, not just miserable. Anyway, I heard she'd learned to fight back. Won a harassment suit against her employer. I wonder if she would have been as intimidated by Serena this time around."

Haley shrugged. "I don't understand what's going on. I wish I did."

I had been wondering if Mona was responsible, but now another idea was starting to form. I said, "Bethann had changed. What if she wasn't willing to put up with this anymore? What if she decided to go public about Serena too? What if she threatened her? Serena would have had plenty to lose this time."

Haley's jaw dropped. "You mean Serena might have killed Bethann? Oh my God. That's . . ."

I raised an eyebrow. "Possible?"

She frowned. "It would explain a lot. But it doesn't explain Tiffanee and Jasmin."

"Maybe they weren't keen on her coming back any more than you were. If there's any truth to the suggestion that Tiffanee had completely changed, that would make sense."

"You mean, maybe they rejected Serena too? And Bethann wasn't a frightened little mouse anymore and said something to set her off?"

"That's exactly what I mean. And maybe Serena didn't like that much. If they pushed back, perhaps that's why they're dead."

Haley hugged herself tightly and said, "I guess that just leaves me."

"Promise me you won't go anywhere alone until this whole terrible situation is resolved."

"Resolved! How can it ever be resolved? My life is in the toilet now." She turned an anguished glance up the stairs to where Brie could be heard loudly weeping.

I called out to Randy. I could tell by his narrowed eyes that he blamed me as he thudded down. But he did commit to making sure Haley went nowhere by herself. I hoped that was going to be enough.

—••—

Jack had his monthly dinner meeting of the WAG'D executive committee, so I dropped into the house first to put the dogs out and feed them. I changed into my new jeans and my favorite hoodie, in soft turquoise cashmere, for my casual dinner with Dean Oliver. I ramped it up a bit with dress boots and silver hoop earrings. I promised the pooches lots of cuddling later. They were already back to sleep, but I hoped I'd reached them at some level.

"New relationship?" Dean said as we settled into a brushed metal table for two at the crowded café. Jalapeño was one of the most popular and relaxed new gathering spots.

"What?"

"Last night, at Al's, you were—"

"Oh no. A friend of a friend. He works at 911. And that's connected with what I want to talk to you about." Dean had absolutely no expression as he listened to my story about Mona and how distressed she was. I suppose they learn to deal with us demented types when they're in the police academy. I launched into my theory of the three hit-and-runs being connected.

When I drew my first breath, he interjected, "If you

don't mind me saying so, Charlotte, you've been known to get things wrong."

"I know. I got it wrong when I talked to Pepper and now she won't give me the time of day. But sometimes I get them right too. I've thought this one through. You're the person that can help me. People are dying in this town and the deaths are connected in some way to the bullies who made Mona's life hell when she was in school. I think you'd be surprised at how attractive and personable those bullies were. And are. Bethann was a bullying victim. Tiffanee and Jasmin were bullies. I think the perpetrator is a woman called Serena Redding, now married to Jerome Zeitz. She was the worst of all the bullies. I know what she was capable of. She's married to a powerful man and she's back in the area. I believe she contacted all the victims. And I have reason to believe that either she, or one of her collaborators, was being treated by Dr. Partridge. I went to him and I explained the problems Mona is having and I could tell that he knew about these incidents back in high school."

Dean's eyebrows were up by this time. "Did he tell you anything?"

"You and I know that a professional counselor wouldn't do that. Serena drives a yellow Hummer and one was seen parked by his house the day of the medication mix-up. Can you make inquiries about exactly what substances were found in his system? Can you—?"

Dean Oliver ran his hand over his forehead. "I can make 'inquiries,' but right now let me tell you, results from the tox lab take months to come back and that's when there's an active investigation. And a body, which there isn't. This is a live person. So no open case and no more than a hunch from a person who is not on the police force. In fact, I'd get my butt kicked for talking to you about it. First of all, it's probably too late to get any uncompromised samples from Dr. Partridge, Charlotte. Second, even if we did, by the time any results came back from the lab, your Dr. Partridge would have died of old age."

"What if it could be an active investigation? What—?"

"Give it up. I'll talk to the principal investigator of the hit-and-runs and—"

"Right. Pepper Monahan."

"Pepper's the best, Charlotte, and you know that. She's under a lot of pressure, but she's one hell of a cop so let's leave it with her."

"I know that, but she's not returning any of my calls. Maybe you could convince her that Dr. Partridge might be in danger. And see what you can find out about his wife. She was killed in a hit-and-run about fourteen years back."

That got his attention.

"Really?"

"I just found that out today. It would be the same time he was seeing one of these bullies." I paused and decided not to leave out key information. "He may have been seeing Mona too."

"But promise me you will not mess around in this thing. If you are right, you could be the next person in the hospital or worse. I'll make a point of checking. I'm on evening shift tomorrow. "

Evening shift tomorrow? I wasn't sure I wanted to wait that long. "I doubt that. Unlike him, I have no idea who's behind all this."

"Maybe they don't know that you don't know. Whoever they are. Thought of that?"

"Two of them are dead already. I'm worried about Haley and I'm terrified that Mona is going to have a complete collapse."

He said, "I know this is hard to accept, but there may be nothing sinister going on. Even with your Dr. Partridge. And a fourteen-year-old hit-and-run? Not much chance. This isn't television. But I'll do what I can."

I must have slumped in defeat. Dealing with this police department was like hurling yourself at a brick wall over and over again. It just stayed unresponsive. A good thing in a brick wall, but a bad attribute when your goal was to prevent more deaths. As much as I liked him, my session with Dean had wasted time I could have used to try to find Mona.

I think we were both glad to say good-bye.

———— ⧉ ————

I decided to return Rose's cookie container, which I'd remembered to put in my car earlier. I was tired and worried about Haley and Mona and didn't feel much like making that stop, but I don't let myself procrastinate. That's just asking for trouble. Unfortunately, there was an unlikely traffic jam on Long March Road. From the blinking lights, it went on for miles, so I made a U-turn and I took the back route, turning at the library. This wasn't the brightest thing I'd ever done, because the hills in that neighborhood were slippery from the new layer on the packed surface. Woodbridge city services were definitely falling down on the job. I finally got the little Miata up to the top of the hill, slowing to make the right angle turn at North Elm Street. The delivery truck behind me had even more trouble getting traction up the hill. The road was so treacherous I was regretting not waiting for the morning. I should have said to hell with the rules and procrastinated my head off. The Miata may not be built for snow, but because it's a stick shift, it's good on hills and has better control than many heavier cars. I geared down and slowed nearly to stop. I wasn't taking any chances.

Just as I slowed to a crawl, foot on the brake, I noticed that the solid guardrail at the edge of the escarpment had been demolished. Had someone else crashed into it earlier? Yellow and black caution tape waved in the wind. I belatedly remembered the news items about the elderly couple who narrowly avoided going over, when I felt a massive crack behind me. The car jolted and my head snapped back with the force. I heard another crack as my air bags inflated. It felt like being smacked in the head by a beach ball traveling fifty miles an hour. The air filled with white powder that stung my eyes. In my shock, I must have lifted my foot off the brake. An explosion? No, a collision. I could feel the Miata moving forward, even though it had stalled. Someone was pushing me forward. I tried to force the air bag away so that I could see. I turned to the rear window and saw the large brown delivery truck behind me. Way closer than he should have been. Had he slid down the road and caused both of us to careen toward disaster? The Miata inched ahead. The air bags were blocking my front view. I leaned sideways so that I could see. The car was being pushed over the collapsed guardrail. I was inching toward the embankment.

I pushed the air bag away from me. They were supposed to save lives, but it sure made it hard to move. As whoever was behind me struck again, I unbuckled my seat belt and pushed again. The Miata jerked forward. I couldn't see past the air bag, but from the side window I could tell I was close to the edge. I decided to take my chances with whoever was behind me. There'd be no way to survive going over the escarpment in the Miata. I pushed my door open and heaved myself out. I tumbled and rolled a few feet, grabbing at snow-covered grass and shrubs to stop my fall. My body was less than a foot from the edge; one foot dangled over. I stared in horror at my Miata as it teetered at the edge, and slowly, almost deliberately, slipped off and plunged. I watched openmouthed as my beloved little car hit the ground below nose first, flopped over, and burst into flames.

I was still on a slippery slope to end all slippery slopes,

with someone who wanted me dead right behind me. Filled with dread, I whipped my head around. Where was the vehicle that pushed me over? I heard shouts. The brown delivery truck rapidly reversed, spun around, and sped away, fishtailing.

A man's voice boomed out to me. "Are you all right? Stay there. We're coming."

Sure thing. Where would I go?

A woman's voice next, high and quavering. "We've called the police. We saw it all! That truck! He tried to kill you."

I was grabbed unceremoniously by lots of arms and pulled up away from the sheer drop. My rescuers were in their late sixties, with kind, creased faces. I tried to stand up, but crumpled into a heap on the road. I stared up at them, bundled in matching blue-and-silver puffy ski jackets. My head was spinning.

"Can we call someone for you?" The woman's voice again, concerned.

"My phone is in the car. And my purse. My briefcase. Everything. Up in smoke."

Thank heavens I hadn't brought Truffle and Sweet Marie. I wouldn't have been able to save them, to get the three of us out of the car. I heard sirens in the distance and thought I saw the flash of red lights. Could the WINY truck be far behind?

"Ask Jack to walk the dogs," I said, before the lights went out.

15

Sometimes a hot bath is exactly what you need, especially if you've been battered and bruised and almost killed. Not to mention hauled off to the hospital, interrogated by Pepper Monahan, and yelled at by Sally and Margaret for not keeping clear of a crime. Oh, and captured for posterity by WINY. My appearance was revolting as always. White powder from air bags doesn't flatter anyone. Let's just say that.

I was so tied in knots, I thought my neck would spasm. Of course, I couldn't relax. Every time I closed my eyes, I saw either the sheer drop off the embankment or Mona's face or Haley or Brie. I was quite prunelike and still grumpy when I got out of the tub. I put on my most cuddly terry-cloth robe. It's much too big and bulky and I feel like a refrigerator in it, but so what. My hair was in a topknot and I had striped socks on *and* my fluffy slippers as I flopped on the sofa to listen to a bit of soothing music. I didn't have the energy to do any of my normal pleasant chores. Naturally, there was a knock on the door.

"Hi," Jack said. "Oh." He followed this with a major grin.

"Oh what, Mr. Grinny Face?"

"Nothing."

"Out with it."

"It's just that you look so—"

"Much like a refrigerator?"

"A refrig—? No I was going to say you looked cute. Is that a polar bear suit? Not everyone would be as cute as you in whatever that getup is."

"Cute? What kind of thing is that to say? I'm a modern woman. We are never cute."

Jack blinked. "So, not a bear suit?"

"Not a bear suit. I've been trying to mellow out in the bath."

"Now that you mention it, you do look a little like a refrigerator. You have that chilly, modern aspect too."

"Very funny."

"You put the idea into my head. I'm suggestible."

"Neither a refrigerator costume nor a polar bear suit. This is a luxurious terry-cloth robe sent by my mother to assuage some kind of guilt. I keep it to wear after near-fatal car crashes. But now I'm truly insulted."

"Cool," Jack said. "I wonder how long you can keep that up. Want to watch television? Catch the news? There's bound to be excellent coverage of your crash."

"I was there. I'm not sure I can bear the WINY take on it. Fine. Oh crap. Where's the remote?"

Both dogs appeared guilty, but the remote turned up under the cushion that Sweet Marie had settled herself on. Jack parked himself next to me on the sofa. If it hadn't been that we were about to watch an item that was bound to be upsetting, I would have been smiling at the warmth of Jack's body next to my refrigerator self. But there was that talk of hit-and-run. I clicked and Todd Tyrell's toothiness appeared. Did the man never sleep?

He appeared to be just this side of gleeful about the burnt-out wreck that had been my beloved Miata. He managed to hold it back, as that was an inappropriate response to what was after all yet another hit-and-run, no matter what the WINY ratings might indicate.

I sat shivering in my cuddly robe, even though I was warm and dry snuggled up next to Jack. Jack who was always there for me. I found it tricky, keeping my feelings under wraps. Jack has a low tolerance for Todd. He'd turned his attention to some paperwork. Not like him in the least.

"What are you doing, Jack?" I asked, with a yawn. Brushes with death make me sleepy apparently.

"Hmm? Oh, just checking over the contractor's estimates."

"Estimates? Are you planning to renovate CYCotics already? You've only been open for—"

"This house. Remember? Converting it back to a single-family home, the way it was when I was growing up?"

"What? Why would you—?"

Jack gave me a strange look. "I told you about it. Don't you recall?"

How could I have missed that? I was sure I hadn't. I'd been busy, sure, but to miss Jack talking about taking my home away from me? My perfect apartment. What the hell was I supposed to do then? Live in my car with my dogs? Oh wait, I didn't have a car anymore.

I stood up unsteadily, feeling a sharp pain in my chest. I was sure that was heartbreak. I would have cried, but who had the energy? "I've had a rough day. I'm going to bed now."

I hoped I sounded brave. And unconcerned.

Jack blinked. "Okay. Sure. See you tomorrow."

As I stomped my homeless, carless body toward my bedroom, I was not unaware that the dogs remained with Jack.

——◆——

Friday started with a headache, a generally sore body, and a bad mood. And that was before I got the call from Mona.

"Charlotte?"

"Mona, you—"

"Don't. I need to talk. I sure hope that one of my alters didn't do that to you. I just saw it on the news. Do you hate Todd Tyrell?"

"Yes, I do, but—"

"Anyway, that's awful about your car and I feel terrible. At least you're not dead. Although if one of my alters is after you, that probably won't be true for long."

I shivered and said, "Mona. Did you ever see Dr. Partridge for therapy when you were being bullied?"

Silence.

"Mona?"

Nothing.

"Please answer the question." I halfway expected a totally different voice to respond. I was that spooked by the possibility of those alters.

"Oh my God. They're almost all taken care of, and now it's starting with Dr. Partridge. I heard he was in the hospital. What happened to him?"

"An overdose of cold medications *and* painkillers. But what do you mean that they're almost all taken care of now? Who? And what does—?"

"Except for Haley, they're dead. Tiffanee and Jasmin."

"But Haley isn't dead."

"Not yet, she isn't. But I guess Rome wasn't built in a day. Serena will finish her off soon. If it's Serena doing it. I was convinced she was behind these murders, but what if it was me?"

My temple throbbed. My own competing theories of Mona's alters versus Serena as the killer were confusing enough without Mona making me dizzy. I said, "Mona—"

"And what about the wife? What if it was happening even back then?"

"What wife? You mean Dr. Partridge's wife?"

"Sure. Who else? I'm pretty sure she died in a hit-and-run too. The same pattern, isn't it? Of course, that could apply to me too. Now that I know about the alters, it's one more thing for me to fear about myself. Maybe this multiple personality disorder has been going on for years."

I stood there, heart thumping. I had only made the connection with Dr. Janelle Partridge and the current hit-and-runs the day before. I'd wondered if that was too far-fetched, but Mona had brought it up too.

"I gotta go, Charlotte."

"No! Wait! You called me. I need to know—"

I wasn't in the mood to listen to the dial tone for long. I stomped into the kitchen to put on coffee. Jack gazed up from the sofa as I passed. He smiled.

"Dogs are walked. Coffee's on."

"Aren't you terrific," I grumped.

He seemed a bit more surprised than I expected. What did he think? Selling my home out from under me and I'm supposed to be Little Miss Sunshine?

He shrugged. "I didn't want to wake you up. It's nine thirty and the contractor's due here soon."

"Nine thirty? Are you kidding? I never sleep that late."

"Apparently, you do now."

I grabbed a coffee, slopping a bit on the counter. The holder toppled over as I grabbed for a paper towel. "I have so much to do today. I need to talk to the insurance company and replace all my cards and . . . What time is the contractor coming?" I managed to keep a tremor out of my

voice when I said that. I didn't want to lose the last vestige
of my dignity.

"Like I said, soon. Any minute."

"I'll get dressed," I said, pivoting on my heel and heading for the bedroom. "I also need to figure out what Dr.
Partridge's wife has to do with all this."

I may have slammed the door behind me. Served him
right, carrying on with a contractor right under my nose.

—◆◆—

My insurance agent was on the ball. He watched the
WINY news and reached me first. I didn't even have to
call. A rental car had been arranged and—Can you believe
this?—dropped off at my house. Of course, I'd had all my
cards and information photocopied and on file and I was
able to arrange for replacements without too much aggra-
vation, if you don't count sitting on hold. At least it kept me
in the office and away from Jack and his contractor. With
any luck, the dogs would give them a hard time.

I'd watched the news too and learned that a brown delivery van had been found abandoned in an alley on the opposite side of town from where it had been stolen two days
earlier. Had I been almost killed by some idiot joyrider?
Somehow I doubted that.

I headed out to do a string of errands, including replacing my cell phone. My new streak of luck held as the library was open that morning and, even better, Ramona
was working. I'd heard nothing back from Dean and figured I should have started with Ramona in the first place.
Some of the usual crowd was hanging around reference. I
got my share of dirty looks when I came flying in. I was
a little bit nervous as I'd been driving a rental car. In this
case, a Hyundai Santa Fe, a large SUV. With the burgeon-
ing accident rate, they were low on choices. I was glad to

have something big and heavy with the roads in their current condition, although I felt like a toy driving it.

I spotted Ramona before she saw me. "Quick, I need to find out whatever you can about the death of a doctor about fourteen years ago. Hit-and-run," I said.

"Hello to you too, Charlotte," Ramona said. "Sorry about your car. I know you two were very close, but you should greet your friends before you demand special treatment."

"Sorry. I'm getting too caught up in this craziness and I'm losing it."

"Think nothing of it. So this query is related to what's happening now?" She smacked her own forehead. "Hit-and-run? Stupid me. Of course it is."

"A Dr. Janelle Partridge."

"I'm on it. I have a vague recollection of that. What am I searching for?"

"Details. Connections. I don't think they ever found the driver of the car that hit her. That has to be linked to the fact that her husband almost died this week, and I am sure both incidents are connected to these hit-and-run deaths."

"You think?" Ramona was already heading off to begin her quest. "I'll call you. As soon as I have something."

"I'll wait."

While Ramona went fact-hunting I sat at one of the solid-wood reference tables and tried to get my head together. I had left the house for the first time in my adult life—maybe in my entire life—without checking my To Do list. I was losing it. But I didn't want to go home and run into the contractor who was plotting to eliminate my home and refuge. I felt a lump in my throat. I grabbed a piece of the library's scrap paper and a pencil and scrawled down a few thoughts. What else to do? My cell phone was gone, my agenda with it. But something that Mona had said was nagging at me. She had said, "They're almost all taken care of." Mona meant the bullies, for sure. But they weren't "all taken care of." Haley remained. If it really was one of Mona's alters, what did that mean? Haley of all of the bullies was the most distressed by Serena's reappearance, the most remorseful. On the other hand, she was definitely not dead.

"Not yet, she isn't," Mona had said.

I stood up suddenly, knocking over my chair. That earned me at least four dirty scowls from the regulars. Ramona was nowhere to be seen. I needed to check up on Haley. I glanced around furtively and took a big chance. I snatched up the phone at the reference desk. I only needed it for a minute.

"Charlotte?" Haley's breathy voice wafted over the phone. "I just left a message at your house! I have such good news. You won't believe it."

I hoped that perhaps there was some positive update on Randy's health. That family could have used a break.

"It's about Mona."

Mona hadn't been such good news lately, so this took me by surprise.

"She's agreed to meet me, to hear me out. I think she is willing to forgive me. I want to make her understand how much I regret everything I did in the past, how ashamed I am of the person I was back then."

I got a sick feeling in the pit of my stomach. "Don't meet with her, Haley!"

Haley plowed on, apparently not hearing. "We're going to get together, for lunch. This will be such a huge weight off my mind. You have no idea how much it bothers me. She picked neutral territory. She picked a spot, more private than the local café, but it's out of town a bit. It's a small family restaurant about ten minutes from my place on Burnt Road. I expect to be pretty emotional and I don't want half of Woodbridge watching me lose it. That diner is such a rambling place; they have booths and they just leave you alone. A lot of people meet there when they want to have private chats without running into half the town."

I supposed this made sense, but not for Haley, not with everything that was going on. "Haley, I don't think you should meet with Mona alone. Those years at St. Jude's and even before, back in the playgrounds, they're all very . . . unresolved for her. She may be a lot angrier than you expect. Why don't I go with you? Mona knows me and she realizes that I understand what she's been through. She'd be all right with that, I am absolutely certain."

"That's real sweet of you, Charlotte, but I have to do this. Anyway, I'm not going to be by myself."

"Yes, but Mona isn't—"

"Not just Mona, but Randy. He's going to drive me in. I am so keyed up that I don't think I could drive. It's snowing out and I'm not real good in that anyway. Told you he's a sweetheart."

"Didn't Mona object?" Randy was linked to the enemy. If Mona wanted to confront Haley and to hear Haley's regrets, she would want to do it in an equal setting. If that was what she wanted.

"To tell the truth, I never mentioned it to her. Randy just offered right now. It won't matter anyway; he'll just sit outside and listen to his music and relax. He knows what I did now, some of it anyway and he's already told me what he thinks of it. He'd be on Mona's side, not mine."

"Haley, please don't—"

"Sorry, Charlotte. Look at the time. I've got to go. Wish me luck."

I didn't have a chance to do that before she hung up. I paced, fuming.

I was in the library, but even that didn't help me find the address of the restaurant without a name. I headed home for reinforcements and burst through the door just as Jack thundered down the stairs. He said. "I was hoping I could talk to you about the reconversion. Because I want to—"

Right. The reconversion. That was the last thing I could deal with. "I have to go out. I need your cell phone. I didn't have a chance to replace mine and I have to drive out to the country. It could be an emergency." I filled him in on Mona's date with Haley and my worries about it. "I think it would be better if they met up with some neutral, professional intervener. Don't you?"

I added, "A shrug is not an answer."

"True, but it's not my business and it's not your business either."

I was outraged enough to stamp my foot. Of course, then I felt like an idiot. Foot stamping at Jack? I was definitely losing it. "It is my business. Mona called me and shared her fears and anger. Then Haley told me they were meeting at some restaurant in the middle of nowhere. I feel responsible for them. I don't want either of them to do any more damage to the other."

"Mona never did any damage to Haley that I ever heard of."

"No, she didn't, but Haley was damaged by her own behavior. She's having a struggle with this. I suppose it's only fair that she suffers some too, but she is having a hard time and I feel for her. I'd like to see them have their meeting in a safe place."

"So you're just going to drive around and see if you can find them?"

"I'm sure I'll find the place. She said it's on Burnt Road about ten minutes from her place. Burnt Road is only a few miles long. Randy's truck's pretty big and so is the sign on it."

"It could be ten minutes in either direction. I'll get my jacket and go with you. Think of me as reinforcements."

I wanted to throw my arms around his neck, but I didn't

want him to know how much I wanted to be with him, especially considering his current plans. "I appreciate that, but it's better if I go alone. There's already a crowded scene. I just need your phone."

"I know Mona. She might be reassured."

"Tell you what, if I find her, I'll ask if she wants you to come over."

Another shrug. "Someone's got to stay here and eat your Ben and Jerry's before it melts. Here's my cell. I'll be here with a landline."

"While you're here, I'd appreciate it if you'd walk Truffle and Sweet Marie. You can work up an appetite that way."

Truffle and Sweet Marie, hearing the word "walk" on a day that should have been too cold to snow, yet it was snowing, immediately attempted to burrow behind the sofa cushions. The idea was that I couldn't see them if they couldn't see me. As strategies went, it needed work.

Jack said, "Don't worry. I'll airlift them."

I bundled myself into my puffy parka, picked a pair boots with more grip than style, and pulled a woolly hat down over my ears. I added a scarf just in case. I hurried downstairs and out to the Santa Fe. The country roads would be worse than usual in this weather and I was glad that I was driving this heavy vehicle.

Fifteen minutes later, I was cruising along, very high off the ground and starting to feel in control of my environment. I was asking myself if it made any sense to show up at this meeting between two old adversaries, if you could call Mona an adversary. She'd certainly been a victim in the past. She might be in full battle mode now, but in my mind she was still a victim. I couldn't believe that a simple apology from Haley, however tearful and remorseful, would be enough. Mona wanted retribution. The positions were reversed now. I didn't want Mona to harm Haley and harm herself by doing that. I figured if I showed up, I could broker a bit. The worst that could happen was that everyone would be mad at me. I could live with that.

I left the twinkly lights of Woodbridge behind and took the interstate. Even that was slippery and I saw three vehicles fishtail before I exited. I hated to get off and drive along gloomy, less traveled surfaces. The snow tires helped and I was glad the Santa Fe was an automatic. Even with this vehicle, I found myself in a skid more than once. My shoulders were aching and my hands stiff from gripping the wheel too hard for too long. I tried not to let my mind wander back to my cozy apartment with Jack and two cuddly dogs and a supply of chocolate. This wouldn't take long and it was the right thing to do. I drove through the gloom with my high beams on. Usually snow brightens and cheers a drive. Not this dreary afternoon. The naked trees cast bizarre and slightly creepy shadows. You could barely see.

I slowed as I approached a small family restaurant. The windows were dark. No cars were parked in the lot. A sign was stuck on the glass of the door. CLOSED FOR THE SEASON. I guess not everyone knew that.

What now? Had Haley and Mona already met up and gone on to some other location? Had I missed them?

I hadn't passed anyone on the road in from the interstate, so Mona hadn't turned around and gone back in that time. Haley would have come from the opposite direction. Had she returned home? Maybe Mona had gone with her. That would have been good. Mona would see Haley's life as a wife and mother in her small, simple home. Mona would realize that it wasn't all roses for the former bully. If Brie was still in her sour mood, Mona might even take some pleasure from that.

I made the choice to drive on and reassure myself that everything had turned out all right. If anything, the winding road got twistier as I made my way to Haley's. I knew it wasn't more than a ten-minute drive, but it would feel a lot longer. I kept my speed down. I turned off Burnt Road and followed the route to Haley's house. The road followed a steep wooded ravine and I didn't care for the idea of sliding off the road and into that. I'd slowed to a crawl when I saw the skid marks ahead. Someone had slid straight off the road and knocked over a wooden guardrail. The local guardrails were not holding up well. I stopped, my heart thundering. What a place to have an accident. There probably wasn't a house for miles. Was anyone hurt down there? Injured? Dead?

Ahead of me, I saw a figure limping along in the dim snowy mist, and then it stopped to lean against the guardrail. I drove forward and slowed. I blew the horn and the figure turned. Haley?

I stopped and jumped out.

She stumbled toward me. Blood and tears streaked her face. Her nose looked like it had been broken. A ragged gash ran along her hairline. She clutched a cell phone in her bleeding hand. I put my arms around her, as she shook.

"You have to help," she managed to say after a minute. "No service here. Randy is . . ." Haley collapsed, racked with deep, shuddering sobs. I managed to help her climb into the Santa Fe. Her leg was obviously injured and she gasped in pain as she struggled into the passenger seat. I was afraid she was going into shock. I backed the Santa Fe up the hill to the highest point, where I was lucky enough to get a signal on the phone.

For once 911 didn't chastise me when I told them about the accident and gave the rough coordinates. "You'll see my vehicle. It's a Santa Fe, an SUV, dark red. There's an injured woman in the passenger's seat. I think she's in shock. Her name is Haley Brennan. I believe her husband, Randy, is in the van that went off the road. She says he's badly injured and possibly . . ." I heard my voice breaking. "I'll try to get down into the ravine to see if I can help him. It could

take me ten minutes or so to make my way down that hill
and then I'd have to climb back up to call back."

I took a deep breath and headed down the steep, snowy
incline, praying I wouldn't find Randy dead. I grabbed onto
the dried grass, brush, and small trees as I slid. At the bottom, I struggled to wade through the snow. Up close, the
van was buried nose first and tilted. Boxes and supplies
had tumbled toward the front seat. The window was broken, probably where Haley had climbed out. I could see her
bloody handprints and drops of blood in the snow.

"Randy? Are you there?"

Nothing.

I could see Randy slumped against the driver's side window. Something was wrong and it took a couple of minutes
to realize that no one ever held their head at that angle. I
gasped before I could stop myself. I forced myself to reach
in and try to see if there was a pulse. There was nothing I
could do for Randy. I turned and fought my way up out of
the ravine and back to the Santa Fe.

It was hard to meet Haley's eyes. As she stared at my
face, her tiny remaining hope was extinguished.

Haley whimpered, "My God, what am I going to do
without him? We have always been together. Always."

"What happened?"

"She forced us off the road."

"What?"

Haley took a deep shuddering breath. "The meeting
didn't happen. Mona was screaming at me from the time
we got to the parking lot. I guess it's a good thing the diner
was closed. When I tried to suggest she come home with
us, she just lost it. Shouting, swearing, kicking the van. She
said she wanted to kill me. Randy got upset and insisted
on leaving. He said I didn't have to take that. Two wrongs
don't make a right. We drove away and she drove off like a

crazy person. Before we got home, someone forced us off the road. It had to have been her."

"Mona?"

"I couldn't see her face, but it had to be."

"Did you see her car?"

"I saw it in the parking lot. A little red thing."

That was bad news. "But did you actually see who forced you off the road?"

"No. We had a lot of new supplies stacked in the back of the van and the boxes were blocking my view. But who else could it have been?"

I had no answer for that.

"Randy's an excellent driver, but she rammed us. I wanted to get out and try to reason with her, but Randy said he was afraid she'd run over me. I think now that he was right. Do you know she actually hit our vehicle? When she came at us, Randy swerved and we crashed right through that guardrail. I can still feel it, the noise, like an explosion. But I thought at least Randy could get us out and . . ." Haley's torrent of words stopped and she started to sob.

"Are you sure it was Mona who hit you, Haley?"

Haley gripped my hand until it hurt. "Of course it was."

"But did you see her? Is there any chance it could have been Serena?"

"Serena? Oh. She's capable of it, but . . ." I could tell she was thinking hard. "No. It had to be Mona. Serena was no-where around. I thought I was going to die. I passed out for a bit. I don't know how long. She left us to die. She killed Randy. She killed him. She did it to hurt me. Oh my God, maybe I deserved that. But he didn't."

16

Although the flashing lights were a welcome sight and the paramedics got Haley out of the Santa Fe and into the ambulance efficiently, I wasn't doing too well myself. I was shaking and my teeth chattered, even though I felt relieved that the team was calming her down. The snow now seemed thicker and wetter and more oppressive. My clothing was soaked right up to my hat. My feet were icy from the snow that had worked its way into my boots during my descent to the van.

A paramedic suggested I wait in my vehicle. He said the police were also on their way and they'd want to talk to me. I supposed the crime scene techs would be there shortly too. I climbed back into the Santa Fe, turned on the engine, and sat there quivering, even after I put the heater on the highest setting and boosted the heated seats. I couldn't get Randy out of my mind. It had been a bad week for innocent bystanders and he was the latest. What would poor angry Brie do now without her father? How could Haley cope with running the business and living without her high school sweetheart and husband? And worst of all, knowing that it was all a result of her actions as a teenager.

I still had a hard time accepting that Mona could do this, but I'd been wrong before. I could never have imagined that I'd be staring at Randy's corpse when I left the house to try to intervene between Haley and Mona.

Mona's life would be over too. I didn't imagine she'd get much sympathy in court, regardless of the background. They'd accept that she'd been the victim and she'd allowed her corrosive hatred and anger to turn her into a villain. Randy had paid the price for that. A gentle man, a devoted husband, and a wonderful father, gone. I kept asking myself if there was any way that it could have been Serena. Haley hadn't actually seen who was driving the car that pushed them off the road. But even I had to admit, it was looking very bad for Mona.

It didn't take the police long to arrive and in short order I was giving a statement. Lucky me, it was Officer Dean Oliver.

"I think we'll just get you home first," he said. "We can do it there. Maybe you need—"

"Never mind me. Check out Haley."

"The ambulance is leaving now with her. She's in good hands. We don't want you to get hypothermia."

Yes, I'd been having a rough day, but I hadn't lost a family member. All to say, I had no choice but to do my session at the library that night. The topic was The Perils of Procrastination. As you can imagine, canceling was out of the question. I would have gone on a stretcher if I'd had to.

"Are you insane?" Jack asked conversationally. "Someone tried to kill you yesterday and today you found the body of someone you know. You have to cancel."

"No. I don't want to lie around and think about Randy. That would be even more upsetting."

"Think of your safety."

"I will certainly be safe at the library."

"And after the session's over? When you have to drive home?"

"I have this huge vehicle now. It will be good."

"This time I am going with you. I shouldn't have let you talk me out of going to hunt for Haley. Look what happened there. Mona could have wiped you out too."

"You're far too busy with your contractor, I am sure." Even I thought that sounded stupid.

Jack scratched his chin and stared at me. "Okay. You are upset about that and I have no idea why. But I'm not going to be sidetracked. I'm following you to the library and I'm following you back. If you don't like it, call a cop."

—◆◆—

On my way out the door, Bethann's brother-in-law called me. It took me a minute to remember that I'd given him my card.

"I thought you'd like to know. You were right," he said. "Bethann did get a call from someone she'd gone to school with. Someone called Serena, who had made her life miserable. She wanted to ask Bethann for forgiveness. Bethann said, 'I'll forgive you after I sue the designer pants off you. See you in court. Or better yet, in hell.' My wife said Bethann said a few other words she wouldn't repeat. I'm not sure if this helps, but I thought you should know."

—◆◆—

My workshop wasn't too bad. Of course, only about half the registrants showed up. That didn't surprise me too much, given the topic. It was too bad, as procrastination is the biggest thief of time. But I was glad to be doing something to take my mind off my aches and bruises and the hit-and-runs. The painkillers helped too.

I glanced toward the back of the room, where I'd first seen Haley sitting less than one week before. I shuddered, then did my best to put her disaster out of my mind and focus on the people who had shown up.

"Congratulations! You've taken the first step toward getting your procrastinating tendencies under control. Now let's—"

Two hands shot up. "Who do you think is behind these hit-and-runs in Woodbridge?" a gray-haired woman wanted to know.

A smiling younger woman with tumbling brown curls said, "What did it feel like to narrowly escape death when your car went over the embankment?"

I managed a grin, and believe me, it wasn't easy. "Let's put off that discussion until later."

Someone yelled. "Procrastinator!"

I faked a chuckle. "Priorities, not procrastination. Hey, there's a slogan." Before I lost control of the group, I launched into a discussion of what to do when you notice you're procrastinating. "First thing. Try to catch yourself at the moment you decide to postpone something. What thoughts are in your head? Let's experiment with, hmm, okay, income tax. That's coming soon. Is everyone on top of that?"

That earned a few groans, a resounding no from most of the group, and one heartfelt, "That's why I'm here!"

"What went through your mind when I mentioned it?"

"Too hard."

"Too complicated."

"Messy."

"I hate that."

"I don't know where all the papers are."

"I'm afraid of doing it wrong."

"I don't feel like it!"

"I hate numbers."

"I hate forms."

I nodded. "Excellent. Now each of you try to find one response that will help combat that thought. How about 'I hate that'?"

Silence. Then the curly-haired smiling woman said, "It won't last forever."

I gave her the thumbs-up.

Someone shouted, "If you hate it, then get it over with."

A small voice said, "Break it into steps."

A nervous woman piped up, "Give yourself a reward for doing the first step."

One of the few men suggested, "Get someone else to do it."

That earned a round of applause.

We were on a roll and the rest of the evening went well. People shook my hand as they filed out. I packed up and was relieved to see Jack, leaning against his dung-colored Mini-Minor in the parking lot. He'd stationed himself there to keep an eye on my SUV and the library doors while waiting for me. He gave me a jaunty wave.

"Great," I said, trying to smile. I had a horrible feeling that things were inching toward an inexorable disaster that I was powerless to prevent. I glanced back at the library. I'd be returning the next morning for my final time-management session. I needed to get some sleep, although that hadn't come so easily lately.

"Nothing unusual," he said, as I opened the door of my rental. "No red cars prowling. All quiet on the western front."

"That reminds me, Jack. What are the chances that the same red car would survive all those attacks? Three hit-and-runs and running Haley off the road. If you hit people and hit cars, like Haley's, wouldn't you have broken glass or dented bumpers?"

Jack had been about to get into his Mini. "I guess you would," he said. "What's your point?"

"My point is that Mona drives a red car, which is missing along with her. If she or one of her so-called alters is behind all this, why hasn't someone spotted that badly battered vehicle? And wouldn't she be better off in a different-colored car?"

"I guess she would be."

"You know what? If you were willing to kill a bunch of people, I bet you'd be willing to steal a car or two as well."

"And?"

"And what if someone is trying to make it seem like it was Mona?"

"You mean someone like Serena?"

"Of course, Serena. Who else? She's always been mean and cruel. I'm not falling for the so-called new her. Mona never was cruel. Why would she turn that way now? I don't believe she tried to push me over that embankment."

"But Mona claims she went after the victims. Some people find that suspicious."

"Very funny. She is saying that she thinks one of her alters did it. I am beginning to wonder if Serena hasn't planted that whacky idea in Mona's head. She'd been a very powerful manipulator. Could she be using Mona as the scapegoat while she gets rid of the very people who know her horrible secrets?"

Jack said, "Wow. Either A, you're losing it or B, this Serena is one magnificent villain."

"My money's on B. Magnificent villain."

"You are prejudiced."

"Maybe, but I've had trouble seeing Mona in this role because of the evidence, including evidence from Mona herself. But I know how all the school authorities were deceived by this smart, pretty girl. They let her get away with her reign of terror. She's all grown-up now, but she's had fourteen more years to practice messing with people's minds while she's torturing them."

All the way home that night, I hoped that Mona would contact me. I worried about Haley too. She had survived an attempt on her life. Would she survive the next one? I wasn't sure if Haley would get a rental as quickly as I had, but she would have to be very cautious. As soon as I was home I made a call to Haley to tell her not to drive anywhere, especially on those lonely roads.

Bric said, "She's sleeping. The doctor gave her something to calm her and some pretty strong painkillers. She's not going anywhere."

"Brie, I am so sorry about your father."

I could hear the catch in her voice. I waited. "Thank you."

"I didn't even get to say good-bye to him," she added with a heart-wrenching sob. I felt my own eyes tear up. "She drove away before I could even see him. She wouldn't let me come along for the ride."

"Your mother had her reasons," I said, not willing to remind Brie of her mother's past behaviors. I wouldn't have had Brie along for that ride either. "She loves you so much, Brie. At least you still have each other."

"All I want is my dad," Brie choked out, before hanging up.

——————

Saturday morning started with twin shocks. When I picked up my home phone at seven thirty the next morning, Ramona said, "Disaster in the library. We have some broken water pipes on the second floor and we have to move a ton of books to save them. I've been here since two a.m. We'll reschedule to next week if that works for you. I bet you can use a day off after what you've been through. And what did you think of— Oh, gotta go. Emergency! Talk later."

Jack had once again walked the dogs and made coffee. I could have gotten used to all this nice treatment in the morning. But was it just a way to soften the blow of losing my home?

I accepted the coffee with a nod. Better not let all that bitterness spoil Saturday morning. Better to make a good plan for surviving it.

Jack settled on the sofa with the dogs, relaxed in his cargo shorts and bright orange-and-yellow Hawaiian shirt. He had the remote firmly gripped. He thought the library closing was a great idea. "You need a break. You've been through hell. We can go out for brunch. We can read and relax. Want to watch the news?"

Before I could say absolutely not, he clicked the remote. Todd Tyrell beamed his phony smile into my living room.

Another tragedy rocks Woodbridge yet again today as a beloved beauty queen dies in a horrific single-car accident.

I gasped and even Jack was suitably quiet. "Who now?"

Authorities are blaming weather conditions on the fatal slide that sent a Woodbridge woman's vehicle plunging into the Hudson River just after midnight.

I watched wide-eyed as the WINY camera panned along a sparkling white stretch of the scenic drive just outside the north end of Woodbridge. The camera lingered over a crumbled railing and focused on a yellow Hummer being hauled out of the Hudson. I thought the camera captured the fate of that Hummer. That shot was replaced by a pair of divers disappearing beneath the icy waters.

Jack and I both shivered.

Todd must have felt the cold as well. He was dressed

in a heavy overcoat and jauntily looped red woolen scarf, probably cashmere. Snowflakes rested on his gelled do. He was practically quivering, whether from excitement or the chilly air was hard to tell.

Police have released the name of the latest victim. This week a deadly combination of bad weather and one or more hit-and-run drivers has claimed five lives in our town. The latest victim, thirty-one-year-old Serena Zeitz, a homemaker and popular volunteer, died when her Hummer plunged into the Hudson River.

As a shot of the Hummer and Serena in happier days appeared, I jerked and spilled coffee on my white fluffy robe. "Serena?"

Jack turned to me. "That's what he said."

Todd burbled. "The former beauty queen is survived by her husband, billionaire entrepreneur Jerome Zeitz—the founder of InZeitz.com, a commodity trading company, and other web-based enterprises—and their eighteen-month-old daughter, Tallulah." He tilted his head as if he was flirting in a bar. "We go now to Sergeant Pepper Monahan. Detective, Serena Zeitz and three of her former classmates, and the husband of another one, have died this week. Was Serena Zeitz another victim of this vicious hit-and-run driver?" Before she could answer, he said, "And what are the Woodbridge Police doing to ensure more citizens are not massacred in this bloodbath?"

Pepper shot him a nasty glance.

I thought, *I'd be very careful not to get so much as a speeding ticket in this town after that, Mr. Todd Tyrell. You've made an enemy.*

Pepper said, "We have put considerable resources into investigating these hit-and-runs and—"

Todd practically stuffed the mic into her mouth. "But

are any of us safe? What about other people in that class? Charlotte Adams was also a classmate and she was nearly killed as well."

From the look on her face, he wasn't all that safe himself. "We do not believe any of these were random attacks. We are making progress and, yes, I believe the citizens of Woodbridge are safe."

"Where are you exactly in trapping this killer?"

I rolled my eyes. Pepper managed not to. "You can count on us for a statement when the time is right."

Once again, the screen filled with a shot of wet suit–clad divers in the cold, dark Hudson.

Jack said, "Huh. So Serena's dead?"

"So it would seem. Why are we still seeing the divers?"

Todd said merrily, "Divers continue to search for the body of the brown-eyed, blond beauty who gave so much happiness back to her community. In a bizarre twist, Woodbridge Police are not offering any advice to citizens on keeping safe during this deadly vehicular rampage. Police are asking the public for information about other vehicles that may have been seen on the road near the accident. Anonymous witnesses report seeing a small red car leaving the scene."

My heart clutched. Small red car? Again. Had I been wrong about Mona?

The scene shifted to a huge and opulent waterside home. A man left the house and climbed into a black hummer, the mate to Serena's. Todd's voiceover said, "Mr. Zeitz refused to comment to WINY about the circumstances of his wife's death."

I said, "I can't believe they are going to chase a man and ask him how he feels about the fact that his wife has just been killed. How ghoulish is that? Even if she was the same miserable bully that put people through hell."

Jack said, "Although, I have to say, that would be a horrible way to die. I wouldn't wish that on her or anyone. Are you still sticking to your idea that she was the killer?"

"I don't know. I was hoping she was behind these other deaths. Manipulating people, causing their accidents, hit-and-runs. But if she isn't, it sure looks bad for Mona."

"Charlotte, I know you care about Mona—"

"I feel responsible for her."

"So do I, but hear me out. One of the things that stuck with me from my studies of philosophy—and by the way, that doesn't mean you can start to bug me about finishing my PhD—one of the main things is to seek the truth. Not what you want to be true or what you believe to be true or what you have been told is true, but to do your best to find what is the truth. The best way you can know it."

"I believe that . . ." I slumped back on the sofa.

"You want to believe that—"

"I believe that Mona was the victim. I saw that. You saw that. We all saw it and we didn't do anything."

"That may be true. It is true. I realize that. We could have done better and we should have done better. But even so, it may not be the whole truth. You have to consider all the facts, Charlotte."

"I prefer the truth where Serena was bumping people off to prevent them—and maybe her new husband for all I know—from finding out what a vile, sadistic person was behind that so-called beauty queen exterior."

"But now it doesn't appear that way, does it?"

"No. Her husband seemed devastated. Not like he'd been living with the queen of mean."

"That's not what I meant. I don't think Serena was the killer."

"No. Wait! Unless Serena was trying to run someone down and the person managed to get away and in the ensuing chase, Serena lost control of her vehicle and got . . ." I almost said "got what was coming to her." But even I didn't believe that.

Jack shook his head. "The truth, Charlotte. Open your mind to the truth. Do you believe for even one minute that's what happened?"

"Well, it's not totally impossible."

"It is highly unlikely. There wasn't any mention of it."

"With all the snow and the condition of the road, they may never be able to tell exactly what happened. That's what I'm afraid of."

"They are looking for that small red car."

"Why are you so down on Mona, Jack? You should want to help her."

"Well, I don't want to help her get you if she turns out to be the person behind these deaths. Or if, as you say, one of her alters is. She has to be stopped. Don't you realize that? You are putting yourself at risk, maybe because you feel guilty, maybe because you have this savior complex. Mona needs to be saved from herself, not from the police."

"Thanks for kicking me when I'm down."

"I'm not trying to kick you. I'm trying to keep you from being the next victim."

"We're out of victims. With Serena's death, all the bullies are gone, except for Haley, and she's injured and had her husband die right in front of her. There's no more reason to kill anyone."

"Except—"

I gasped. "Except you think someone will go after Haley again? It's not enough she's been left alone with a resentful teenager and a failing business and without her husband? You think someone still wants her dead? You're right. We have to warn her."

Jack put his hand on my shoulder. "Charlotte! It's not only bullies who are dying. Bethann wasn't a bully. Randy wasn't. You definitely weren't and yet someone tried to kill you. Something else is going on."

"We all graduated in the same year. Except for Randy, but I think Haley was the target there and Randy was—"

"Collateral damage."

"Like Dr. Partridge. He has a connection, but it's not because he was in our class."

"Face it, Charlotte. There's a terribly angry soul out there who doesn't care who gets caught up in all this. You can't keep stirring things up."

"Someone has to get to the bottom of it."

"Let the police do it. In the meantime, I'm not going to let you out of my sight. Two people are harder to get rid of than one. I'll close up the store or I'll leave the part-timers in charge, and I'll stick by you. Whatever you decide to do. Wherever you plan to go, I'll be there."

"Why?"

Truffle and Sweet Marie both took that moment to snuggle up to Jack, indicating that in any argument they'd be voting with the guy who first rescued them. Jack stroked them absentmindedly and stared at me. Truffle stretched up and kissed Jack's nose. "Because I don't want anything to happen to you. I don't want to be without you. Ever. I can't imagine a day without you. I'm surprised you would even ask that, Charlotte."

I blurted out, "Then why are you trying to change the house back to a single unit? Displacing me."

Truffle and Sweet Marie snapped to attention. Truffle uttered a cautionary bark as he does when voices are raised. Jack stared at me. "What do you mean?"

"What *could* I possibly mean? You are talking to contractors about converting the house back to a single family home again. Where is that going to leave me?"

We both jumped as the phone rang. BLOCKED NUMBER.

I let it go to message. Before Jack could answer my question, it rang again. BLOCKED NUMBER. I still figured our conversation was much more important.

"So, Jack, my question was, where does that leave me? Looking for a new home?"

Sweet Marie whimpered. Probably a coincidence, but still. I felt like whimpering myself.

Jack said, "But—"

The phone trilled again.

At that moment, I felt that Jack's response would be more important than anything else in the world. I did *not* want a phone call from anyone to interrupt it. I said, "Still blocked number. Answer the question. She'll keep calling."

"Just take the call. It must be important to your old friend Blocked Number."

What was that? A lame joke to disguise the fact he didn't have the courage to answer my question? I took the call.

Mona Pringle shouted in my ear, "I knew you were there. I knew you were avoiding my calls."

Defensively and not quite truthfully, I said, "You're blocking your number, Mona. How could anyone ever figure out it was you calling?"

"Well I *am* in hiding. Do you think I'm going to rent a billboard that says 'find me here and arrest me while you're at it'?"

"You have to turn yourself in, Mona. Too many people have died. This has to end. You must realize that."

"They all had it coming."

"They didn't deserve to die and Randy didn't have *anything* coming. He was an innocent bystander, a decent man, and now his daughter will grow up without support from her father. And what about Dr. Partridge? Such a kind person. He could have died."

"I know, that was bad. It's not me really. I would never

have done that. It has to be one of my alters. I can't control them. I can't reach them to reason with them."

"Then your alters have to be stopped. You are the only person who can do that. Go see Pepper. She likes you. And Margaret will make sure you get help. She's a terrific lawyer and she is your friend."

"There's more to do."

"What more? Serena's dead. She was at the heart of it. Don't you understand that it's over now?"

"Yeah, right. Did you see a body?"

"I saw the police pull her vehicle from the water. I saw the divers."

"Big deal. You know the Woodbridge Police. Do you think they couldn't be fooled by a manipulator of Serena's caliber?"

Of course, I knew very well that the Woodbridge Police could be remarkably thickheaded. "Are you suggesting that Serena isn't dead?"

Jack's head jerked. "Not dead? How?"

Mona raised her voice. "I'm not suggesting anything. I am *telling* you that woman isn't dead. She's far too smart and sneaky to get killed that way."

I would have completely dismissed that as more Mona nuttiness, except for the fact that prior to this week, Mona had always been a decent citizen while Serena had been a devious and sadistic witch. But still, it was off the wall.

I interjected, "What way was that, Mona?"

"By having her vehicle run off the road and into the river. Didn't you see the footage?"

"Yes, but—"

"But what?"

"How could she escape? The river is freezing. If she didn't drown, she would have succumbed to hypothermia in minutes."

"I repeat: Did you see a body?"

I said, "They haven't found it yet. But the divers are searching."

"Plenty of current at that point of the Hudson. She'll be counting on that."

"But why would Serena stage her death, if that's what you are suggesting?"

"So she'll be free to go about her evil business. Why else? If she's dead, no one will be watching her, will they?"

"What evil business, Mona?"

"To get rid of everyone who is still around and connected with her rampage back at St. Jude's."

I was worried that my head would explode at this point. "I thought one of your alters was behind the rampage."

"So what? I still don't trust Serena. Even if it was one of my alters, she's still the one who got that whole alters business going. All that trauma messed up my head. She'll want to finish me off now."

Mona needed a lot more help than I could give her. "Mona. Whether it was one of your alters or Serena, it's over. They're all dead."

"Haley isn't. You're not. I'm not. Kristee's not. Think about it. Lots of scope left."

My heart was beating fast. This was crazy, but was it also true?

"Here," I said. "Explain your theory to Jack."

Mona was squawking that it wasn't a theory when I handed over the phone. I sat there trying to analyze everything she'd said. Could Serena have staged her own death? I didn't know and would have to talk to the cops to get details about the so-called accident. If it was true, would her death give Serena free reign to continue to wipe out people who had the potential to reveal the truth about her? Logically, yes, but there were big holes in the idea.

I took the phone back from Jack. He had a totally

stunned expression on his face. It was sort of cute in a de-feated philosopher way.

"Mona. If Serena appears to be dead, what difference will it make to her if people damage her reputation? She's 'dead.'"

"So far. I haven't got all the details worked out yet."

Conversations with Mona were challenging at the best of times, which this definitely wasn't. I rubbed my temples. The dogs were back to snuggling with Jack. Jack continued to look puzzled, confused, and, yes, defeated.

"So far? Oh. You think she'll surface later?"

"Sure she will. She could claim to have been kidnapped by me. Or perhaps she'll be found wandering, suffering from amnesia, poor pretty thing. That will be because of something that I've done. You watch."

Was this any more bizarre than the things that actually had happened? One thing I knew, we couldn't leave Mona on the loose.

"You have to give yourself up, Mona. It can all get sorted out afterward. Call Pepper. Or let us meet you before—"

"I may be crazy, but I'm not stupid," she yelled before she hung up.

Our game plan included "stay alive" ourselves. First I needed to check with a member of the police force to see if there was any way that Serena could have survived in that Hummer. On WINY we'd heard about witnesses who had seen her zoom by. Wouldn't someone have seen a woman walking away from something like that? Of course, it had been in the night. Even so, I told myself that Serena had to be dead and Mona had to be paranoid and dangerous. That was the only thing that made sense. I had been deluding myself that I could help Mona.

Pepper wasn't going to cooperate, but I knew two who

might. Make that three. I called Margaret and asked her to sound out her husband, Frank, on Serena's tragic end. "Sure," she said. "And I'll even attempt to sound broken up about it. By the way, anything new on my 'client'?"

"I still don't know where Mona is and if I find out, I'll get you on the line right away. Thanks for digging around about the witnesses. Let me know. You're a bud. I'll call you later."

Next I contacted Dean Oliver at home. Before I could ask him anything, he said, "Listen, I can't help you out with Mona anymore. I have explicit orders from Sergeant Monahan not to encourage you."

Take fifteen minutes a day to chip away at a large or overwhelming project that you've been neglecting. In a few weeks, you'll be amazed at the results.

17

Jack insisted on following me to the scene of Serena's so-called fatal accident. Neither one of us was staying on top of work this particular week. Jack slipped a winter jacket over his parrot-festooned shirt and I managed to bite back any comments about his baggy, all-season shorts. I was glad to have him with me. I didn't want to find myself in the river like Serena. It hadn't been long since someone had tried to kill me. I noticed the police seemed to have forgotten about that.

The police were gone, although yellow police tape still fluttered in the wintry wind. The brush along the side of the river was seriously flattened out where Serena's vehicle entered the water. Even if we hadn't seen the distinctive clump of broken branches on the WINY broadcast, we would have known that this was the spot. She must have been struck, and spun partway around before she headed straight into the water at high speed.

Jack and I stood there on the frigid snow-covered roadside, stamping our feet. The Hudson is deep and dangerous at this point. Puffs of our frozen breath decorated the air in front of us. I said, "How long do you think it took for her to land in the water?"

"Seconds. Not enough time to get out if she was buckled in, but an eternity once she realized what was going to happen to her."

I shivered and not just because of the Siberian landscape that had taken over poor old Woodbridge.

Jack said, "I guess I do feel sorry for her. That was an awful way to die. I think it would take minutes under water. It would seem like forever."

"What about Mona's theory that she's not dead?"

Jack shook his adorably spiky head. Sometimes it's hard to believe he's a philosopher of sorts. "There would have been footprints or marks from the impact of her body if she'd flung herself out and let the Hummer go in without her."

I said, "If that happened right there in the middle of the road where the car headed straight into the water, any signs would have been quickly eliminated by cops and the elusive witnesses, even though there's not much traffic around here. It's so farfetched. How would she get away? It's miles from anywhere. Can you imagine Serena Redding walking back to town? Oh wait, what if she had an accomplice?"

Jack thought for a second. "To do what exactly? Oh, you mean pick her up once she got out of the car, and then ram the car into the river and make it seem as if someone had killed her?"

"Exactly."

"But what good will it do for her to appear to be dead?"

"Mona believes that it's intended to target her. She's convinced that Serena will reappear miraculously and then claim that Mona tried to kill her."

"We both know that Mona's behavior is bizarre."

"No arguments on that, Jack. But didn't you tell me to open my mind for the truth?"

"I did, but—"

"Then let's not close our minds before it's too late."

"Fine. So to sum up what happened: Either Serena's dead and her body has yet to surface, or she's alive and hiding out for some purpose, which might be to incriminate Mona. Or she's alive and hiding out because she's afraid of whomever tried to kill her. Might be Mona; might be someone else."

I exhaled. "Way too many choices. And we still don't know whether Serena had changed her ways."

Jack shivered in the wind. "That complicates it, but even so, I can't think of any other alternatives. That's a good thing, because it's hard to know what to do with what we have."

I gazed out over the cold and deadly river. Was Serena down there? I leaned into Jack as we turned and trudged back to the SUV. I was glad of his friendly arm around me. That felt good. But it didn't change the fact that we were just good friends. Or that I would soon be moving.

"If Serena hadn't changed her ways, and I don't believe for one minute that she had, then considering that might help us figure out what is going on."

"Accept it, Charlotte."

"But how do we even know it was her driving? Maybe she wasn't anywhere near that river. Maybe she had an accomplice. Maybe—"

"Let it go."

Jack and I took some time to pick out a replacement cell phone for me after that. It had lots of nice features and a touch screen, plus I was able to keep my old number. It was an easy and pleasant task compared to everything we'd been grappling with that week. After that we headed for the Woodbridge Police Station and sat lurking in the Mini, waiting for Dean Oliver when he pulled into the police department parking lot to begin his shift. I used the time to enter all my contact numbers into the new phone. Jack spotted Dean arriving. "Here he is."

I hopped out and scampered across the lot.

"So," Dean said as I tapped on his window. "What is it now? I'm not supposed to talk to you. Remember?"

"This is something completely different. Just a quick word about Serena Redding. I was wondering if there's any way she could be alive."

"What?" That took him by surprise.

"Seriously. Do they have a body?"

He shook his head. "They don't have to find your body to know that you're dead if you shoot into the Hudson in winter conditions. Give me a break. There's no way she survived."

"Makes sense." I nodded. "I suppose that witnesses confirm that she went in?"

He frowned. Didn't care for the direction this chat was going in. "There were no witnesses to the accident, but she didn't survive. Trust me."

"I saw the Hummer being pulled out. She wasn't in it."

He shook his head sadly. "They think she was able to open the door and get out, but when you're under water you can lose all sense of direction. It's deep in that section of river and it would have been dark. Hypothermia would set in very fast, maybe a minute. No one saw her."

"How do you know it was Serena driving that vehicle? Maybe it was some unlucky joyrider who stole it and—"

Dean stared at me like I'd sprouted horns or something. "She was seen. Okay? Enough of this."

"But you said there weren't any witnesses."

"They came along minutes afterward. But they saw her

before. There was a young couple whose GPS had misdirected them. The county changed the names of some back roads a bit back and the online maps haven't caught up yet. They were parked about a mile away, trying to get back to VanKleek Road. They'd been all over the place, just missing it. So they were checking their print map and one of the locals stopped to give them directions. They all saw Serena drive by."

"How did they know it was Serena?"

He sighed. Deeply. "They saw a woman of her description drive by, not going too fast."

"They described her to you?"

"That's right and they were able to identify her from the photograph that her husband provided."

"I don't know if I would notice that much detail if a person in a monster car like that sailed by me. And it was late, wasn't it?"

Dean rubbed his upper lip. Finally, he said, "The two couples were out on the road talking and she practically ran them over. They had to jump out of the way."

Ha. That was the Serena I knew, not Mrs. Goody Two-Shoes. "That sounds like her."

"Whatever. All four of them saw this battered red compact car zoom down, right after the Hummer. It almost killed them."

—♦—

I realized that I was being scattered with all this murder and mayhem. My normal routines were disrupted, my thinking was chaotic, and there was no way to simply relax and enjoy a Saturday afternoon. I said as much to Jack.

"And other people are even worse off than I am. I have to keep that in mind."

He glanced at me warily.

"So I think we should check on Haley again. She's the

one who is in danger." I tried calling her using my new cell, but no one answered.

"She'll be at home, resting," Jack said. "No one is likely to attack her there. The weapons of choice seems to be vehicles."

"True. But don't forget Dr. Partridge."

Jack sighed. "Let me guess where we're going. Although she probably needs to be left alone."

"Just a quick visit to be sure. But first Kristee's Kandees for something to take with us. I lost some excellent fudge when the Miata went over the escarpment."

Aside from being gleeful over Serena's apparent death, Kristee had no news or information. I got out of the shop as fast as I could. Jack had stayed in the car.

⁕

As we drove into Haley's driveway, we saw Brie sitting alone on the front steps. She jumped to her feet and stomped up the stairs to the house. She turned to glower at us and headed into the house, slamming the door so hard that it rattled.

"Haley won't sleep through that," I said.

Haley was awake and her bruises were starting to bloom. She now had two black eyes from the impact of the crash.

I didn't waste time. "You shouldn't be here alone."

"I'm not alone. Brie is with me."

"You both need protection."

She sighed. "You're right. I'm going to put this house on the market and go stay with relatives as soon as I can. I have cousins in Pennsylvania."

From upstairs, Brie shouted, "Well, I'm not coming with you." A door slammed again.

A flash of pain crossed Haley's battered face. "She's so angry. I can't say I blame her."

"Why don't we find you both someplace to stay that's

not quite so isolated? Can you even get out of here in an emergency?"

"I have an old beater that Randy kept for errands. It's ancient, but it runs. And my cousin and her husband are on their way from Pennsylvania to help me. They'll be here later tonight. I'll be fine."

"Okay, but you still have to be careful. Promise me that you'll call me if anything odd happens at all. No matter how small. And dial 911 too. You are the last one of your group alive, Haley."

She nodded and stared at me out of swollen eyes. "Believe me, I am aware of that. But I must have left my phone book in the van with . . . You know what? Maybe I don't deserve to be alive."

Jack said, "Your daughter needs you, even if she doesn't realize it just now. You have to stay safe for her. Take my number too." He scrawled both numbers on a scrap of paper.

As tears welled up in Haley's eyes, she reached over and gave me a powerful hug. Jack got one too.

I felt depressed and hopeless as we drove off into the misty darkness. It wasn't until we were halfway back to town that I remembered the black-and-white fudge. I was truly not myself lately.

—••—

We picked up Chinese on the way, walked the dogs, and watched the news. WINY had nothing useful to offer. I don't even remember what the food tasted like. Somewhere during the weather—light snow, big surprise—my restless nights caught up with me and I fell asleep on the sofa with the dogs. I dreamed of endless ringing. Finally I swam back to consciousness and sat up with a jerk. I was alone with the dogs. The home phone was ringing.

"Jack?"

Silence.

I stumbled to the phone, but missed the call. The message light was flashing. I could hear my new cell phone ringing by now. I raced to my handbag, but missed that call too. On the handbag was a scrawled message from Jack.

Had to check the shop. Attempted break-in. Back soon.

That must have been him on the phone. I was so groggy I could hardly remember my name. I headed for the bathroom and splashed cold water on my face to wake myself up.

I sat on the sofa again, scratched the dogs' ears, and played my messages.

Not Jack at all.

First Ramona. "Sorry, Charlotte; with all the fuss over the burst water pipe, I forgot to tell you that I found a bit of info about your fourteen-year-old hit-and-run. The police wanted to talk to a blond woman who'd been seen in the neighborhood that night. My money says you can chalk another one up to Serena."

Serena was conveniently dead, of course, or at least missing. But would anyone have noticed mousy little Mona hanging around that wintry night so long ago?

Speak of the devil. The next message was from Mona. Her voice was hoarse and rasping, showing the stress she was under. "Charlotte? It's Mona Pringle. I can't wait anymore. I think the police will be closing in. There's no point in letting Haley be the only one who gets away with it. They'll get me for the others, so why should she be the only one to live? Poor Randy wouldn't have died if it wasn't for her. I have a weapon. It will be easier to get it right with a gun than with a vehicle. Thank you for trying, but there's no hope for me."

She must have been crying, she sounded so choked up. I could hear her blowing her nose, strangely comic for someone announcing a planned murder. But I could only imagine the amount of anguish that had reduced her to this state. Even so, despite everything Serena and her followers had done, Mona was once again going to lose out because of them. I couldn't let her kill again.

I said out loud, "Oh no, Mona. You can't do this."

I stared at the receiver and listened to the dial tone. My hand shook as I checked my call display just in case. Of course it said BLOCKED NUMBER. The dogs lifted their heads sleepily as I paced, thinking hard. Where would Mona go? To Haley's home?

I had to warn her. The phone rang on and on. I hung up. Then redialed it again. After the twentieth ring, a bleary voice answered.

"Brie," I shouted, "it's Charlotte Adams. Is your mother still there?"

"What? You woke me up. I'm so tired. Why can't you leave us alone?"

"Is your mother still there? I urgently need to speak to her."

There was a long unsettling silence before Brie said, "Well, you have a problem, I guess. I don't see her. She's not in the house, so she must have gone out."

"Do you know where she went?"

"I don't know and I don't care. My father is dead and it's her fault. Do you think I want to follow her around?"

"She's not to blame, Brie, please. Help me here. I think she's in danger."

"Tell that to someone who cares."

"I think you do care. I need to know where she's gone."

"I *don't* know. She didn't tell me anything. She must have gone out when I was asleep. And I'm going back to sleep now."

"What is she driving? Hello? Hello? Brie?" I listened in despair to the dial tone. I tried again, but the phone rang on and on. Brie might be a teenager, and an angry and grieving teenager at that, but I couldn't imagine how she'd feel if her mother was killed and she'd done nothing to prevent it.

Had Mona tricked Haley into meeting her? I couldn't see how that could happen twice. Or had she just parked and waited until Haley left to get food or something? But Mona had sounded like she knew where to find Haley.

It couldn't be anywhere with a crowd or surely someone would stop Mona. That left out the shopping areas, uptown and downtown, the library, and most cafés and restaurants. No, it would have to be slightly private. The type of place where you might have a face-to-face meeting with someone you hated. A park? Lots of bad things had happened to Mona in the parks. But that could hardly be it this time. The weather continued to be vile. You couldn't talk without your teeth chattering violently, extinguishing your dignity. Of course, they could always talk inside a vehicle, but I didn't think that Haley would get into a car with Mona.

Mona had said go back and put things right. Where had most things gone wrong for Mona at the hands of the four bullies?

Of course. St. Jude's.

Where else? If we had done a better job of keeping Mona safe when she was attending the school, we wouldn't be faced with this tragic, murderous rampage now.

I dialed 911 and got Brian.

"Mona's at St. Jude's school with a gun. She said she's going to kill Haley. They're both on their way now. Please get the police there as soon as possible."

"Oh my God, she wouldn't do that."

"She said she would. She said she has nothing more to lose. She thinks she'll go to jail anyway because of the others."

"I'm calling it in."

"I hope they can stop her in time."

I called Jack. His cell phone went straight to message. I tried Pepper immediately.

No answer, of course. I left her a message. "I hope you get this, Pepper, because Mona's heading to the school to kill Haley. You have to take this seriously. I know you think she has a solid alibi but I've learned that a coworker may have covered for Mona when Bethann was killed. He's covered for her before. Now Haley isn't answering her phone and her daughter doesn't know where she is. Haley thinks that Mona is willing to forgive her. I'm sure she has no idea of Mona's plan. She'll walk right into a trap. It's horrible. Please get over there. You know them both. You know what Mona went through. You can make a difference. You could stop this."

Was there anything I could do myself to stop it? I figured if I went to the school, the police would keep me away, but maybe I could be helpful in some small way. I knew Mona pretty well and I had the background. And she'd called me with that message. Deep down I wondered if she didn't want me to stop her from killing Haley.

I had no choice. I grabbed my jacket and purse and took the stairs two at a time.

In the car, I left a message for Margaret as well. I had a feeling she'd be needed this time.

— ❦ —

By the time the Santa Fe squealed into the parking lot at St. Jude's, the lot was jammed with emergency vehicles, parked every which way. Roof lights were flashing and armed officers made sure that no one got in or out of the school yard.

I parked and stepped out of my car. I approached the nearest cop, the smart young officer, Dean Oliver. "I need you to get back in your car," he said.

"I know the two people involved," I said. "They're—"

"In your car. Now, please."

Pepper hadn't returned my call. I hoped she'd respond if

one of her own officers called her. "Listen, Dean, I called it in. You have to hear me out. Mona Pringle has threatened Haley. Can you call in Pepper Monahan? She knows them both and she likes Mona and understands what she's been through. It could diffuse the situation if Pepper speaks to them. She—"

"In your car, Charlotte." It seemed to have more impact when he used my first name.

"But—"

"I'll speak to the officer in charge and I'll make sure he contacts Sergeant Monahan, but right now, I need you to stay out of harm's way. We have a report of a weapon on the school site."

"Yes, you have that report from me through 911."

"Doesn't matter. I can't keep arguing with you. You'll end up getting arrested."

"Okay, okay. I'm getting in. But please make sure you contact Pepper."

A commotion near the school caught our attention. The cluster of cops surrounded a pale, blond woman, who was huddled near the side door.

"That's Haley," I said. I fought back tears of relief. "She's the one who Mona is planning to shoot. Thank God she's still alive."

Haley appeared to be dazed by the collection of law enforcement, particularly the response team with their high-powered weapons.

She followed instructions and put her hands over her head.

"What's going on?" I heard her say. "Charlotte? Is that you?"

"First her husband is killed and now Mona's after her," I said to Dean Oliver. "Can you make sure those SWAT guys don't brutalize her any more?"

Dean Oliver moved decisively toward the scene of the

action. I followed in his wake. "We have to find out where Mona Pringle is. She called me and told me she was going to kill Haley. You can listen to the message on my phone if you want to. Here. I can access that message from the . . ."

He gestured toward Haley, who was lost and bewildered in the face of all those cops.

"Charlotte," Haley shouted through chattering teeth when we approached. "What is going on? Where have you been?"

"What? What do you mean?"

"I got your message to meet you here and when I got here, I couldn't find you. Mona had a gun. She said she was going to shoot me, and then, thank God, the police showed up."

I said, "But I didn't leave you a message, Haley. Wouldn't you recognize my voice?"

"Oh. It wasn't you. One of your friends said you'd asked her to call because there was a problem with your new cell phone."

I said, "It wasn't me. Must have been Mona."

"I didn't recognize her voice or I never would have come."

I wasn't sure I wanted to explain about the alters. Haley wasn't listening anyway.

"Oh my God, she set it all up and I fell for it. She killed my husband, didn't she?" She turned a tear-streaked face to the cops. "You have to find her and stop her."

Dean took out his radio and spoke into it. I couldn't quite hear what he'd said. Before I could ask, a dark sedan arrived and Pepper Monahan stepped out, all grace and danger.

"Pepper!" I yelled across the parking lot. "Haley's okay. We have to find Mona."

Pepper shot me one of her famously dangerous scowls. I had to ignore it.

I turned to Dean. "I need to talk to her. You did say that you owed me."

It was somewhat unfair to keep playing the "you owe me" card, but I had to do what I had to do. The bright young officer squared his already square shoulders and we elbowed our way over. "Important information for Sergeant Monahan," he muttered as we approached.

"Now what?" Pepper said.

"Did you get my message?"

"Of course, I get all your messages, including the last one. Why else would I be here at this time of night? I have a life, you know. Now, where's Mona? Is she inside?"

"Let's ask Haley."

"Let's? You mean let the police ask. I imagine that's what you meant to say."

"Works for me," I said.

Pepper had the clout to work her way past all the SWAT types, although they kept their weapons trained on me, Haley, the parking lot, and the school. Haley had her jacket clutched tightly to her. She was still shaking. I glanced at Pepper, who was gazing impassively at Haley's damaged face. I wondered if the sight of Haley's bruises and black eyes brought back memories of Pepper's own trauma the previous June. "I hope they're not going to drag her in to the police station and grill her after what she's been through."

Pepper shook her head. "They'll be easy on her. I'll make sure of it. But she does need to make a statement. And so do you. We'll get to the bottom of this."

Of course, in the drama of the moment, I had forgotten that if you make a call to 911 announcing an impending murder, they will insist that you provide details and sign your name.

"See you at the station," Pepper said.

"But where's Mona?"

Pepper glanced around. She obviously didn't want to be

seen giving information to the enemy. "No sign of her. And don't you even think about driving around Woodbridge looking for her. We'll find Mona and if your allegations are correct, we'll deal with her. We'll be searching the school too. If she's hiding in there, we'll find her."

"Wait! You want substance. Listen to this." I used my new cell to dial into my home phone messages. I handed the phone to Pepper so she could hear for herself the message that Mona had left. It went without saying that her expression changed.

"Maybe now you believe," I said.

She gave it her best scowl. "Officer Oliver will take you to the station and take your statement. And after that I want you to keep your nose out of this whole thing before it gets shot off."

"That's hardly fair. You wouldn't even know about the danger to Haley if I hadn't told you. Haley would have been killed right here tonight. Mona told me what her intentions were for a reason. She wants to be stopped. She needs to be stopped."

Pepper turned away and strode off. She hates it when I'm right.

18

It felt like days later when I emerged from the police station after yet another statement in yet another interview room. Of course, it was only about an hour. But time behaves differently inside the thick walls of the Woodbridge Police Station. Haley was also emerging at the same time, frowning as she sent a text.

She smiled wanly. "Brie must be frantic. I sent her a message."

Haley looked a lot worse for wear. I probably did too, but at least I couldn't see myself. Her bruises continued to emerge, the new ones like dirty smudges on her cheeks. Of course, the black eyes took your mind off that. They were getting worse with every hour. I gave her a hug.

"Why is this happening?" she said, her voice breaking.

I shrugged. "St. Jude's. Symbolic for Mona of all the—"

She glanced at me, shame and guilt on her face. "Of course, I should have thought of that. All of this is my fault. Randy is dead because of me."

She absentmindedly pushed a stray lock of hair and flicked a puff of dust from it. Haley was a mess. She needed to be home, in the shower, getting cleaned up, and then sleeping for however long it would take to get over this strange night.

She wrinkled her nose. "Little Mona, always such a . . . a mouse. How could she manage to kill everybody?"

"I can't imagine," I said. "Now, where did she go?"

"I'm not sure. She got into this little red car and drove off." Haley pointed down Church Street. "She must have just turned the corner onto Hillside when all the cops showed up. I didn't know what was going on. They gave me a real fright."

Not as much as if Mona had stayed there, I thought.

"Thank you for saving my life. I am sorry I fell for that trick. I have a lot on my mind. I still have to make all the arrangements for Randy's . . ."

"And you have to be careful. Maybe you should take Brie and go somewhere to be safe until the police track down Mona."

"I think I will, as soon as the funeral's over."

I put a steadying hand on her arm. I realized that she was alone dealing with the death of the man she'd loved since high school. Brie wouldn't be much help. In fact, she'd most likely add to her mother's grief.

"I'm okay," she said.

"I am good at making arrangements and organizing things. Let me help."

"Thanks. I will probably take you up on that as soon as I know exactly what to do. I have to meet with the funeral home tomorrow morning, even though it's Sunday. Do you want to meet me there?"

"I'd be glad to."

She flashed me a sad but luminous smile. "My appointment's at McNally's at nine thirty."

Haley's shoulders slumped as she headed toward an elderly black Honda Accord. She was still limping from the accident that killed Randy. How could anyone continue to function after what she'd been through? I walked slowly back to the Santa Fe, which was parked at the other end of the police station, shaking my head in astonishment at everything that had happened that day. I got into the car and spotted the black-and-white fudge in its attractive glossy box. I'd forgotten to give it to Haley earlier and now I'd missed another chance. Of course, it hadn't exactly been a social event. I figured she could use it now, maybe share with Brie. I tooted the horn, but Haley obviously didn't hear me. She pulled out of the lot. I felt a wave a fatigue sweep over me. Why not wait and give her the fudge some other time?

"Don't put things off. You know better," a voice in my head said.

Haley would be heading home to a house without the love of her life and with an angry teenager who held her responsible for her father's death. I had to listen to that little voice.

I eased the Santa Fe out onto the road and followed her. I figured I'd have to be out of sight of the police station before I could speed to catch up. I wasn't ready for a ticket on this night. I could still see the lights of Haley's Honda up ahead. As long as I could get her attention before she got on the highway. I gunned the SUV. Haley was driving pretty fast too. As she neared the turnoff for the interstate, I figured I'd lost her. But she turned left instead of right. Maybe there was another way to her place. Whatever, that was good. I had a chance to catch up and do something nice for her. Five blocks later, I realized that Haley wasn't heading for the country. She was driving back toward St. Jude's. I thought I must be mistaken, but soon she was slowing near the school. The police had left the parking lot. They'd had plenty of time to clear the school while we were giving statements. I pulled over, cut the engine, and turned out the lights. What was going on? What was Haley doing? Had she forgotten something? Dropped something in the school yard? Received another call from Mona and been stupid enough to meet her? That did not make sense.

She was just far enough ahead for me to see her glance over her shoulder and drive into the school yard. She parked around the corner and soon emerged on foot and headed for the side door. I turned on the engine and inched forward. Haley seemed different somehow. Straighter, more determined. She checked around, but didn't see me parked out on Church Street.

I forced myself to breathe deeply and think hard.

With a final glance over her shoulder, Haley bent forward. She opened the door and stepped in. I gasped. Why was the school unlocked in the night? Haley had mentioned that Office Cleaning Specialists did some work for St. Jude's. She must have had a key. But why would she have it with her? This put a new spin on things. Why was she returning to St. Jude's now?

Of course, I reminded myself that she wasn't just visiting; she was trespassing. That didn't make any sense at all. But then, so much didn't make sense. There were so many small oddities. I had believed Haley. The police believed her too. I felt the first glimmer of an idea that I should have had much earlier. *Of course* everyone had believed Haley. She was very credible. And she had been when we were in high school too. Pretty, popular, and bright. No one in authority had ever been convinced that she was also cruel. People like Mona didn't even bother to try anymore. Naturally, no one had paid any attention when Mona had tried to explain her situation. Everyone had believed the girls who were tormenting her. Had I missed the boat completely? Fallen for a ploy again? I'd sworn I wouldn't abandon Mona this time, despite her bizarre behavior, but I'd fallen for it. I'd wanted to help Haley make amends. But what was going on? A number of small discrepancies clicked in my brain. For one thing, Mona's so-called message to Haley, about my new cell phone not working. Mona didn't know I had already replaced my cell phone, but Haley did. Another thing: Why had Haley's face been dirty? And what about the clump of dust in her hair? She hadn't mentioned à scuffle. The police certainly hadn't tackled her. A vision of Haley struggling with Mona flashed through my brain. Sometimes, your subconscious is smarter than the rest of your brain.

Then I knew. Every small niggling worry I'd had about Haley began to surface. I could see how I'd been tricked yet again. Mona wasn't stalking Haley. Instead, Haley had plans for Mona. But why Mona? If Haley wanted to torment people, she could find lots of potential victims. No, Mona was special for some reason. And I knew intuitively that Mona had to be in that building. I just didn't know why. I did know this was all about Haley and Mona.

Jack's cell phone went right to message yet again. I figured the police would not be happy to hear from me, but what choice did I have?

I called Pepper. Of course, that also went to message.

"Pepper, please listen to this. Haley has just returned to the school. She unlocked the door and went in. She must have a key. I've misjudged the situation and misled you. There's something not right about Haley. She'd been in a struggle. There's no sign of Mona being here. No other car or anything, but I'm worried. Please call me back. I'm phoning 911 in case."

Brian was still on duty. He sighed and said, "They are treating you as a nutcase and I am telling you that as your friend."

I wasn't so sure that Brian was my friend, but I had to admit he had a point about my reputation with the cops.

I said, "I can deal with them. It's good that Mona isn't the villain of this piece, but it will be very bad news if Haley gets to have her way."

"Sorry. Nothing I can do." Brian broke the connection.

I was alone in the parking lot. If Mona was in the building, where was her vehicle? How had she gotten there if not by car?

I called Jack once more. No answer. I left a message for him to call me.

No sooner had I hung up than my phone vibrated. Jack. A text.

Meet me at St. Jude's. Urgent. Come alone. I know what is going on.

But I was already at the school and Jack was . . . Where? I glanced around, but there was no sign of him. The Mini certainly wasn't in sight. The parking lot at St. Jude's was empty, except for Haley's Honda in the shadows. I edged the Santa Fe toward it and locked the doors, as it definitely felt creepy. It was hard to be inconspicuous in it. Had Jack gone into the school with Haley? Why would either of them enter the building in the first place? I cruised carefully around the perimeter of the school searching for something that would shed a bit of light on this. Nothing. There was, however, a sliver of light shining from one of the windows. It hadn't been there earlier.

I got out of the SUV and walked to the nearest window. The gravel crunched under my shoes. I stood on my tiptoes and tried to peer through the window, but the light seemed to be coming from the corridor beyond the class. No one was visible in the room. The door was closed and I couldn't see anyone passing by the interior window. What to do?

I found Jack's Mini on the far side of the school. I touched the hood. The engine was still warm. Why would he go to the school alone? I thought back to the evening

years ago when he'd returned and found Mona a prisoner
in the locker. Was he trying to rescue Mona again? But how
would he know that Haley was here? Had she contacted
him? How? Of course she had. In a moment of sympathy,
he had given her his number. Somehow she'd tricked him
into meeting her.

I proceeded to the side door and clicked the latch. Haley
had left it unlocked. I swung the door open and listened for
voices. But all I heard was silence. I stuck my nose inside.
Where would Jack go? Inside? Had I missed him when I
was searching for his car? Where would Haley be? Was
Mona there too?

Empty schools are among the creepiest places on earth if
you ask me, but at least I could see a bit because there were
lights on in the next corridor. I wished I hadn't seen the dark
spots on the shining tiled floors. Red? I bent forward and
touched the first bloody puddle with the tip of my finger.
Wet. I sniffed my finger and recognized the metallic smell
of blood. Someone had been injured, just inside the school
by the door. Who? Was it my imagination or was the blood
still warm to the touch? I stared around. What looked like a
spray of blood had dotted the institutional green walls. My
heart thundered for Jack. Had I brought him into danger yet
again? The trail of drops zigzagged toward the double door
leading into the next corridor. I tried to remember the layout
of my old school. If you walked through those wide doors
and turned, you'd pass the science labs. Around the next corner were classrooms and the banks of lockers we'd all used.
That was where the light was coming from. I stared down at
the tiles and followed the drops. They'd turned into streaks
as though someone had been dragged.

Hugging the wall, I tiptoed down the hallway past the
labs. As I reached the corner of the hallway with the lockers, voices drifted out. I stopped. Listened. One of them

was definitely Jack. But who was he talking to? Not Mona. The pitch was wrong. Haley? A confident, powerful version if so.

I scrunched down and peeked around the corner. I could see halfway down the long hallway. Jack was kneeling, facing me, hands in the air. The person whose back was to me seemed to be pointing a weapon at him. Haley. Jack didn't react to me, didn't give my presence away, although he did shake his head. Even from that distance I could see that Jack winced as he did. While I watched in horror, he quickly touched the back of his head and stared at his hand as it reappeared, covered in dark blood. I realized that was a message to me and now I also knew whose blood I'd seen back by the door. Haley had a physically demanding job. She was strong enough to have dragged Jack along the hallway to this location. But why?

Jack was using his best, most persuasive yet utterly hypnotic boring voice. He'd read passages from leading nineteenth-century philosophers to me in that voice for years. I practically used to go into a trance on the spot. Jack's tactic seemed to be calming Haley, slowing things down. I ducked back the way I'd come and scurried out of earshot. I keyed in Pepper's number. Again.

Not answering.

Fine. 911. I didn't give Brian a chance to protest.

"Don't think I'm crazy, but my friend Jack Reilly is being held at gunpoint by—"

"Sorry. I've been told to ignore your calls. You have to stop pestering us."

"You have to listen to me. This is serious. I was wrong before, but I'm right this time and it's really life-or-death. Mona's life too."

It wasn't easy for Brian. "I have to hang up now. Please stop calling."

"I'd like to speak to your supervisor."

"Well, who do you think made that decision?"

Margaret and Sally's phones went straight to message. Why is no one ever available in an emergency? I left them each the same message: "Haley is holding a gun on Jack at St. Jude's. Mona Pringle may be dead. I haven't been able to get the cops to come or 911 to listen to me. If anything happens to me, let them know what I told you. I believe Mona was a decoy in all this. She's been tricked and so have we."

Next I called Lilith and gave her the short version.

"Unbelievable. What can I do?"

"You and Rose have to convince the cops to come. I have to go back in before she shoots Jack or something."

"Don't go in!"

"No choice here. But here's something you can do. Rose has one of those ancient answering machines that takes long messages, right?"

"Right."

"Can you hear the message the caller's leaving as they leave it?"

"Are you kidding? You hear every word, whether you want to or not."

"Great. Use your cell to contact the police and leave Rose's line free to take my message. At least there will be a record of what's going on here. That's the record 911 would have had, if they'd taken my calls."

I dialed Rose's number again, tucked the cell phone into my front pocket, hoping the receiver would pick up enough sound. Time to get moving. I hustled back along the corridor, staying close to the walls.

Too bad there was nothing around I could use to take Haley down. Nothing at all. The only weapon I had was the element of surprise. That wouldn't last long. And I didn't have much time. Whatever she was planning with Jack, she wouldn't take much longer to do it. What about something in the labs? Perhaps I could have a MacGyver moment. But, naturally, the doors were locked.

I peered around the corner. Haley seemed to be dragging Jack, facedown now, farther down the hall. I noticed a long smear of blood on the floor. I hadn't heard a shot, so I had to assume that this time she'd hit him hard in the front of the head with the butt of the gun. I shuddered at the thought of my brilliant Jack with two head injuries. What was she planning next? She didn't look in my direction, where she might have spotted me peering around the corner while I crouched by the wall in the dim light.

There were smoke detectors and sprinklers. That could bring the fire department, but I had no matches or flammable materials. I needed something.

Over the thundering of my heart I heard a strange pounding. I held my breath and listened. It sounded like someone kicking at metal. It was rhythmic and getting louder. Was someone arriving? Help? I glanced around, but the sound was definitely coming from the corridor in front of me. Haley paid no attention. Then it hit me. Of course, that was the sound of a person banging inside one of the lockers. Haley wasn't startled or surprised because she had put that person in the locker. It began to fall into place. Mona was back in her nightmare prison again. And Haley had been behind everything. I didn't understand why and I didn't care at that moment. All that mattered was saving Jack and Mona, if I was right about her. I'd let too much time elapse already. At that moment I had no choice.

I needed to go forward, but my knees were trembling. I had nothing to face off with and Haley had a weapon. I could see that she wouldn't be afraid to use it. She had used it to knock Jack out. Would she be able to shoot him too? By this time, I was convinced she would and I also knew he wouldn't have been her first victim. The thumping continued as Haley tugged at Jack's feet.

Why was I frozen? Unable to move? I shook myself. This would be one of the most important moments of my life. I couldn't let Jack die. I couldn't live my life without him. I cast one more frantic glance around for a weapon, or even a shield. There was nothing except a solitary free-standing metal trash can just ahead. I stared at it. Well, it was better than nothing. And it was cylindrical. Perfect for rolling. But rolling it would make a racket and that would give Haley too much warning. Lucky for me, Haley chose that moment to turn her back to me. I tried not to grunt as I picked it up and tiptoed forward around the corner, staggering under the weight. I did my damnedest not to make a sound. Six feet away from Haley, I raised it higher and heaved it with all my might. All that airlifting two thirteen-pound dogs up and down stairs and over snowdrifts had improved my upper body strength. The trash can flew through the air and I lunged behind it. All I needed was to get control in those first surprising seconds. The trash can hit Haley behind the knees. I threw myself on her, grabbing for her gun.

To my relief, Jack raised his head, opened his eyes, and managed to lurch unsteadily to his feet. I got my mitts on the gun. Haley snarled and glared at both of us. "Don't count on getting away with it. I'll tell the police you attacked me. They think you're psycho and they'll believe me. I'm a widow and my husband is not even buried yet and you are trying some weird teenage revenge. You and Mona are totally deranged. Jack's just your patsy."

"Yeah, give that a try, Haley, and see how it works out for you. Jack, are you all right?"

"She must have whacked me twice." Jack touched the front of his head this time. He flinched and then stared at the blood on his hand. "I never saw it coming either time."

"She's devious. We were all fooled."

"As soon as the cops get here, you'll be marched away. I can show the damage where the trash can hit me. That's assault. The only prints on that gun will be yours. Explain that."

Sure enough, Haley was wearing gloves.

"That would work, Haley, except that I figured it out before I set foot in here. I knew that Mona didn't kill those people. And I understood why you did. I made sure that Pepper Monahan knew too. You mean girls caused her some grief too. She believes me this time and she won't give your latest smear campaign one second's thought."

"She didn't seem to believe you when you spoke to her earlier this evening." Haley's pale eyes glittered. "They all think you're a fool."

"You didn't think I was a fool. You thought I was getting too close. You must have been following me. Did you see me meet with Dr. Partridge at the hospital? Did you also watch while I checked out Bethann's street? What else? My guess is that you stole that brown van and hid it near your home, maybe in the shed or in that nearby car graveyard. You could use it to follow me around, because I might have been watching for small red cars, not vans. They didn't take me seriously, but you were worried about me, weren't you, Haley? That's why you needed to kill me."

"No one could worry about you, Charlotte Adams. You are a self-important, conceited little bulldozer. I would have enjoyed watching you go over that escarpment."

I said, "Jack, can you open that locker door, please? I don't want to take my eyes off our blond villain here."

Jack was slipping down the wall, like he was about to pass out. He barely stopped himself. "It's just like when were kids."

"Exactly. Haley and Serena and the rest of the mean girls were brilliant not only at humiliating people but also at redirecting suspicion and fooling the authorities. How many times did that make life even worse for the victims?"

"No kidding," Jack said as he steadied himself and put his hand on the lock. Lucky for us, Haley had unlocked it already. I doubt if there would have been any way to get the combination out of her if she hadn't.

Jack swayed, held his head.

"But the others had actually changed. Tiffanee and Jasmin had turned into basic, decent people, but Serena had to be special. She'd made a bargain with the Almighty to save her daughter. As part of that bargain, I think you all had to make amends. Not a problem with the others, but not you, Haley. I think Serena knew your darkest secret and that secret was big enough to ruin what was left of your life. It wasn't just that she'd tell your clients about your nasty sadistic side, but she had the goods on you. Information that could send you to jail. She knew what happened to Dr. Partridge's wife. I heard tonight that police had been interested in talking to a blond woman, a witness who was seen near Dr. Partridge's place that night. Serena wasn't the only blonde, was she?"

Haley sneered. "Don't make me laugh. You won't get anywhere with that."

I said, "Sure, that's not enough to convict you or even get you charged, but if Serena went to the police, it would be a bit of extra evidence. She knew that Dr. Partridge had been the real target even back then. And why was Dr. Partridge a target, Haley? Another of your cruel jokes? A power play to show the others that you could get away with anything? Or were you angry at him? Did he cause you to look at yourself in a way you didn't like? Did you worry that he might find a way to end your reign of terror? Never mind. The police will get it out of you. Too bad his wife had borrowed his car that snowy night. You were the one who hit her. The other three could testify to that. At the time you were all in it together, although I am guessing they didn't realize you'd actually murder someone. But now, they'd changed. You couldn't trust them not to betray you. You had to get rid of them, but you also needed to make it look like someone else killed them. Depending on what information Serena left behind, you might still be implicated. How did you trick Serena into going by Dr. Partridge's house when you visited him to drug him? Offer to meet her? Knowing that someone would see that giant yellow Hummer? I am surprised he let you in. He had a pretty good idea that you were a psychopath. Did you pull your seeking-forgiveness act?"

"I never liked his face," she said, with an evil grin. "He thought he was so superior, but he was stupid, or I couldn't have dropped anything into his coffee."

I felt shivers run down my spine. Poor Dr. Partridge, so kind and correct.

I shifted gears. "It was brilliant sending Mona over the edge. Setting her up, planting the idea of the alter egos. How did you achieve that? Did you leave messages for her as if from those alters? You always did have a knack for imitating voices. That worked on our friend Margaret when you made a fake call supposedly from her teacher saying she'd cheated on her Regents exam."

Haley laughed at that memory. "Conceited bitch. It was good to take her down a notch."

I managed to keep my cool. "I think with a warrant, the police will be able to document your calls to Mona. And your calls to me, pretending to be her, all stuffed up from crying. And to Jack pretending to be me. Everyone. You may be able to block your number from me, but they have ways of getting past that."

She smirked. But she seemed to have stopped implicating herself. I needed to appeal to that monstrous ego again.

"Let me guess. Somewhere in Serena's property, someone will find Dr. Partridge's missing appointment book. That was brilliant. I have to admit it."

"You are wrong. It's in Mona's dreary little apartment," she said. "I am proud of that and I'm not worried. You can forget your talk of the police. No one else will ever know because you won't get out of here alive. You'll be dead and so will your useless little friends."

I knew I had to stall until someone got there. I might have been holding a gun, but I had no idea how to use it. Just a matter of time until Haley realized that.

I said, "I think when the police check that junkyard I spotted down the road from you, they'll find a collection of badly damaged small red cars. I suppose county records might show that the property belonged to Randy. And the cars will turn out to have been stolen recently. You were good at that. I suppose you and your friends did quite a bit of joyriding as teenagers. You can probably hot-wire anything."

So help me, she seemed flattered.

I kept talking. "Plus when they comb the inside of the brown van you hit me with, they'll find some trace evidence linking you. Your DNA may not be in the system, but they'll have a good reason to get a warrant for it now. You're not quite as smart as you think. I've been able to figure out everything."

I knew I'd gotten that right by the look on her face. Haley tensed. I figured she had nothing to lose at this point and she would try to overpower me as soon as Jack's attention was diverted by whoever was in that locker. Two could play that game. I needed every scrap of attention and strength that I had to try to keep us both safe.

"This was planned too, wasn't it? Everything to throw suspicion on your targets," I said. It had come together so easily now, once I knew it was Haley. When I'd been focused on Mona and Serena, of course, none of these clues fit in. I felt like kicking myself now.

"You can babble all you want to, but people will regard me with sympathy. 'Poor thing, she just lost her husband.'"

"Oh right, your husband. Would that be the same husband you killed?"

She blanched.

I said, "I guess that wasn't supposed to be as obvious as it was. But I started to ask myself why all this was happening. What was to be gained? Mona wasn't in your life. I wasn't in your life. Yet you sought me out. You signed up for my workshop, even though clutter and time management were not your problems. Money and health were. You insinuated yourself into my life. You asked forgiveness. You didn't want merely to torment people this time. You had an elaborate plot. Same old manipulative Haley."

"You'll never prove that."

"Was it fun getting into Mona's place and taking her things? Leaving a scarf or a hat or something that belonged to Mona near each hit-and-run and planting something from each victim in her apartment. You were toying with her, but I actually think that was a bit stagy, self-indulgent. It would never have worked. You're not as smart as you think you are, Haley."

"Shut up! The police will fall for it."

"It's too late to shut me up, remember? And they won't fall for it. I've already filled the authorities in on what you did. You won't get away with it. Trying to pin your crimes on Mona ruined any chance you might have had of cutting some kind of a deal."

Out of the corner of my eye, I could see Jack turning to stare at me. As if Haley could ever cut a deal with what she'd done, he must have been thinking. I turned my gaze back to Haley. "So what triggered this rampage? Serena wanting to come back and make amends for the harm she'd done? Was that it? She was such a public person. You couldn't afford to have people know the kinds of things you'd done. My guess is Randy didn't know. Is that why Bethann had to die? She was going to take Serena to court, as I imagine Serena told you. A lot would come out then, not just about Serena, but about you. Was Serena holding that over your head too?"

"That stupid bitch Bethann. She'd won some kind of Mickey Mouse legal case and it went right to her head. She must have thought she was a superhero. When she heard Serena was back, she decided to make her, and the rest of us, pay. She told me if I didn't make amends, she'd go to our clients and tell them . . . things that I'd done. Then she said the court case would make national news because of who Serena was married to. Serena was pressuring me too. She didn't want some of these things to get out. She wouldn't let up. As if I didn't have enough trouble."

"Right. Of course, Bethann might have been more careful if she'd known you'd actually killed somebody. It must have been easy enough to trick her into coming out on to the street. Pick a lock, let the little cat out and soon enough she'd come looking for it and bang! Bethann's dead and there will be no court case. But that was just one problem, wasn't it? Life was far from perfect. Randy wasn't quite the great catch he had been. First he lost his job, then the house and the cars, and finally all those terrible health problems. Now your only child hates you, although I'm betting she has reason. You, Haley McKee, blond princess, end up cleaning the very school where you once made life hell for so many. Oh, the irony."

"I said, shut up."

More desperate kicks at the door.

"Now your life was hell. And there was no way out. Except, of course, for that life insurance."

"How did you—?"

"I figured Randy would take care of that. He cared about his family. Didn't he say he always took care of his girls? Once you started on this path to get rid of Serena and the others, you also found a solution to the problem of your ailing, failed husband without ending up broke and divorced. I bet he was starting to look more appealing dead than alive. But of course, you couldn't just kill him. Too obvious. No you had to arrange to have him die in a way that wouldn't draw any suspicion to you. Mona could be framed for that too. Too bad you didn't wipe me out, Haley. Nice try, though."

"I'm not done yet," Haley said.

Jack, swaying, managed to lift the combination lock from the hasp. He yanked the door open.

"Mona!" he yelled as Mona tumbled out, writhing as if in pain. She must have been in agony being crouched in that small space. Had Haley drugged her and put her there earlier? If she'd been unconscious and quiet, the police wouldn't have done more than check that the lock was engaged.

Too bad I took a moment too long staring at Mona.

Haley took that moment to head butt me. The gun tumbled to the ground and I dropped like a stone. I managed somehow to roll over and land on top of it. I screamed as Haley yanked my hair with one hand and grabbed for the gun with the other hand. I found myself flipped on my back and saw Haley raise the gun high. The corridor echoed with a roaring shriek straight from a nightmare. Was that me facing death?

Haley's eyes widened and she landed splat on top of me. The air shot out of my lungs with a whoosh. The howling continued. Mona had jumped on Haley. I struggled to breathe with Haley's, and now Mona's, weight pushing down on me. I gasped in relief as Haley was heaved off me and slammed against the nearest locker wall. Her head hit the metal with a bang. But it took more than that to stop Haley. As Mona lunged at her again, Haley lashed out with her hand. Mona grabbed it and bit it. Haley stopped, stunned. That gave Mona the chance she must have been waiting for: Her fist connected with Haley's jaw. Haley's eyes rolled back when her head clanged against the metal locker again. As she dropped to the ground, I knew it couldn't have been slow motion, but it seemed that way. Mona leapt on Haley's unconscious body and continued to pummel her. Jack stood in frozen astonishment. It took me a few seconds to catch my breath and pull myself together. We reached Mona. I put my arms around her and said, "Now it can stop."

Jack added his arms to the mix and together we seemed to be enough.

By now Mona was weeping, soundlessly. A torrent of tears, years of misery and desperation pouring out. Jack lifted Mona off Haley. He caught a clip on the ear. Jack yelped. Mona gasped, I suppose just realizing what she had done. I did my best to keep an eye on the unconscious Haley, because nothing would have surprised me. We had no weapons except for her gun. Haley would try to recapture it if she woke up. And it was entirely possible that she was faking it. I couldn't imagine Jack or me being able to shoot her, but I had no doubt that Mona could. As much as I hated the woman for all the harm she'd done, I hoped she wasn't dead. That could be her final act of bullying: having Mona convicted of her murder. She'd probably mock poor Mona from beyond the grave. I shook my head to rid myself of that thought. Jack continued to hold on to Mona, rocking her back and forth and muttering soothing words. Mona's tears had soaked the shoulder of his Hawaiian shirt.

"Mona," I said. "It's over. We've got her now. She can't hurt you or anyone else anymore." I was praying that was true. The sound of "Police! Hands in the air!" sounded like music. My own personal hit parade was playing.

Pepper, wearing a bulletproof vest, led the charge, but I noticed she was accompanied by a bunch of cops who seemed to be Darth Vader look-alikes.

"I'm glad you're here," I said. "You almost had a triple murder. Thanks for ignoring all my information."

"What the hell happened to you, Jack?" she said, ignoring me one more time.

Jack said, "Bit of bad luck running into Haley. Fell for an old trick."

Pepper bent down and felt for Haley's pulse. I said, "I sure hope you can get her locked up forever."

Pepper straightened up and turned to the nearest uniformed officer. "Call for extra paramedics. What happened?"

"She lured Jack to the school by pretending to be me."

Jack said, "I'd nod but I believe my head would fall off."

"And she had Mona trapped in a locker. The same thing she did back in school. Mona must have been drugged and unconscious because your cops didn't find her."

Pepper scratched her head. "Why would Haley do this?"

"She planned to blame Mona for everything. Haley was going to kill Jack and blame it on Mona. She'd knocked him out and dragged him in here. I am not sure how she managed to get Mona into that locker. Mona will have to tell you that. Haley planned to let Mona out, then kill her and claim self-defense. After all, everyone believed that Mona was a homicidal maniac."

I could see the uniforms making eye contact with Pepper. Pepper had developed a massive scowl by this time. "No small thanks to you, Charlotte."

I felt like hanging my head. "I let myself be manipulated just like when we were kids. I didn't see how information was being used to twist the truth."

"So all the phone calls and the entreaties, the pleas to arrest Mona, to stop her, they were because Haley was pulling the strings?"

"Yup."

"But there is no proof of any of this."

"If everything went well, you'll hear her incriminating herself via my cell phone on Rose's ancient answering machine."

"They've been in touch, but you shouldn't have meddled, Charlotte. I told you that. How many times?"

Jack said, "I told her the same thing, but I was wrong. If Charlotte hadn't gotten involved, Haley would have gotten away with multiple murders. Including mine."

Pepper sighed.

I got in my two cents' worth. "It's good news, Pepper. You're going to clear up five hit-and-runs, Dr. Partridge's nearly fatal medication mix-up, the hit-and-run that killed his wife fourteen years ago, and now this. You see, Haley was behind all the hit-and-runs. They were a smoke screen to get rid of the other girls."

"But why?"

"I'm guessing the plan was to get rid of Dr. Partridge because he knew too much about Haley. The girls had to go because Serena was threatening to expose Haley for killing Dr. Partridge's wife. If he recovers, you may be able to get him to talk about it. I think he knew that Haley was a psychopath even then. She was also drunk on power and making a point. And possibly trying to make sure that Dr. Partridge didn't share what he knew, not that he could have done that. She more or less admitted that she killed the wife thinking it was Dr. Partridge. Of course, she didn't think she'd ever get arrested. What a comedown."

"With the three of you here and beat-up the way you are, I figure I can buy this. But what about Randy? Come on. Let's not go completely insane."

"Oh, Haley wasn't off her rocker. She planned and orchestrated this from the beginning. You'll want to question her daughter, Brie. She wouldn't let Brie say good-bye to Randy. Perhaps he was already dead when they drove away from the house that day. I should have caught on when she wasn't worried about Brie's safety. Of course, she loved Brie as much as she could love anyone. And Brie had nothing to fear from her mother."

Pepper said, "My head hurts. It's so complicated."

Jack put his hand to his head and wiped off a trickle of blood. "Yeah, tell me about it."

For the first time, Mona spoke. She seemed small and broken crouched on the floor, but as she struggled to her feet, she seemed to get her strength back. "It is complicated. They created a world of pain and misery for other people."

I said, "Mona, I am so sorry that I wasn't there for you when we were in school. The nightmare could have been prevented if we had gone to the principal or just stood up to the bullies."

Jack said, "Honestly, except for that time with the locker, I didn't even know it was going on. Guys are kind of stunned about girls and their politics, I guess."

Mona managed a weak smile. "I don't think so. They had the school authorities eating out of their hands, just like Haley had you eating out of her hand."

I said, "You're right."

Mona shook her head. "But you guys were never the problem. You helped me and Sally did too. You were the only people who had any use for me at all. If it hadn't been for the times you stepped in, I don't think I ever would have been able to value myself enough to get a job and have a life. I think I would have killed myself."

I felt a lump in my throat, as a brigade of paramedics showed up and bent over Haley. Pepper said, "I'll take your statements personally at the hospital. Paramedics will have to check out the three of you first."

Mona said, "Did I kill her?" She pointed to Haley out cold on the floor, surrounded by emergency workers.

19

"She's breathing," one of them said.

Mona said, "That doesn't make me happy."

I stepped forward. "I think it should, Mona. You stood up to her and you fought back even when she'd convinced you that you had done these terrible things. She manipulated you and sent you practically over the brink, and yet, you are okay and she'll be going to prison."

A pair of paramedics approached Mona and another pair was busy taking a close look at Jack's head.

As the first group loaded Haley up on a stretcher, I said to Pepper, "She's extremely dangerous. I hope you're going to keep her under guard. Oh. Sorry. I guess I got a little bit bossy again."

Pepper actually snorted. "A little bit? Okay, I'm going to need your story and you're the only one who's well enough to go to the station."

Jack said, "I'm all right. I'll go with her."

"Down, boy. You wait until you're cleared by the hospital." Jack earned a smile from her, at least.

I blurted, "You got whacked on the head, Jack. You need X-rays and scans. You need to be seen by specialists right away."

"All thanks to you," Pepper said to me.

Jack flashed her a dirty look. "I told you, it's not Charlotte's fault, Pepper. She's not the bad guy here."

Pepper stepped back in surprise. That had been pretty un-Jack-like behavior. "Yeah, well, you wouldn't have needed help if Charlotte hadn't stirred this up. We were on it."

I said, "Yes, but—"

Jack said, "No, you weren't. Mona was almost killed. I was almost killed. If Charlotte hadn't followed up, we would have been. She should have been listened to instead of discounted."

Pepper rolled her eyes. "Sure. Stick together. Whatever. But she's right about one thing—no statement until you've been checked out."

Jack was muttering about hating ambulances as the paramedics prepared to bundle him off to Woodbridge General. Then he said, "Charlotte, why are there two of you?"

I gasped and Pepper did too. "Concussion," we said in unison. "Hospital now."

I said, "I want to go with him. And Mona needs someone with her. I'll keep an eye on her as well."

Pepper pulled me aside and spoke in a low tone. "There will be an officer doing that. Mona's probably going to be facing a ton of charges." Pepper didn't seem happy about that, which was a good thing. "I don't know if we can avoid it. She did some crazy stuff."

"When the information comes out about Haley impersonating her, I think it would be hard to prove that Mona did anything, except run for her life."

"But she wasn't running for her life."

"She sure was. And I bet any jury will believe that too. Just saying . . ."

Pepper glanced over to where the uniforms were watching the paramedics with interest. "I always liked Mona and I'll be happy if we don't have to charge her with anything."

"And she can't lose her job."

"I don't control that," Pepper snapped.

"You certainly could influence the outcome. You can put in a word for her, explain the situation. She was manipulated and terrified by a vicious criminal."

"Don't get ahead of yourself. I haven't even heard anyone's statement yet, let alone conducted an investigation. You seem to think that because you have come up with a wild-ass theory, that it's settled. Trust me, it isn't. And it's way too early to decide what happens with Mona."

That reminded me of something important. "She already has a good lawyer. I want to call Margaret again. That can be my one phone call."

"Make all the calls you want. I'm not arresting you. What would the charge be? Being a pain in the butt?"

"You did say you could charge me for interfering in your investigation."

"Don't tempt me."

"You should be happier about what I found out. Check out the life insurance on Randy, and when that policy was taken out. I bet there's one held by the business too. That's common practice. I believe Haley planned to take that insurance and head out for a new life that didn't involve cleaning toilets in the school where she was once part of the ruling party or working nights or any of the other things she's had to do this past while. She was going to be free. She needed a fall guy, as she would have been an obvious suspect. Mona was perfect. And Mona could be used to take care of her pesky problem with Bethann, Serena, and anyone else who got in her way, like me. Haley was a one-woman murder machine. I'm pretty sure she enjoyed it."

Pepper went back to scowling. "Something tells me it won't be easy to prove. She's a lot of things, most of them bad, but she's not stupid."

In the end, still scowling, Pepper let me follow Jack to the hospital and took my statement there.

I couldn't imagine going home without Jack, even though everyone at the hospital seemed determined to get rid of me. He needed X-rays. He needed a scan. He needed to see a neurologist. How could I leave him there? What was home without him? How many more days and nights would we have before I had to move? When would I find the guts to tell him how I felt about that? Murderers are easy compared dealing with complicated emotions.

Throughout the long night, there was a steady stream of visitors. Margaret and Frank came by. Margaret said that if anyone in Woodbridge Police thought they'd be charging Mona with anything, she'd make them sorry they'd ever been born. That was quite a long statement from Margaret. I noticed that Frank turned pale. He did have one piece of news: Serena's body had washed up on the icy shore and had been identified by her husband. Another part of the story had come to an end. I figured I would never know if Serena had been sincere and repentant in the end.

Sally slipped into the room in the middle of the night. A doctor's wife has her privileges. Jack was snoring softly and I was dozing in my chair. "Benjamin's with the kids," she said. "I just had to see for myself that you were both all right. Charlotte, I am so sorry I didn't support you more in this investigation. I didn't take you seriously. I don't know why. I guess I let myself be manipulated by those mean girls too. It will never happen again. And tell Jack the kids send their love. He'd better be all right, or else."

Lilith and Rose also managed to sneak in past a phalanx of nurses. Rose brought a huge batch of sugar-and-spice cookies, minus what had been used to bribe the staff.

"The police have the tape," Lilith said. "Pepper came by herself and picked it up."

Rose added, "Aren't you glad I kept that old answering machine instead of trading it in?"

"You saved the day, Rose. Lilith too. That reminds me, Lilith. Haley's daughter, Brie, is now without two parents. She's already troubled and angry. I think she was bullied too."

Lilith nodded. "Oh boy. She'll end up in the care of the state. Let me see what I can do. Seth will help me."

Rose said, "What about me? Can I help? Cookies of any use these days?"

Kristee actually had a jumbo package of black-and-white fudge delivered with a note expressing gratitude. That told me that Todd Tyrell was on the story. I tried not to think too much about what he could do with that.

The last visitor in was Ramona, who looked like she hadn't slept for two nights, which I guess she hadn't. "Sheesh," she said. "I let you down."

"You didn't."

"Did. Well, I finally tracked down the distant relatives, where Mona had been staying and, of course, I was too late for that to be useful. Is there anything I can do now?"

"You always go the distance. And you know what? You'd better get some rest, because Mona's going to need all the help she can get rebuilding her life. Maybe you can talk to Brian at 911 too. I am persona non grata there and probably always will be. But she'll be under psychiatric observation for a while and she'll need support and visitors. Oh, and Mona's upstairs neighbors, Caroline and Tony, need to know too. They'll want to drop in and let her know how the animals are doing."

"I'm on it. We might be up to our patooties in leaks, but this is a priority."

—••—

It was morning before Jack was cleared to leave the hospital. Although I'd been told I should go home, I was unable to do that. After all, what was home without Jack? I slept in the chair next to his bed, although "slept" would be an exaggeration.

As usual, Jack slept like a nursery full of babies. Takes more than murder to keep Jack awake. His eyes popped open when the neurologist came in to announce that he was going to be fine. The specialist was a plump fiftyish motherly type. She was accompanied by Sally's husband, Benjamin. He said, "If you let anything happen to this guy, my wife will kill me. He spends a lot time with our kids."

"Then you're lucky. He got off easy," she said to him. "Blows like that can do a lot of damage. Got a guardian angel, Mr. Reilly?"

"More like a hard head." Jack glanced at me. "And, of course, I have my own lucky charm."

"Off you go then. You're taking valuable space from sick people," she said, grinning.

Jack grinned back. "Okay, Charlotte. Time to go home."

I took the opportunity to ask Benjamin what Dr. Partridge's prognosis was.

"He seems to be improving. I would say there's some guarded optimism there."

That was more good news.

—••—

We took the Santa Fe as Jack's Mini was still at the school. Lilith had offered to pick it up with Seth and drop it off for us.

Jack said, "Now that all that's over, we can get started on planning to put the house back the way it should be: a family home. And before you start fussing and fuming, you need to accept that."

"Accept that—?"

"That we are a family. You and me and the dogs. We are all we need and it's time you realized it."

I sat in silence for a while as I struggled to keep my eyes on the road.

"You're not planning to sell it?"

"What? Sell my parents' house? The place I grew up in? I'm the one with the head injury and you're the one talking crazy."

"I thought—"

"I figured out what you thought. How could you ever believe for even a minute that I would send you away? That I would want to live without you? That I could live without you?"

Tears filled my eyes. "Oh, Jack, that's so—" I was trying to finish the sentence with a word like beautiful or wonderful or romantic, when he added, "Don't I put up with all your bossy little ways and obsessions?"

"Excuse me! Is this from the man with bike parts in the oven?"

"I'm willing to compromise over that. There are quite a few things you need to compromise over too. I can wait until you're ready. However long that takes. And I'm not planning to back down because I love you. Don't even think about making a joke about it."

For once I couldn't think of a single thing to joke about. "I love you too."

"It took you long enough to figure it out."

"I had bad influences and I blame my parents. But now that I've said it out loud, I hope you're happy."

Jack said, "I am."

"Me too." I was. Not only would I finally have a real life with Jack, but also a major renovation. That offered wonderful organizing possibilities.

I said with a delicious shiver, "We'll need charts, schedules, priorities, lists—"

Jack said, "I guess we'll need a new bed. King-size, because I'm tall."

I felt myself blushing. "That would be good. High-thread-count sheets."

A small voice in the back of my head said, *What took you so long?*

We drove on through the clear, bright morning. For the first time in two weeks, Woodbridge was blessed with blue skies, fluffy clouds, and warming temperatures. Around us the snow was melting furiously. The Santa Fe splashed though puddles the size of lakes. Spring was on its way. New beginning. New life. And whatever else that would hold for us.

Mary Jane Maffini is a lapsed librarian, a former mystery bookstore owner, and a lifelong lover of mysteries. In addition to the five Charlotte Adams books, she is the author of the Camilla MacPhee series and the Fiona Silk adventures. She has nearly two dozen short stories published in anthologies and magazines such as *Ellery Queen's Mystery Magazine*. She is a former president of Crime Writers of Canada and has won two Arthur Ellis awards for best mystery short story as well as the Crime Writers of Canada Derrick Murdoch award.

Mary Jane is a frequent speaker on crime fiction and the writing process. She lives and plots in Ottawa, Ontario, along with her long-suffering husband and two princessy dachshunds. Visit her at www.maryjanemaffini.com.

WELL-CRAFTED MYSTERIES
FROM BERKLEY PRIME CRIME

- **Earlene Fowler** Don't miss these Agatha Award–winning quilting mysteries featuring Benni Harper.

- **Monica Ferris** These *USA Today* bestselling Needlecraft Mysteries include free knitting patterns.

- **Laura Childs** Her Scrapbooking Mysteries offer tips to satisfy the most die-hard crafters.

- **Maggie Sefton** These popular Knitting Mysteries come with knitting patterns and recipes.

- **Lucy Lawrence** These brilliant Decoupage Mysteries involve cutouts, glue, and varnish.

- **Elizabeth Lynn Casey** The Southern Sewing Circle Mysteries are filled with friends, southern charm—and murder.

M5G0610